A Gentleman
of Courage

A Gentleman of Courage

A Novel of the Wilderness

James Oliver Curwood

MINT EDITIONS

A Gentleman of Courage: A Novel of the Wilderness was first published in 1924.

This edition published by Mint Editions 2021.

ISBN 9781513280691 | E-ISBN 9781513285719

Published by Mint Editions®

 MINT
EDITIONS

minteditionbooks.com

Publishing Director: Jennifer Newens
Design & Production: Rachel Lopez Metzger
Project Manager: Micaela Clark
Typesetting: Westchester Publishing Services

Contents

I

Pierre Gourdon had the love of God in his heart, a man's love for a man's God, and it seemed to him that in this golden sunset of a July afternoon the great Canadian wilderness all about him was whispering softly the truth of his faith and his creed. For Pierre was the son of a runner of the streams and forests, as that son's father had been before him, and love of adventure ran in his blood, and romance, too; so it was only in the wild and silent places that he felt the soul in him attuned to that fellowship with nature which the good teachers at Ste. Anne de Beaupré did not entirely approve. Nature was Pierre's God, and would ever be until he died. And though he had crept up the holy stair at Ste. Anne's on his knees, and had touched the consecrated water from the sacred font, and had looked with awe upon mountains of canes and crutches left by those who had come afflicted and doubting and had departed cured and believing, still he was sure that in this sunset of a certain July afternoon he was nearer to the God he desired than at any other time in all his life.

Josette, his wife, slender and tired, her dark head bare in the fading sun, stood wistful and hoping at his side, praying gently that at last their long wanderings up the St. Lawrence and along this wilderness shore of Superior had come to an end, and that they might abide in this new paradise, and never travel again until the end of their days.

Back of them, where a little stream ran out of the cool forest, a tireless boy quested on hands and knees in the ferns and green grass for wild strawberries, and though strawberry season was late his mouth was smeared red.

The man said, pointing down, "It makes one almost think the big lake is alive, and a hand is reaching in for him."

"Yes, they are Five Fingers of water reaching in from the lake," agreed Josette, seating herself wearily upon a big stone, "though it seems to me there should be only four fingers, and one thumb."

And so the place came to be named, and through all the years that have followed since that day it has tenaciously clung to its birthright.

The boy came to his mother, bringing her strawberries to eat; and the man, climbing a scarp of rock, made a megaphone of his hands and hallooed through it until an answering shout came from deep in the spruces and balsams, and a little later Dominique Beauvais came out to the edge of the slope, his whiskered face bright with expectancy, and with him his little wife Marie, panting hard to keep pace with his long legs.

When they were together Pierre Gourdon made a wide and all-embracing sweep with his arms.

"This will be a good place to live in," he said. "It is what we have been looking for."

With enthusiasm Dominique agreed. The women smiled. Again they were happy. The boy was hunting for strawberries. He was always empty, this boy.

Pierre Gourdon kissed his wife's smooth hair as they went back to the camp they had made two hours earlier in the day, and broke into a wild boat song which his grandfather had taught him on his knee in the wicked days before he had known Josette at Ste. Anne, and Dominique joined in heartily through his whiskers.

The women's smiles were sweeter and their eyes brighter, for fatigue seemed to have run away from them now that their questing men-folk were satisfied and had given them a promise of home.

That night, after supper, with their green birch camp-fire lighting up the blackness of the wilderness, they sat and made plans, and long after nine-year-old Joe had crawled into his blanket to sleep, and the women's eyes were growing soft with drowsiness, Pierre and Dominique continued to smoke pipefuls of tobacco and to build over and over the homes of their dreams.

Young and happy, and overflowing with the adventurous enthusiasm of the race of *coureurs* from which they had sprung, they saw themselves with the rising of another sun pitched into the heart of realities which they had anticipated for a long time; and when at last Josette fell asleep, her head pillowed close to her boy's, her red lips that had not lost their prettiness through motherhood and wandering were tender with a new peace and contentment. And a little later, while Pierre and Dominique still smoked and painted their futures, the moon rose over the forest-tops in a great golden welcome to the pioneers, and the wind came in softly and more coolly from the lake, and at the last, from far away, rose faintly a wilderness note that thrilled them—the cry of wolves.

Dominique listened, and silently emptied the ash from his pipe into the palm of his hand.

"Where wolves run there is plenty of game, and where there is game there is trapping," he said.

And then came a sound which stopped the hearts of both for an instant, a deep and murmuring echo, faint and very far, that broke in a note of strange and vital music upon the stillness of the night.

"A ship!" whispered Pierre.

"Yes, a ship!" repeated Dominique, half rising to catch the last of the sound.

For this was a night of forty years ago, when on the north shore of Superior the cry of wolves in the forest was commoner than the blast of a ship's whistle at sea.

The pioneers slept. The yellow moon climbed up until it was straight overhead. Shadows in the deep forest moved like living things. The wolves howled, circled, came nearer, and stopped their cry where the kill was made. Mellow darkness trembled and thrilled with life. Silent-winged creatures came and disappeared like ghosts. Bright eyes watched the sleeping camp of the home seekers. A porcupine waddled through it, chuckling and complaining in his foolish way. A buck caught the scent of it, stamped his foot and whistled. There were whisperings in the tall, dark spruce tops.

Caverns of darkness gave out velvety footfalls of life, and little birds that were silent in the day uttered their notes softly in the moon glow.

A bar of this light lay across Josette's face, softening it and giving to its beauty a touch of something divine. The boy was dreaming. Pierre slept with his head pillowed in the crook of his arm. Dominique's whiskers were turned to the sky, bristling and fierce, as if he had taken this posture to guard against harm the tired little wife who lay at his side.

So the night passed, and dawn came, wakening them with the morning chatter of a multitude of red squirrels in a little corner of the world as yet unspoiled by man.

THAT FIRST DAY FROM WHICH they began to measure their new lives the axes of Pierre and Dominique struck deep into the sweetly scented hearts of the cedar trees out of which they were to build their homes at Five Fingers. But first they looked more carefully into the prospects of their domain.

The forest was back of them, a forest of high ridges and craggy ravines, of hidden meadows and swamps, a picturesque upheaval of wild country which reached for many miles from the Superior shore to the thin strip of settlement lands along the Canadian Pacific. Black and green and purple with its balsam, cedar and spruce, silver and gold with its poplar and birch, splashed red with mountain ash, its climbing billows and dripping hollows were radiantly tinted by midsummer sun—and darkly sullen and mysterious under cloud or storm. Out of these fastnesses, choked with ice and snow in winter, Pierre knew how the floods must come roaring in springtime, and his heart beat exultantly, for he loved the rush and thunder of streams, and the music of water among rocks.

At the tip of the longest of the five inlets which broke like gouging fingers through the rock walls of the lake half a mile away they decided upon the sites for their cabins. Against those walls they could hear faintly the moaning of surf, never quite still even when there was no whisper of wind. But the long finger of water, narrow and twisted, as if broken at the joint, was a placid pool of green and silver over which the gulls floated, calling out their soft notes in welcome to the home builders, and in its white sand were the prints of many feet, both of birds and of beasts, who played and washed themselves there, and came down to drink. Between these two, the open and peaceful serenity of the inlet and the cool, still hiding-places of the forest, were the green meadowland and slopes and patches of level plain, a narrow strip of park-like beauty at the upper edge of which, in the very shadow of the forest, Pierre and Dominique struck off their plots and squared their angles, making ready for the logs in which the afternoon saw their axes buried.

The days passed. Each dawn the red squirrel chorus greeted the rising sun; through hours that followed came the ring of steel and the freedom of voice which is born of love and home. Pierre sang, as his grandfather had sung long years ago, and Dominique bellowed like a baying hound when the chorus came. Women's laughter rose with the singing of the birds. Josette and Marie were girls again, and the boy was forever leading them to newly discovered strawberry patches hidden among the rocks and grass and ferns.

It was a new thing for the wilderness, this invasion of human life, and for a long time it fell away from them, listening, frightened and subdued. But the birds and the red squirrels gave it courage, and softly it returned, curious and shy and friendly. The deer came down to drink again in the dusk, and moose rattled their antlers up the ridge. Pop-eyed whisky jacks began to eat bannock crumbs close to Josette's hands. Jays came nearer to scream their defiance, like wild Indians, in the tree-tops, and thrushes and warblers sang until their throats were ready to burst, and twenty times a day Pierre would pause in his labor and say, "This is going to be a fine place to live in, with the sea at our front door and the woods at our back."

He called Superior "the sea," and twice in the first week they saw far out in its hazy vastness white and shimmering specks which were sailing ships.

Log upon log the first of the cabins rose, until the roof was covered, and scarcely was it done when Josette and Marie were planting wild morning glories and crimson splashes of roses about it, and were digging in the dark, cool mold of birch and poplar thickets for violet roots, and out in the sheltered fens and meadow-dips for hyacinths and fire-flowers; and in the hour before dusk, when the day's work was over and supper was eaten, they would go hand in hand with their men-folk to study and ponder over the fertile patches of earth here and there where next spring they would plant potatoes and carrots and turnips and all the other fine things they had known back in the land of Ste. Anne.

It was August when the two cabins were finished, small in dimensions but snug as dovecotes, and in the eyes of Josette and Marie grew a deeper and more serious look. For they were housewives again, with little to do with, but with a world full of endeavor and anticipation ahead of them. And it worried them to see that the fruits were ripening, red raspberries so thick the bears were turning into hulks of fat, black currants and saskatoons among the rocks, and all over the ridgesides great trees of wild plums and mountain ash berries, waiting for the first frosts to make them ready for preserves and jams.

So Dominique, one day, set out to blaze a trail to the nearest settlement, thirty miles away; and thereafter their men-folk took turns, one and then the other, going with empty pack and returning with sixty pounds of burden, and berries were put into cans and dried and preserved—until Pierre and Dominique began to tease their wives and ask them if they wanted their husbands to turn into bears and sleep on their fat all winter. It was this banter which reminded Josette of candles, and in September they killed two bears and made several hundred of them.

With the first frosts of autumn Pierre said even more frequently than before, "This is a fine place to live in," and Josette and Marie, seeing what the frosts were doing, rose each morning with new wonder and new joy in their eyes. For if these frosts were giving to the waters of the lake a colder and harder sheen, with something of menace and gloom about it, they were also painting the ridges and hollows and all the forest land as far as they could see with a glory of color which they had never known at Ste. Anne.

Breath of winter came in the nights. Higher grew the great birch piles of firewood which Pierre and Dominique dragged close to the cabin doors, and very soon came the days when the carnival of autumn color was gone and all but the evergreen trees assumed the ragged distress of naked limbs and branches, and winds broke down fiercely over the wilderness, and the moan of the lake, beating against its rock walls, grew clearer and at times was a muffled and sullen roar half a mile away.

But these changes were not frightening to Pierre and his people. Canadian winter was, after all, the heart of their lives; long months of adventure and thrill of deep snows and stinging blizzards on the trap lines, of red-hot stoves, and snug evenings at home telling the tales of the day, and appetites as keen as the winds that howled down from the north.

This season, of all seasons, they would not have changed. It was then the wolf howl took on a new note, the foxes cried out hungrily at the edge of the clearing in the night. The call of the moose floated awesomely through the frost of still evenings, and the bears hunted their dens. One after another songbirds departed, leaving the whisky jacks and the jays behind, and the ravens gathered in flocks, while in the thickets and swamps the big snowshoe rabbits turned from brown to gray and from gray to white. All hunting things were astir, from the wolf and the fox and the little outlaw ermine to the owl and the dog-faced fisher-cat, and in November Pierre and Dominique dipped their traps in hot bear grease and prayed for the first snow.

It came in the night, so quietly that none heard the breathless fall of it, and the world was white when little Joe got out of his bed at dawn to look at his rabbit snares in the edge of the timber. That was the beginning of their first winter at Five Fingers. It was a cold, dry winter, and there was never a day that a haunch of venison or moose meat was not hanging behind the cabins. Trapping was good, and the store of pelts grew as the weeks went on, until Pierre and Dominique both swore in the same breath that it was a paradise that they had found on this north shore of Superior, and each day they made new promises of what they would buy for Josette and Marie in the spring. The snow piled itself deeper, and the lake froze over. In January it was thirty degrees below zero.

The white world, Josette called it, and at times they all played in it like children. There was Christmas, and then New Year's, and a birthday for Marie, and games and stories at night round the crackling stoves in the cabins. Pierre and Dominique built toboggans, and from the crest of the ridge where they had first looked down upon the Five Fingers they sped in wild races over the open and halfway across the snow-crusted ice of the middle finger. And yet when Dominique came in one day and said quite casually that he had heard the chirp of a brush warbler back in the big swamp Marie gave a little cry of delight and Josette's eyes grew suddenly bright.

It meant spring. A day or two later Pierre said the coats of the snowshoe rabbits were turning rusty, which meant early spring. Then came discovery of the first bear track, the track of a foolish bear who had come out hungrily, like a woodchuck, only to hunt himself a den again when he saw his shadow freezing in the snow. After this there was more sun in the morning and less of the cold of sullen twilight each night, and before even the crust of the snow had begun to thaw Pierre brought in a poplar twig to show how the buds were swelling until they seemed ready to pop. "I have never seen them fatter," he said. "It means spring isn't far away."

When the first robin came Josette told her husband she could already smell the perfume of flowers. He was a cold-footed and crabbed-looking bird, forlorn and disappointed at the world's chill aspect, and for a few minutes he sat humped up on the roof log and then flew away.

This was the beginning. The snow began to thaw on the sunny sides of the slopes, and after that the change came swiftly. In April a steady and swelling murmur ran through the forests, the music of the gathering waters. Meadows and flats became flooded, little creeks changed suddenly into rushing torrents, lakes and ponds crept up over their sides, and the tiny stream which passed near the cabins, quiet and gentle in summertime, was all at once a riotous and quarrelsome outlaw, roaring and foaming in its mad rush down to the Middle Finger. Half a mile away was a larger stream whose flood sounds came to them like the distant roar of a cataract. It was glorious music, with something in it that stirred the blood of Pierre and his people like tonic and wine. Pierre, in his optimism and love of life, explained it all by saying, "It is good to have a long, cold winter that we may fully enjoy the spring."

The birds seemed to return in a night and a day—robins perky and glad to get back from the lazy southland, thrushes and catbirds and a dozen kinds of little brown warblers and brush sparrows whose voices were sweetest of all the spring songsters. The earth itself began to breathe with swelling roots and tips of green; the first flowers popped up; the poplar buds exploded into fuzzy leaves, and Pierre and Dominique worked from morning until night, clearing the patches they were to plant this year, and spading up the rich, dark soil.

It was about this time Pierre gave voice to a thought which had been growing in his head all winter. He was standing with Josette at the tip of the green ridge from which they had first looked down upon Five Fingers.

"Ste. Anne was never as fine as this, *chérie*," he said.

"No, not even before the woods were cut," agreed Josette.

He took her hand and held it softly in his own, and Josette laid her cheek against his shoulder so that his lips could touch her smooth hair. Pierre always liked it that way.

"I have been having a dream," he said, his voice a little queer because of its secret, and because he knew how its confession would thrill the one at his side, "and I have said nothing about it, but have done much thinking. Would not a little church look pretty down there, just where the tip of the evergreen forest reaches to the Middle Finger?"

"A church!" whispered Josette, her heart giving a sudden swift beat.

"Yes, a church," chuckled Pierre softly. "And over there, in that green bit of meadow—what a place for a home for our old friend Poleon Dufresne, and Sara, and all the children. And there is room for the Clamarts, too, and Jean Croisset and his wife. It is a big land, with plenty of fur and game and good rich soil underfoot, and I have thought it is not right to keep it all to ourselves, *douce amie*."

From the door of her cabin some distance away Marie Beauvais wondered just why it was that Josette threw her arms so suddenly round her husband's neck and kissed him. And Pierre, with a heart full of happiness, little guessed that with the fulfilment of his dreams would come tragedy into the wilderness paradise at Five Fingers.

II

It was five years later that Simon McQuarrie and Herman Vogelaar came to Five Fingers. They were a queer but lovable combination. Simon was a Scotchman, tall and spare, with a thin face which seldom broke into a smile and which had the appearance of being made of flint. His companion was a Dutchman, short and round as a dumpling, with a pink, smooth face, light blue eyes and a great habit of puffing when he exerted himself a little, which came, Simon said, from overeating. They had been boys together more than thirty years ago in a little Ontario town, and now they were partners, timber-looking, prospecting and bartering and saving a little money as the years went on. Herman was a widower, and his only daughter, Geertruda, had married Jeremie Poulin back in Quebec, and Jeremie was a cousin of the Clamarts and lived now at Five Fingers. It was Herman's first visit. He had come to see the new baby and had brought Simon along with him.

The instant Simon's shrewd eyes came upon the clearing and the little settlement, with the fingers of water reaching in from the big lake, he began having thoughts which he did not at once announce to Herman.

The years had brought changes to Five Fingers. The single-room cabins which Pierre and Dominique had built were gone, and in their places stood larger buildings of clean-cut and nicely squared logs, with flowers and garden plots around them, and rows of smooth stones painted white. Josette, now almost forty, was still slim and pretty, and Pierre was more than ever her lover, in spite of a great disappointment which he kept shut up in his own heart. He wanted children. His love for them was a passion, but for him stalwart young Joe, now fourteen years old, was the first and the last. Pierre had implicit faith in prayer, and ever since that first summer at Five Fingers he had prayed devoutly that God might send more children.

And God answered, though somewhere there was a slip that puzzled Pierre, for the more he prayed the more children came to Dominique and Marie. First there was a pair of them, Louis and Julie, then three singles as regularly as could be—Aimé and Félipe and Dominique— and with each one of them Marie grew plumper and jollier and began questing about in her head for a name to be given the next.

But Pierre was happy, for if they were not entirely his own there were at least children all about him. Poleon and Sara Dufresne had come with three children and had built their cabin a stone's throw away; Jeremie and Geertruda had a baby, and at the edge of the green bit of meadow which he had pointed out to Josette five years ago were the homes of Jean Croisset and Telesphore Clamart, and Aleck Clamart was courting Anne Croisset. With Pierre he was secretly making plans for a home the following year, after one more season of trapping.

And right at the tip of the evergreen forest, where Pierre had promised, was the little log church in which they gathered each Sunday, and to which Father Albanel, a wandering minister of the forests, came once and sometimes twice a month.

As the population had grown, so had the clearing expanded. There were a good dozen acres or more under careful tillage, and in the open were cattle and several horses, and in every wild meadow for miles about a stack of harvested hay in season. There were chickens and geese and a community flock of turkeys, and at all seasons plenty of eggs and milk and cream and the sweet butter, and the dug-out cellars were filled to the brim with good things to eat when the first cold blasts of winter came. Pierre and Aleck had built a boat, and the six families had combined in the purchase of two nets, so there was no lack of fish either winter or summer at Five Fingers.

For two winters, much against his desire, young Joe had been sent back over the new Canadian Pacific to attend school at Ste. Anne.

Simon McQuarrie made note of all these things with the judgment of a fox and the keenness of a weasel. No one would have judged Simon for what he really was, at least not on short acquaintance. In him was a heart so honest he would have cut off a little finger before taking a mean advantage of any other man or woman. But, as Herman put it, he was always looking around to see what he could pick up. Herman furnished the laughter, the jollity, the never-ending good humor and four-fifths of the stomach of the partnership, and Simon was the ferret who smelled out the dollars; so when Simon said one day, "I never knew a better place than this for a little mill, Herman," the proud grandfather of baby Tobina knew something was in the air.

First of all, with his native shrewdness, Simon took stock of the happiness at Five Fingers. This contentment, the community affection which brought all together like members of one family, was a big asset in the very beginning. The mill itself could be made a sort of family

JAMES OLIVER CURWOOD

affair, and a boat arranged for twice or three times a year to run up from Duluth or Fort William and carry away the lumber. There was enough fine birch and cedar and spruce right about them to keep going for years, and the mill would bring even greater prosperity than trapping, which was sure to wear out now that the settlements were filling up rapidly along the line of the railroad.

At last he talked over the matter with Pierre, and Pierre called in Dominique, and there was a meeting of all the men-folk of the families at which it was agreed nothing could be finer for Five Fingers than a mill. Simon promised the first thing to be made from its lumber should be a schoolhouse, and they would have to see to it the schoolhouse had a teacher, for if Dominique and Jeremie and Poleon kept up the pace they were going there surely must be teaching at Five Fingers.

This was on Saturday. The next day Father Albanel came, a little, gray-haired, rosy-cheeked man who loved life and all living things, and who had no settled church because he saw in nature a greater God than he had ever been able to find in the Book written by man, a freedom of thought which had been labeled heresy by those who traveled the old and unchangeable paths. But Father Albanel was loved by every man, woman and child who knew him, and while his stricter brethren chanted and prayed in their vaulted cathedrals and little mission houses, his Church was ten thousand square miles of forest land. And on this Sunday Father Albanel prayed that Simon McQuarrie might be able to keep his promises.

So the mill came. There was not much to it, but when on a certain September afternoon a tug and a scow came creeping up the middle inlet every soul in Five Fingers was down to meet them, and every heart was beating with the biggest excitement that had ever come into the lives of Pierre and his people. With the tug came Simon McQuarrie, proud as an admiral in command of a fleet, and with him a Norwegian engineer and his wife, two mill-hands, and a sallow-faced, anemic-looking young man who was to teach Jeremie Poulin's children and Dominique's kindergarten during the winter for fifteen dollars a month and board.

The mill was set up, with only pieces of tarpaulin for roof at first. Axes rang merrily in the woods, and the three horses at Five Fingers dragged in the logs at the ends of chains. Even the women were excited, and the children waited eagerly for the set day when smoke would pour from the tall boiler stack and the saws would begin to hum and grind.

This happened on the fifth day, and when at last steam was up, and the long belt began to turn, and the big, shining saw to whirl, there rose a great hurrah, and even Baby Tobina waved her tiny fists and crowed as loudly as she could. Then the sharp teeth of the saw touched the end of the first log, and there came the first of that beautiful, droning song—the song of live steel cutting through sweet wood—which was to last for many years at Five Fingers, and which may be heard at times to this very day.

No one, not even his sweetheart wife, Josette, was permitted to look deeply and completely into the heart of Pierre. As time passed he saw his beloved forest dragged in, a log at a time, to be cut into pieces by that droning, merciless saw. He watched the life's blood of the timber pile up in great golden heaps of sweet-smelling sawdust in which the growing children loved to play, and down on the shore he saw his wilderness garnered in huge piles of boards, waiting for the little black tugs to come in and drag them away. He knew that it was all as it should be, for new prosperity came with the mill, more comforts and happiness for the women and children, and a few more people to Five Fingers. This was progress. Yet an ache was in his heart which he kept to himself, and which would never quite die away. For with a passion next to his love for children he loved his forests, and with him every tree was a word of God.

Yet he would not have changed conditions, for he knew it was himself who was wrong. Everything told him that. Even the wild things seemed to love this more intimate companionship with man, for the birds and squirrels were never more numerous about Five Fingers. They sang and chattered with the music of the mill, ran over the roofs of the houses and built their nests under the eaves, and in winter came to the very doorsteps to eat crumbs and grain thrown out for them. It was Pierre whose word was unwritten law at Five Fingers. One of his laws was that no living thing that was not a pest should ever be harmed near the settlement, and when ice and snow were heavy in the hills and between the ridges deer came out shyly to eat with the cattle.

Pierre went no more on the trap line but attended to the business of the mill, and Josette pleased him by saying this made her happiness complete. In spare hours one could always find children about him, and in the evenings, when the droning of the mill saw had ceased, there were games and races and fun among the sawdust piles, and never a day passed that the home of Pierre and Josette was not filled with childish laughter and the patter of little feet, although the little girl they prayed for never came to bear their name. "But she will," said Pierre, keeping up that undying hope in his heart. "Some day, my Josette, there will come a little girl to be a sister to Joe."

Even Joe, his one child, seemed to be getting farther away from him, for as time passed the boy needed no urging to return to Ste. Anne, but was restless and ill at ease when back home from school, and was excited when the day drew near that would take him from Five Fingers again. He was eighteen when Josette learned his secret, and she laughed softly, and kissed him, and told Pierre so that he would not worry any more. The girl was none other than Marie Antoinette, the beautiful little daughter of Jacques Thiebout, whom they had known years ago on the St. Lawrence. She was a year younger than Joe, and had told him he must wait until she had finished completely with the school of Ste. Anne de la Perade, for that was her ambition, and her father's, too. Then she would come with him to Five Fingers.

Tears of joy filled Pierre's eyes the night Josette whispered the secret to him, for if the little girl they both wanted persisted in not coming they would at least have grandsons and granddaughters to make up for it.

"And it may be this is the answer to my prayers," Pierre said to himself. "For Joe's children will be of our own flesh and blood, and we shall love Marie Antoinette as our own. And as Joe is younger and stronger than Dominique, who is growing fat, I do not see why he should fall behind him in the matter of family."

Few changes came to Five Fingers as the years rolled on. The little mill continued to hum and the axes to ring farther and farther back in the forest, and twice or three times in a season the boat came up with loads of supplies and carried away the lumber.

Not a single year did the stork fail to build his nest somewhere about the sawdust piles. Twice he visited Aleck Clamart, who married Anne Croisset; two little Dutchmen he brought to Geertruda Poulin, and there were nine pairs of feet to shoe in the home of Dominique and Marie when young Joe Gourdon brought Marie Antoinette to Five Fingers as his wife.

The mill did not run that day, for it was a day of feasting and rejoicing, and all the world held no prouder monarch than Joe. Marie Antoinette, tall and slim, with her great dark eyes, her glad smile and her outreaching arms of love for the people who had now become her own, was as sweet and beautiful as his mother had been in the days of her youth. And Pierre, in his joy, found in her a rival, for the children gathered round her in dumb worship, and in her pretty arms Marie Antoinette gathered every one, kissing each in turn, even to bashful Louis, the eldest son of Dominique. And when, in their cabin, she flung those same pretty arms around Josette's neck and called her Mother, Pierre winked hard and went outside to puff at his pipe, for he felt like a boy who wanted to cry.

God had been good to him. God had blessed Five Fingers. In the going down of the sun his eyes rested upon a green slope where no plow had touched and no cabin had been built. Religiously that sacred little plot had been held for the time when death might find its way among them. And death had not come. Gratitude welled up in Pierre's heart and choked him—gratitude and pride and faith, for all this was the handiwork of the great and good God he believed in, the God of his forests, the open, the sun and the sky. And the thought came to him that when at last there was a break in the little green slope it was only right that he should be the first to go, for God had filled his measure to the brim, and it seemed to him he could hear the whisper of a message from the violets and red roses of that little knoll in the setting of the sun.

Marie Antoinette, coming to him so quietly he did not hear, put her little hand in his and whispered, "It is beautiful here, my father!"

III

As long as men remain to tell the story of the Inland Seas the great autumn storm of 1900 will not be forgotten. It has been set down as a matter of history, and a hundred tales could be told of the ships that went down and the men who died in those days when the Five Lakes were like five mighty churns, whipping and tossing their waters in maelstroms of destruction.

It was not cold. A part of the time the sun shone brightly, and back in the woods from the Superior shore birds sang, and flowers still bloomed. To Pierre and his people this was of strange and mysterious portent, for though they had seen many storms at Five Fingers there had never been one like this, with that terrific roar of enraged waters against rock walls and birds preening themselves and chirping in the sunshine of the forest.

On the second day Pierre took Josette and Marie Antoinette down to the tip of the wooded peninsula that lay between the Second and Middle Finger that they might see the lake as they had never seen it before. It was fun for the women. The wind choked them at times, and they had to scream to be heard, and it whipped their long hair loose until they were like panting naiads, clinging to Pierre's hands, their eyes shining and their hearts thrilled with the excitement of the adventure. Pierre, laughing, told Josette she was as lovely as a girl with her shining hair all about her in a windblown tangle and her cheeks as pink and soft as Marie Antoinette's. But he was only half heard, for the seas were roaring among the rocks below them like the steady thunder of countless guns.

When they came out of the last rim of sheltering spruce and looked beyond the black and dripping rampart of rock that held back the raging waters Josette clung to him in sudden fear, and Marie Antoinette gave a cry that cut like a knife above the wind.

Pierre's heart went dead and still as he stared gray-faced out to sea. There was a twist on his lips where laughter suddenly died.

Out from the shore lay an entanglement of reef and rock, jutting up like great heads of sea-monsters in the quiet and calm of summer, a resting-place for gulls, and strangely quiet and beautiful at times when the water rippled between them in wide paths of green silver. Through this network of waiting traps ran the channel in which the tug made her way to and from the Middle Finger. But there was no channel today. It was lost in a fury of thundering flood, lashing itself into ribbons, and among the rocks, half a mile from where Pierre and his women stood, a ship was beating herself to pieces.

In his first moment of horror Pierre knew they had come just in time to see the end. She was a schooner of possibly three hundred tons, and had plunged broadside upon the long, low reef which Josette herself had named the Dragon because of the jagged teeth of rock which rose from it like the spines of a huge fin. Her tall masts were gone. A mass of wreckage tangled her deck, and Pierre fancied that even above the roar of the surf he could hear the crash of her rending timbers as she rose and fell in mighty sledge-hammer blows upon the reef. As he waited, struck dumb with horror, the vessel was raised half out of the sea, and when she fell back her stern split asunder and the foaming water engulfed her until only her bow was held up by the projecting spines of the Dragon.

Marie Antoinette cried out again, and her face was waxlike in its fear and horror, for very clearly in that moment they saw a moving figure in the bow of the ship. In an instant the figure was inundated and gone.

Life leaped back into Pierre.

"If any live they may sweep into this pit of the Middle Finger," he shouted. "We must help them." Then he turned to Marie Antoinette and placed his mouth close to her ear. "Go back," he cried. "Go back and bring help as swiftly as you can!"

Scarcely were the words spoken when Marie Antoinette was gone with the quickness of a bird, her long hair streaming about her like a veil as she ran. Pierre looked at Josette. She was not frightened now. Her face was white and calm and her eyes were pools of steady fire. She was looking on death. She could almost hear the cries of death. Her glance met Pierre's, and her lips moved, but he did not hear her words. It was then, looking again toward what little remained of the schooner, that they saw something sweeping in toward them among the nearer reefs. It came swiftly, now almost submerged, then popping up for an instant, and was swept at last upon a rock where the waters split like a mill race at the very edge of the smoother sea that ran through the mouth of the Middle Finger.

"It is a raft," shouted Pierre, "and someone is on it!"

Josette's cry rose shrill and piercing:

"It is a woman!"

　　　　　　　　　　　　　　　　　JAMES OLIVER CURWOOD

They could see the figure flung upon the rock, with a hand clutching at its slippery sides, and Pierre's breath came in a sudden gasp of despair when he saw it was a woman. Her face was a ghost's face in the surf mist, and her drenched hair streamed upon the rock as the water ebbed away. She seemed to see them as they stood at the cliff edge, and Pierre thought he heard her voice rise faintly above the thunder of the water, crying out for her life.

He turned and ran to a ragged break in the cliff and climbed down swiftly to the narrow shore line at the edge of the Finger, shouting for Josette to remain where she was. But Josette was close behind him when he began tearing off his clothes. She was terribly white. Blood streaked one of her soft cheeks where she had stumbled against a sharp-edged rock coming down. But her eyes were filled with a strange and unchanging fire, and she fell upon her knees among the stones to unlace one of Pierre's boots while he freed himself of the other. She looked up at him. A glory of strength shone in her face even as her heart was breaking in its agony. For she knew that Pierre Gourdon, her husband, was going into the pit of death; and she tried to smile, and Pierre kissed her lips swiftly and sprang into the sea.

She stood up straight and watched him as he fought his way through the shore surf toward the seething maelstrom where the woman lay upon the rock. Josette could see her clearly. She could see the water and white spume leaping up about her, reaching for her, thrusting her up and then dragging her back, and almost she prayed that God would take her and cover her completely with the sea so that Pierre might turn back. For a little her courage left her and she called wildly upon Pierre to return, telling him she was his wife and that the woman on the rock was nothing to him. And then the woman who was fighting for her life seemed to look into the eyes of Josette through the distance that separated them—and Josette held out her arms and cried encouragement to her.

All sound but the roar of water was lost to Pierre. He was swimming now, and a hundred forces dragged at his body, beating him one way and then the other, while with all his strength he fought to keep himself in the right direction. He knew what it meant to be carried beyond the rock into that deadly place which they called the Pit. There he would die. He would be pulled down by the undertows, and a little later, when they were done with him, his body would be thrown up at the foot of the cliff. The thought did not fill him with fear. It gave him strength to know Josette was watching him in this struggle against death, and that she was praying for him—and for the woman on the rock.

Only Josette and the other woman could measure the eternity of time it took him to win the fight. In the last moment a mighty hand seemed to gather him in its palm and sweep him up to the rock, and he found himself clinging to it, facing the woman. She was as white as he had seen Josette. Her eyes were as dark, and there was something in them that was more terrible to look at than fear. Pierre was exhausted. He drew himself up a few inches at a time, trying to smile the encouragement he could not speak. His eyes reached the level of the rock, and he looked over and down—and saw then what it was the woman was holding in the crook of her arm.

It was a little girl, six or seven years old, and forgetting in his amazement the thundering menace of the sea Pierre thought that in all his life he had never seen anything so beautiful as this child. She was not hurt. Her eyes were wide open—great, dark eyes that were velvety pools of terror—and her face, lovely as an angel's, looked at him from a mass of jet-black hair that dripped with water and clung about her neck and shoulders like silken strands of seaweed. It was as if a vision had crept up from the foaming surf to taunt him, a vision of a face he had painted in his dreams and had prayed for and hoped for all through the years of his life, and he dashed the water from his eyes to see more clearly. Then he reached down and drew the child to him and held her fragile, slim little body in his arms. The woman's face changed then. Its fierce resolution died out. She became suddenly limp, and seeing her weakness Pierre caught hold of her so that the surf would not beat her from the rock.

"I will get you ashore," he shouted. "You must not give up! You must hold to the rock!"

He bent his face to the child's.

"And you—"

She lay against his breast. Her eyes were looking up at him steadily, and words choked in Pierre's throat. Those eyes, it seemed to him, were too beautiful for a child's eyes. Her lips were still red. But her face was the color of a white cameo in its frame of wonderful black hair, and the thought came to him again that it was an angel the storm had blown in from the sea.

The woman was drawing herself up beside him. Another wave broke against the rock, smothering them in its surf. Out of it came her voice.

JAMES OLIVER CURWOOD

"I am Mona Guyon," she cried, so close that her head touched his shoulder. "This is my baby. Her father—went down—there—beside the rock—a few minutes ago. Take her ashore—"

A roaring flood inundated them. When it was gone Pierre drew in a deep breath.

"You must hold to the rock," he shouted again. "I will come back for you. It will be easy—easy for all of us to get ashore—if you will hold to the rock!"

When the roar of the surf died away for a moment he told the child what to do. She must put her arms round his neck and ride ashore on his back and draw in deep breaths whenever her face was out of the water. They would swim to the shore very quickly, and then he would come back for mother. He even laughed as he told her how safely and quickly it could be done. And then he kissed her; there on the rock Pierre Gourdon kissed the soft little mouth he had prayed for so many years, and bowed his head a moment, asking God to help him. Then he lay flat on his face and drew her into just the right place on his back, and when her arms were round his neck he tied her hands tightly together under his chin with a strip which he had torn from his shirt. She could not get away after that. They would go ashore together, one way or the other.

Slowly he lowered himself over the slippery lee of the rock, and again he smiled at Mona Guyon. The hour of his Calvary had come, and his heart beat fiercely with the strength of two praying women as he slipped into the sea with his precious burden. The twisting undercurrents reached out like the tentacles of an octopus and tried to drag him into the doom of the Pit. But it was not Pierre Gourdon alone who was fighting for the right to live. The woman on the rock was fighting for him, and the woman ashore—standing to her waist in the boiling surf—no longer had heart or soul or strength of body, for all had gone to him; and about his neck were the arms of a child that gave to him the courage, not only of those who loved and prayed, but of the good God who had called upon him to play his part in this day and hour.

So he fought, and won at last to the place where his beloved Josette reached out and caught him and helped him to the stony shore, where he sank down weakly, with the child in his arms and her face looking up at him from his breast. He had kept her above the water—that had been the never faltering thought in his mind; and now there seemed to be something of awe, of reverence, of unspoken worship in those strangely beautiful eyes of l'Ange, as Pierre called her in his heart, and suddenly her arms tightened round his neck and with a little cry she kissed him.

Then she was in Josette's arms, and Pierre rose to his feet.

A sudden dread swept over him as he looked out at the rock again. It seemed to him the seas were higher, and the woman was not as he had left her. Her face was down, she was limp, a dark blot without life or resistance, and he saw a huge wave drive up and move her like a sodden chip a little nearer to the edge of the Pit. She was not *holding on*, as he had prayed God she would! A few more waves like that last one, a taller crest, an angrier thrust from the sea—and she would go.

He turned to Josette. She was on her knees among the sharp stones with her arms about the child, and both she and little Mona were looking up at him, waiting, knowing that only Pierre Gourdon was master of himself and of life and death in this hour. He had never seen such eyes as theirs—Josette's in their agony of fear for him, little Mona's so strangely, gloriously beautiful, saying more to him in their childish terror and entreaty than human lips could have spoken.

"I am going back," he said. "It will be easy this time!"

They heard him above the smashing fury of the Pit, and Pierre, catching an unknown note in his own voice, knew that he was lying. As he faced the beat of the sea he made as if he did not hear Josette calling wildly to him that help would surely come in a few minutes, and he must wait. A few minutes and it would be over, for he could see that with each thrust of the frothing surf over the crest of the rock the woman was a little nearer to death.

It was a harder fight this time. At least it seemed so to Pierre, for the old strength was no longer in his limbs, and something seemed to have gone out of his heart. If he could reach the rock, just reach it and cling to it and hold the woman until Marie Antoinette's message brought the men! That was all he prayed for now, all he hoped for. It was inconceivable for his imagination to go beyond those things—the rock, the woman, a jutting tooth of reef to hang to for their lives. He could feel death all about him as he fought and swam. It struck at him, choked him, blinded him, dragged at his breath until it seemed as if he must give up and go riding with it into the maelstroms of the Pit. It laughed and jeered at him and roared in his ears, but through it all he saw the rock, and at last the same strange current caught him with the force of a gargantuan hand and flung him to it.

He tried to climb up, and slipped back. He tried again and again, and then began to make it, an inch at a time. Something was singing in his ears. It was like the droning hum of the saw in the mill. For a moment he rested. He could not see the top of the rock, but he could see the shore, and there were many figures on it now—men running down to where Josette was again standing waist-deep in the water.

With new courage he pulled himself up, and then he gave a cry—a madman's cry of horror, fear and futile warning. The woman had slipped to the very edge of the rock—the edge that lipped the fury of the Pit. She was half over. And she was slipping—*slipping*. . .

He scrambled toward her, flinging himself down the treacherous dip to catch at her long hair. He caught a strand of it, but it pulled away from him—and he thrust himself another foot and buried his fingers in the wet mass of it. In that moment the sea took her. It dragged her down, and Pierre, holding fast to her hair, went with her into the black death of the Pit; and as he went his wide eyes saw once more the blue of the sky and the tops of his beloved forests, and out of his soul came a soundless cry, the faith and gratitude of a man who was not afraid to die, "After all—God has been a long time good to me—Pierre Gourdon!"

Even then, in that roaring baptism of death, his mind was on the woman. It would not do to let her body beat itself among the rocks alone, and in some way—as they were twisted and torn by the rending currents—he got his arms about her. He made no effort to fight, except to hold her. To fight against the forces which had him in their power was impossible. He was like a chip in a boiling pot, twisted and turned, now thrust downward and then up, but never far enough to snatch a breath of air. He felt the blows of the rocks. Then he began going down, until it seemed in the last moment that he was falling swiftly through illimitable space. Consciousness of the woman's presence was gone, but he still held her in his arms.

Only the strong hands of Joe Gourdon and Simon McQuarrie held Josette from joining her husband in the heart of the Pit. She struggled against them, crying out her right to go to him, until they brought her to the narrow rim of beach under the cliff and her eyes fell on little Mona. The wind had blown the child's wet hair back from her face, and a bitter cry came to Josette's lips and resentment burned in her for an instant like a fire. Pierre was gone because of *her*, because of this beautiful, star-eyed child and the woman! They had taken him from her. And here was the child, living, staring at her with those eyes which had made Pierre call her *l'Ange*—staring at her—while Pierre—and the other woman—dead and beaten among the rocks. . . And then. . .

"*My mother!*"

It was the child's voice, two words crying out to her, faint and yearning and filled with agony above the lash of the sea, and with an answering cry Josette fell down sobbing upon her knees and opened her arms and held the little stranger tightly against her breast. For a space after that she was blind to what happened about her. Dominique stood between her and the sea, even as he saw the grim joke which the fiends of the Pit were playing upon them this day. For these fiends were seldom known to give up their playthings, whether logs or sticks or living things. Once he had known them to keep the body of a dog for days, and at another time a strong-limbed buck had died there, and it was a week before they had tired of him and had thrown him ashore. But this day there was a change. Joe Gourdon and Jeremie Poulin and Poleon Dufresne had leaped waist-deep into the surf and were bringing out the bodies of Pierre and the woman!

It was Marie Antoinette who knelt beside them first, and unclasped Pierre's arms from about the woman. And then Josette saw them. She staggered to her feet and ran past Dominique, and the first she looked upon was the white, dead face of the mother. Very tenderly then she took Pierre's head in her arms, and bent her own over it until both their faces were shrouded in her long hair.

"He isn't dead," she whispered. No one heard her, for she was saying it only to herself, and then to Pierre. "He isn't dead. He isn't dead." She repeated the words, swaying her body gently with Pierre, and the others drew back, and Marie Antoinette hid little Mona's face against her while Simon McQuarrie and Telesphore Clamart bore the dead woman between them round the end of the cliff. And Josette kept repeating, "He isn't dead, he isn't dead," and she kissed Pierre's lips, and pressed her cheek against his cheek, and the women and men of Five Fingers stood back and waited, none daring to be first to break in upon these sacred moments which belonged to Josette and her dead.

At last Marie Antoinette came up softly and knelt beside Josette and put a loving hand about her shoulder. Josette's eyes turned to look at her and they were soft and glowing and so strange they frightened Marie Antoinette. "He isn't dead," she was still saying, and she bowed her face down again to Pierre's.

Choking the sob in her throat, Marie Antoinette put her hand to Josette's face—and a great shock ran through her. She had touched Pierre's cheek. She felt with her other hand, and drew back Josette's hair, her heart suddenly throbbing like an Indian drum. Then she saw it was not the madness of grief that kept Josette repeating those words, but the intuition of a soul which had felt the nearness of its mate, for Pierre's eyes slowly opened and the first vision which came to him out of a roaring sea of dreams was the face of his wife.

From the group of tensely waiting people Mona had come, sobbing in a strange, quiet way for her mother, and as Marie Antoinette drew a little back Josette caught the child close to her, along with Pierre, and as Pierre reached his arms up weakly to them both the thought came to him again, "*God has been a long time good to me—Pierre Gourdon!*"

IV

It was the blue jay that mellowed the fear of death in the swiftly beating heart of Peter McRae. He had always been a friend of the blue jays, and this particular bird had perched himself in a spruce top a hundred feet away, screaming defiance at Peter's enemies and telling him to keep up his nerve and not be afraid.

Without going beyond his fourteen-year-old power of reasoning Peter had a strange and abiding faith in the Canadian blue jay tribe. He was a boy's bird, if there ever was one, with his everlasting cocksureness, his persevering courage and his hundred and one little tricks of outlawry and piracy—a bird who was always ready for a fight, never ran away from trouble, and who lived up beautifully to the man-made law, "Do others before others do you." He was a gentleman and a sportsman even if he was a robber and a pest, and Peter loved him.

He could see this particular blue jay very clearly. Shouting voices and the crack of rifles had not frightened him away, and he was making a great commotion in the spruce tops, screaming until it seemed his raucous cries must split his throat. Then, too, there was the cheerful little sapsucker who persisted in pecking for grubs in the end of the big log behind which Peter and his father were hidden, and two newly mated red squirrels who chattered and ran up and down a tree a little farther on, one chasing the other. A big yellow butterfly slowly opened and closed its fan-like wings almost within reach of Peter's hand.

These things kept the madness of utter fear out of the boy's brain. His thin, rather frail face was very white; his blue eyes were round, and staring; his body, not so strong as it should have been, was doubled up behind the log, and his heart throbbed like a hammer inside him—but his courage was not gone. There were no tear stains about his eyes. In one of his hands he clutched a twisted stick.

From the blue jay and the sapsucker and the yellow butterfly his eyes rested upon the face of Donald McRae, his father. That father, so far back as Peter could remember clearly, had been not only a father, but mother and brother and pal as well. "One thing you must live up to all your life, Peter," this father had told him a hundred times, "and that is to be a pal to your own boy when you have one, just as you are now a pal of your dad's. If a dad and his boy are not pals they shouldn't have been born." So they had been that, with no secrets between them except one that had led up to this tragedy of today, and which the boy had not yet begun to understand. All he knew was that for some mysterious reason they were fighting for their lives, and were now sheltered behind a log, and that men a little distance away were watching and waiting to kill them with guns.

The man smiled at him and chuckled in a way Peter loved. But the smile and the chuckle did not hide the flame smoldering deep in his eyes, nor the pallid tenseness of his face, nor the trickle of blood that persisted in running down his cheek and wetting the soft roll of his collar. He was bareheaded and sweaty; his blond hair, very much like Peter's, was wildly disheveled; his hands gripped a gun, and lying on his stomach, he had made himself a loophole by digging leaves and mold from under a crooked elbow in the log. Through this he had watched for his enemies. His grin was chummy and companionable as he turned to Peter.

"Everything all right?" he asked. "Not afraid, are you?"

Peter shook his head. "I'm not much scared."

"Getting hungry?"

"No."

"Thirsty?"

"A little—not much."

The man laughed. He did not feel like laughing. But he laughed, fighting to make it appear natural and unstrained.

"You're a trump, Peter. God knows you're a trump!"

A rifle cracked in the thick fringe of balsams and jack pines a hundred and fifty yards from them, and a bullet struck the log with a sodden *chug*. The man wiped the blood from his cheek with a handkerchief that was stained red.

"Does it hurt, dad?"

"Nothing but a scratch, Peter."

He put his face to the ground and peered under the log again.

Peter changed his position, uncramped his legs and doubled himself up in another fashion, hugging the earth closely. The blue jay was having a fit, and the sapsucker perked his bright-eyed little head at him not more than a dozen feet away. He could hear a bird singing, and one of the red squirrels was chattering his late afternoon song in a mountain ash tree overhanging the river. Between his knees was a clump of violets.

The log was almost at the edge of the river, which was a swollen flood, and the stream bent itself around like a hairpin, shutting them in on three sides. That was why they were safe, Peter's father had told him. No living thing could swim it to get behind them, and in front of them was a narrow neck of land which was open and clear right up to the thick edge of the swamp a rifle shot away. Across that open no one had dared to come.

A dozen times during the past hour Peter had wished the river was not there, for it held them prisoners even if it did keep their enemies back. Across it, not much farther away than he could have thrown a stone, was a deep, dense forest of primeval darkness, low and swampy, in which he conceived a thousand hiding-places for himself and his father. Peter's mind sometimes traveled beyond his years, and as he looked at the stream, yearning for the safety of the other side, he wondered why the blue jay and the sapsucker and the singing brush sparrow should have wings while they had only legs and arms.

Only wings could carry them over the stream. In the dry months of summer it was not much more than a creek, with sand bars and pebbly shores and polished rocks sticking out of it. Now, in this flood time of spring, it had no shores and was a thing gone mad. It was deep and black, and swept past with a steady, growling roar, eating into the banks on its way, uprooting trees and slashing itself into caldrons of boiling fury where the channel narrowed or where it leaped over the great boulders and rock débris of rapids. From where he crouched Peter could see one of these places a quarter of a mile below, and there the water was not black but white, and leaped and spouted as if huge monsters were churning it. Under ordinary conditions the swollen stream would have lured and fascinated him. It came out of a vast and mysterious Canadian wilderness, and it disappeared into an adventure land of forests equally vast and strange. With it rode many things of interest—huge piles of driftwood, shooting down on the crest of the flood like islands; big logs that sped with the swiftness of monster serpents; and great trees, freshly torn out by the roots, and with their tops trailing and swishing like whips urging on a living thing.

Peter was staring at it when a hand rested itself gently on his head. Donald McRae was watching him, and a slow torture had burned itself like the scar of a living coal in his eyes and face. More than the earth he walked upon and more than the God he believed in, he loved this boy. It was Peter, with his thin, quizzical face, and his mind and courage developed beyond his strength and years, who had made life bearable and joyous for him. As he had worshiped the mother, linking his soul with hers until it had been taken away, so he worshiped this one precious part of her she had left to him. Without Peter. . .

He choked back the thickness in his throat as he placed his hand on the boy's head. It was a habit with him to talk with Peter at times as if he were a man, and the man-way in which Peter's eyes met his now gave him courage.

"They won't try to cross that open before dark," he said. "They're afraid of us in the light, Peter. But they'll come when it's dark. And we can't wait for them. We've got to get away."

The boy's face brightened. He had a consummate faith in this father of his. He waited, keenly expectant, twisting one of the blue violets between his thin fingers.

"Does the creek frighten you, son?" asked the man.

"It's pretty swift, but I'm not much scared of it."

"Of course not. You wouldn't be your dad's boy, if you were. See that log down there, the big dry one, half in the water?" He pointed, and Peter nodded. "When it begins to get dusk we'll crawl down and take a ride on that. It won't be hard to get away."

For the first time a tremor came in the boy's voice.

"Dad, what are they trying to shoot us for? What have we done?"

Donald McRae made a pretense of peering through his loophole again. He wanted to cry out with the sickness that was in his heart, and in the same voice call down the vengeance of God upon the makers of that grim and merciless law which at last had come to corner and destroy him where he had built his little cabin home in the edge of the wilderness. It was impossible—now—to answer that question of Peter's, "*What have we done?*"

He raised his head, and faced his boy.

"It's five o'clock. We'd better have a bite to eat. When we take to the water it will spoil our grub."

From the pocket of a coat which lay at his side he took some biscuits and meat. Peter made a sandwich and munched at it, yearning for a little of the black river-water to go with it. When the man had finished he drew from an inside pocket of the same coat a wallet, a pencil and a corked bottle half filled with matches. In the wallet he found a sheet of paper, and on this he wrote for several minutes, after which he folded the sheet of paper very tightly, thrust it into the bottle with the matches, and corked it in securely. Then he gave the bottle to Peter.

"Put that in your pocket," he said, "and remember what I'm telling you now, Peter. We're going to make for a place called Five Fingers. A man lives there whose name is Simon McQuarrie. Don't forget those two—Five Fingers and Simon McQuarrie. What I have written and put in the bottle is for him. If anything should happen to me—" He broke in upon himself with a cheerful laugh. "Of course nothing *will* happen, Peter, but if it should—you promise to take that bottle to him?"

"I'll take it."

"Where?"

"Five Fingers."

"Who?"

"Simon McQuarrie."

"Right. Now keep watch through this hole while I cut some leather strings out of the tops of my boots. We may need them to harness the log with when we go to sea. Won't they be surprised when they come and find us gone—eh—Peter?"

"You bet they will!" agreed Peter fervently.

Quietly he began watching the open through the hole which his father had made under the log. He breathed a little more tensely, for he realized the deadly importance of his vigil. Yesterday one of his ambitions had been to wear a uniform when he was old enough, one with stripes and brass buttons, and with a big revolver fastened to a cord hung around his neck. He had looked upon the wilderness police with the awe of a youngster who loved romance and adventure. Today he hated them. Only a little while ago he had waited for his father at their cabin, with a good dinner ready for him. Then his father had come, galloping on a horse Peter had never seen before.

"I've had a little trouble with the police, Peter, and we've got to hit into the woods," he had said.

The suddenness of it had taken Peter's breath away. They did not wait to eat any of the dinner he had prepared. Even then the police almost caught them before they reached this log. There were four of them. His father had kept them back with his rifle, and Peter was disappointed in his marksmanship. He was sure he could have done better himself. His father missed every time, even though his bullets did go close enough to make their enemies dodge behind trees. And always before that he had been proud of his father's shooting!

His hand touched the cool barrel of the rifle, and a thrill ran through him. It was a thing he had never felt before. He was sure *he* would not miss if he could only be given a chance, for he had often hit rabbits at that distance of a hundred and fifty yards, and a man was many times larger than a rabbit. An inch at a time, slowly and carefully so that his father would not notice what he was doing, he poked the barrel of the rifle through the hole. He would be ready, anyway. He had forgotten fear. His blood was hot. His father had always talked to him about playing square, and never taking a mean advantage, and always to fight for women, no matter who they were. Well, there were no women here, but it wasn't playing square when four men came after his father like this. If they would come out, clean and sportsmanlike, one at a time, and fight with fists instead of guns. . .

"You see, Peter," his father was saying as he cut a thin strip from his boot top, "I couldn't leave you in the cabin alone. I've got to get you down to Five Fingers. If Simon McQuarrie isn't there, you wait for him. And don't show anyone else that paper in the bottle!"

Peter was not listening. His heart had given a sudden terrific jump and was half choking him. In the edge of a clump of dwarf banksians something had moved. And then his father turned—just in time to catch his hand, to stop his finger at the trigger, to drag him back from the hole. Never as long as he lived would he forget the terrible look that had come into his father's face. To hide it Donald McRae leaned over his son and hugged him close to his arms, and for a space the law might have descended upon them without resistance.

From the shelter of the evergreens Corporal Crear of the Provincial Police was looking toward the log. His men were lying close about him.

"We've got to go out and get him when it's dark enough," he said. "Don't shoot unless you have to, but if that happens—shoot straight. Only be sure it's not the kid. That's what puzzles me—why McRae has the kid with him out there behind the log!"

Only Donald McRae and Peter could have solved that mystery for Crear, and even then Crear might not have understood. It was something which belonged entirely to Peter and his father. As they waited for the sun to dip behind the tall evergreen forest across the river, they lay very close together, and their eyes met frequently and their hands and bodies touched.

There was something pathetically doglike in the man's dependence upon his boy. Take Peter away from him and his heart was gone, for Peter was the one thing he had left of a great faith and a great love that would never die. More than once a cold fear had swept over him at the thought of something happening to him, and he had always prayed that if anything did happen, it would come to both at the same time. Even now he would not have sent Peter back to the safety of the cabin. That would have meant dissolution for himself—and strangers and a heartbreaking tragedy of aloneness for Peter.

Across the river there was hope, and a refuge for Peter at Five Fingers with Simon McQuarrie. A woman had put an undying faith in the justness of God in Donald McRae's soul, and always there were two things in his breast, faith and memory of the woman, like stars which no darkness could dim. Their glow lay warmly in his eyes as he saw the courage with which the boy waited for the setting of the sun.

As the long shadows came creeping across the river Peter no longer felt the fear which had made his heart beat so uncomfortably fast. His father's presence and the touch of his hand filled him with an utter confidence. The man even pointed out to him the mysteries of an ant home which they had accidentally destroyed in the log, and told him a story of how once upon a time he had gone down a flooded stream like this, and what fun it had been.

Then the shadows came more swiftly. The sun at last left only a golden glow above the forest. The blue jay and the sapsucker were gone. Out of the woods came the melodious dusk song of many red squirrels. A flock of crows sailed overhead on their way to the evening roosting place. The rush of the river seemed more gentle and lost its menace for Peter. The churning turmoil of the distant rapids was mellowed in a soft mist, and a little later they could not make out clearly the driftwood going down with the stream.

"Now is our time," said Peter's father. "Creep after me, flat on your stomach."

It took them only a minute to reach the big dry log. They could move freely here, for the upward dip of the bank concealed them. Donald McRae did not let Peter guess the tension he was under as he worked. He stood his rifle where the police would easily find it and laughed softly as he tied one end of a stout leather thong about Peter's wrist and the other end about his own. After that he rolled the log into the water and tested it to get its proper balance and tied the other leather thongs to a projecting stub.

"It's just right," he announced cheerfully. "A canoe couldn't have been better built for us, Peter. Are you ready?"

"I'm ready," said Peter.

JAMES OLIVER CURWOOD

He was in the water to his knees; now he went in to his waist. It was cold, biting cold; his teeth clicked, but he did not say anything about it. He looped his arms about the stub and through one of the leather thongs, and from the opposite side of the log his father twisted the fingers of one hand tightly in his coat. Then they began to move. His feet lost bottom and the cold water shot up to his armpits, taking his breath away. His father grinned cheerfully at him and he tried to grin back. In a moment they were in the current and the shore began to slip past them with amazing swiftness. It was not unpleasant, except for the icy chill of the water, which seemed to take the place of blood in his veins. There was no resistance against his body; the log carried them buoyantly and smoothly, so that after a little he had courage to look about him.

Their log had swung quickly into mid-stream, and they were overtaking a more slowly moving mass of driftwood. The thought came to Peter that it was like a race. Then something alive caught his eyes on the flotsam. It was a furry, catlike creature with short, perky ears and a fox's face, and he could almost have touched it with his hands when they passed.

"A fisher-cat," said his father. "He will have a nice swim when he hits the rapids!"

Peter was wondering just how much of a chance the fisher-cat had when something drifted against him. It was a drowned porcupine, floating belly up. The porky must have had a nice swim, too!

He shivered. The roar of the rapids was growing, and it was no longer pleasant to hear. The musical cadence which distance had given it was gone, and a sullen, snarling undertone of menace and wrath began to pound at the drums of his ears. In the twilight it looked as though they were racing straight into the mouth of a huge churn out of which milky froth was spouting.

Then two things happened which seemed odd to Peter. The dead porcupine was clinging to the log as if some sort of life held it there, and the fisher-cat's raft of driftwood which they had overtaken and passed was now *passing them*. To Peter this last was unaccountable, but to Donald McRae, who understood the whims and caprices of flood currents, there was no mystery about it. For a moment the fisher-cat seemed about to make a leap for the log. Then he huddled back and disappeared with his raft in the rougher water that preceded the gray wall of spume.

The man's hand tightened its hold on Peter.

"Hang on and don't get scared," he cried. "We'll go through this like a rubber ball!"

That was the last Peter heard of his voice, and suddenly his father's face was blotted out from his vision. A huge mouth opened and engulfed them. He could feel himself going down it, with roaring gloom and mighty explosions of water bursting itself against great rocks all about him. For a space which seemed an eternity he gave himself up for lost, and he wanted to scream out to his father. But the water smothered him. It thrust him under, buried him, then tossed him up to breathe. He hung on, as his father had told him, and after three or four minutes which were so many hours to him he could breathe easier and the roaring grew less.

They had come through a half-mile of the rapids then. The last of the rocks snapped at them, like growling dogs at their heels, and suddenly the water grew deep and smooth where it swung shoreward in a great eddy. For the first time Peter felt a hurt. It was his father's hand, holding him in a grip that only death could have broken. And then he saw his father's face. Donald McRae was gasping for breath. Even Peter would never know the fight he had made to keep the log running right during those three or four minutes in the rapids.

Slowly the current brought them to the shore. It was the shore they wanted, too, with its deep evergreen forests and its hundreds of miles of untrailed hiding-places. The big pool was dotted with drifting masses of débris. One of these, very near to them, Peter was sure he recognized. But the fisher-cat was no longer on it.

He was terribly cold, and when at last his father brought the end of the log to the shore and helped him out to dry ground the boy fell down in a sodden heap. He was ashamed of himself and tried to get up.

Donald McRae took one of his hands.

"You must walk, Peter—run if you can. Come on!"

He almost dragged him into the darkness of the forest, and Peter began to use his legs. It made him feel better. But his teeth chattered and his body shook as if he had the ague. Two or three hundred yards in the shelter of the timber they came to an overturned spruce tree, and near this was a birch with festoons of loose bark hanging from it.

Donald McRae stripped off an armful of the bark, and one of Peter's blue hands fished out the precious bottle of matches from his pocket. Very soon the flames were leaping up joyously, and he felt their warmth

JAMES OLIVER CURWOOD

entering into his body. He helped to gather wood. In a quarter of an hour there was a glow in his face, and the big backlog of pitch-filled cedar was a flaming furnace. Darkness settled heavily in the forest, and he was no longer afraid or uncomfortable as he continued to dry his clothes. His father, in a period between wood-gathering, cleaned his pipe and began to dry out some of his soaked tobacco. That was cheerful and inspiring. It always seemed chummier and more homelike to Peter when his father was smoking his pipe.

Later they broke off cedar and balsam boughs until they had a soft bed two feet deep within the warmth of the fire. When the last thread in his clothing was dry Peter crept into this bed. He had no idea of sleeping but made himself a comfortable nest and sat bright-eyed and watchful while his father rested with his back against the log and smoked.

A hundred times they had made camps together that were very much like this one. On hunting and fishing expeditions, and when berries were ripe, and on the trap lines, they had slept out many nights with boughs for a bed. But there had never been the thrill of tonight. The cumulative significance of what had happened was just beginning to find itself in Peter's head. This night was different from all other nights. The darkness which had gathered heavily about them was different, the fire did not seem as friendly, and his father, smoking his pipe, was changed. Always in their adventuring they had been in quest of something—fish or venison, berries or fur. Now something was after them. It was this slow process of mental and physical change from the hunter into the hunted, and its understanding, that was creeping into Peter's soul.

He loved night with its mystery of darkness, its stars and its moon, but now he could feel and hear it breathing secret plottings and danger. When the fire crackled too loudly or its flames leaped too high he shivered, fearing it would betray them. He wondered why his father remained in the light now that they were warm and dry, for there were safer hiding-places in the great pits of gloom that encompassed them. But he said nothing, feeling strangely that even to voice fear would bring reality upon them.

He watched his father, and the brightness in his eyes—something new and strange that lay in them—was like a stab to Donald McRae. In this hour he saw the boy's soul changing. Peter, at last, was beginning to build up the truth. Something terrible must have happened—somewhere—or the police would not be after his father. He had believed the police were omniscient, that they hunted only bad people. That was what they were for—to shut bad people in prisons, or hang them, or shoot them. *And they were after his father!*

The man saw these things in Peter's eyes and in his pale, thin face. And suddenly a revulsion of horror and of rage swept over Peter. If the police said his father was bad they were liars. He hated them, and if the chance came to him he would get even with them. He would beat out their lives with a club. He would kill them—if they didn't leave his father alone!

He said nothing. But he got out of his nest in the evergreen boughs and sat close to his father against the log, and Donald McRae put his arm around him and puffed hard at his pipe to keep the firelight from revealing what was in his eyes. The world might be against him, but Peter would be like this, his friend and pal to the last. He knew it, and thanked God.

V

Peter did not know when he fell asleep. He was buried in the sweet-scented cedar and balsam when his father awakened him. He sat up and rubbed his eyes, and it came to him quickly where he was. The fire was out and dawn was breaking up the gloom of the forest. He missed the fire, and the bacon frying over it, and the pot of coffee steaming in the coals. Those were the usual things that greeted him when he woke up in camp. And this morning he was hungry.

They headed straight into the heart of the unexplored timberlands south and west, and with empty hands and no pack on his back Donald McRae talked as cheerfully as though they had a week's rations with them. But his eyes were constantly questing for something to eat, and it occurred to him as a sort of tragedy that he had not tied his rifle to the log. He did not explain to Peter just why he had left it where the police would easily find it.

By midday their hunt for food had become a thrilling adventure to Peter. It stirred his blood even more than thought of their enemies, for the police seemed an interminable distance away now, shut out by miles of wilderness. There was something fascinating about it, too. There were birds about them and rabbit runways in every dip and swamp they came to, and deer and moose and caribou tracks so plentiful in places that they made trails like the hoof-beaten paths of cattle.

But there was nothing they could get at, except porcupines. During the morning they could have killed half a dozen of these animals with clubs, but each time porcupine flesh was suggested for dinner Peter made a grimace of revulsion. Twice they had tried it experimentally on their camping trips and both times it had nauseated him. He insisted he would rather starve than eat any more of that ill-smelling, fatty stuff the porcupine was made of. He would chew spruce gum instead. There was plenty of it on the trees they passed.

"If you get too hungry we'll roast some lily roots," said Donald, "but if you can hold out until night we'll have the feast of our lives."

Peter held out. The sun was still up when they came from heavy timber into a long, narrow meadow running into a swamp on the other side. This was the sort of place Donald McRae had been looking for. In the edge of the swamp were rabbit runways beaten fresh and hard. They chose the site for their camp in the rim of the high timber, and while

Peter brought in firewood Donald made snares from another section of boot top. These he set in the runways. It was scarcely more than dusk when the first big snowshoe ran his head through a noose and found himself swinging at the end of a sapling. An hour later he was roasted, and in the light of their fire they divided the feast between them. Peter didn't mind the absence of salt and bread and potatoes. Nothing he could remember had ever tasted quite so good to him as the unseasoned rabbit.

Food and the warmth of the fire made him drowsy, and very soon after they had finished their supper Donald tucked him snugly into the bed of evergreens they had made and covered him with his coat. Peter fell asleep instantly, and for several minutes the man remained on his knees at his side, the smile of tenderness in his face changing slowly into a look of haggard grief. When he rose to his feet the luster had died out of his eyes and years had fallen upon his shoulders. He caught his breath sobbingly as he stared into the wall of chaotic darkness beyond the firelight. It was only Peter who counted now, and this night was the last Peter would be with him. Tomorrow he would be alone, an outlaw, a hunted man running away to save his life. And Peter. . .

A moan came to his lips, a dry and broken cry of hopelessness, and his eyes fixed themselves in their anguish upon the heart of the fire. Without Peter, would God give him strength to live? What would the days be like—and the nights—and the months and years to come without Peter? For Peter was not only Peter. In taking the mother, God had given her soul back to him in the body of her boy. She was a part of him, speaking with his voice, looking out of his eyes, loving with his love, a comrade and pal to the man in spirit even as she had been in her own sweet life. And now—tomorrow—he would lose them both. The law was after him. Its hounds would follow him from hole to hole, like foxes after a rabbit, and probably in the end they would get him.

He closed his eyes to shut out the thing that was hurting him. When he opened them a face seemed to have taken form in the glow of the fire like a soul come to give him courage and resolution, sweetly sad in its inspiration, glorious in its consolation and cheer. Every day through the years this visioning of his wife had come to him; through those years she had walked hand in hand with him, she had been with him in the upgrowing of Peter, had helped to teach him the love of God and the glory of nature, and had laughed and cried and sung with them as

JAMES OLIVER CURWOOD

sunshine and shadow came. And always, in the darkest hours, Donald McRae saw her face, sweet and strong and never afraid. And so it was tonight.

"This is your last great fight for our Peter," her eyes seemed to say to him. "You must be strong."

And then she was gone. Slowly the fire died out, and he put no more wood upon it, but sat motionless and silent until it was only a red glow of ember and ash.

He did not sleep. The moon rose and the clear sky above was filled with stars. In their light he walked back and forth in the open, a solitary figure with a thousand still shadows about him. It was the sort of night he loved, a spring night breathing and whispering of summer and sweet with the perfumes of balsam and spruce and growing things under his feet. These things were a part of his God, and of Peter's God. Just as the woman had built up his faith in him, pointing out its truth and beauty and glory, so had he built up in Peter an illimitable faith in this God which was nature. It strengthened him now. The glow of the moon, the softness of the stars, the gentle whisperings of the wind, the low music of running water and the thrill and tremble of inanimate and voiceless life about him were a part of his religion.

"Love a tree and you love God," had been his text for Peter. And as long as there remained trees and flowers and the songs of birds and eyes and ears with which to see and hear, hope could never die. His brain cleared and his heart grew stronger as he paced more swiftly through the moonlight. The world was gloriously big, he told himself again and again. Somewhere in it was a place for him and Peter, and when he found it, far away from the menace of the law, Peter would not fail to come when he called. But tomorrow he must be strong enough to lie and strong enough to leave Peter at Five Fingers with Simon McQuarrie.

Toward dawn he built up the fire and cooked another rabbit which he caught in one of the snares. It was ready when Peter crawled out of his balsam bed. He did not know his father had not slept during the night. Donald McRae began to whistle when he saw the boy was awake, and though an uncomfortable thickening, persisted in his throat he fought to make the whistling cheerful just the same.

He announced his plan to Peter as if it were born of sudden inspiration and happily solved a temporary problem for them. He told him about Five Fingers and their old friend, Simon McQuarrie. Peter could just remember the Scotchman and Simon's fat Dutch partner and friend, Herman Vogelaar. Donald McRae seemed to recall them now with great pleasure, and he was sure Peter would enjoy his little visit with them, especially as there were several boys and girls of his own age to play with at Five Fingers. Of course he would come back soon, and maybe they would live at Five Fingers, if Peter liked it there. He continued to build up the lie, but something of trouble remained deep back in the boy's eyes. Donald tried not to see it too much, for it was the look he would have seen in the woman's eyes, if she had been in Peter's place.

They traveled until noon and ate their lunch. The afternoon was well gone when they heard the striking of an axe ahead of them. A quarter of an hour later they could hear several axes, and the distant crash of a falling tree. Donald McRae steeled his heart, and stopped. Yet in this moment he was smiling.

"That is Five Fingers," he said. "Can you go on alone, Peter?"

Peter nodded. "But I don't want to," he said. "I want to go with you, dad."

"You must go to Five Fingers, Peter. I'll come back soon. I promise that. I'll come back—soon."

A gulp came in Peter's throat.

"I'm not tired. I can go a long ways yet, dad. I'd rather go with you."

The man drew him into his arms.

"I'll come back tomorrow," he lied, fighting to speak the words calmly. "And you must get the paper in the bottle to Simon McQuarrie as soon as you can. You aren't afraid to go alone, are you, Peter?"

"No, I'm not afraid."

"Then—you must go." He hugged him close for a moment, and rested his cheek on Peter's disheveled hair. "Maybe I'll come back tonight," he whispered desperately. "Good-by, little pal. Hurry—and give Simon the paper—and—good-by!"

His lips burned against Peter's forehead. It was that kiss which startled Peter, and when his father turned away, and then looked back, smiling and waving a hand, a suffocating feeling remained in Peter's heart as if he could not get all the air he wanted to breathe. He tried to wave his hand in response, but in a moment it fell limply to his side. Donald McRae saw the gesture and a sob came in his breath. He disappeared behind a windfall, stopped and looked back. Peter was slowly turning toward Five Fingers. The small figure was pathetic in

　　　　　　　　　　　　　　　　JAMES OLIVER CURWOOD

its aloneness. Twice it paused and turned, and then went on, and was hidden at last by a screen of evergreens.

"God be with you and care for you, Peter, and give me strength to bear this parting," sobbed Donald McRae.

With white and haggard face he turned into the North.

VI

B eyond the thicket of young jack pines Peter did not hurry. His feet dragged, and he listened, hoping he would hear his father's voice calling him back. In half an hour he did not travel far beyond the evergreens. Then he knew his father was gone. He continued in the direction of Five Fingers, recalling his promises. Tonight or tomorrow his father would return. He hoped it would be tonight, for there was a lump in his throat which he could not get rid of, and something in his heart which frightened him with suspicions and fears which he was too young to analyze. But he knew his father would not lie. He would come back. He wondered what was written on the paper he was taking to Simon McQuarrie. Probably it told about the wickedness of the police, and Simon would help in some way. Other questions came into his mind now that he was alone. Why hadn't his father gone on to Five Fingers with him?

The chopping of the axes had ceased, but he knew he was heading in the right direction. He came into openings filled with the stumps of trees that had been cut down, and these clearings were carpeted with white and pink spring flowers and masses of violets. He had never seen such beautiful violets, or so many birds at this season of the year. There were robins and thrushes and dozens of little warblers and brush sparrows, and the cutting down of trees seemed to have brought all the sapsuckers and woodpeckers and gaudily colored blue jays in the woods. The sun was delightfully warm, too, though in another hour it would be settling behind the tree tops. In this glory of peace and quiet he proceeded quietly and cautiously, for his father had taught him always to do that in the forest. So he came without sound of footfall or crackling brush to the edge of a little opening beyond a thicket of poplars and birch, and here he stopped suddenly and his heart jumped up into his mouth.

Standing in a warm pool of sunlight not twenty feet away from his concealment was a young girl. She was almost as tall as Peter and so lovely to look upon that he stared at her in amazement and admiration. He thought she had seen him, and his first vision was of her face and a pair of beautiful dark eyes, laughing up at a red squirrel, chattering in a tree top a few paces away. Then she sat down, gathering her flowers about her, and eyes and face were lost to him in a mass of shining, black

JAMES OLIVER CURWOOD

hair that fell quickly about her, almost touching the ground she was seated upon.

At first he was astonished. Then timidity and fear crept upon him and he wanted to steal away as quietly as he had come. He drew back a step and was preparing for the next when an unexpected interruption rooted him to the spot. The wild and agonized yelping of a dog came from the thick brush beyond the girl. Instantly she was on her feet, her slim body quivering with the tension in which she waited. And then she called, "Buddy—Buddy—come here!"

With a series of pain-filled yelps the creature called Buddy responded. He darted out of the brush and came like a streak across the open. It seemed to Peter the half-grown pup was all legs and head and tail, and that from the sounds he made he must be mortally hurt. Whimpering and crying, he cringed at the girl's feet and kissed the hand she reached down to him. But she did not look at him. She had dropped her flowers and her attitude was fierce and expectant as she waited.

Peter could see the bushes moving across the open and in a moment a boy burst through them. He was half again as big as Peter, and he had a stick in his hand. He followed the dog, half running, and Peter began to hate him as he came. "Any person who will strike a dog should never have been born," his father had taught him from the beginning; and this boy with his thick red face and hulking body had been beating the pup. He was panting triumph when he came up, and the pup slunk closer between the feet of his mistress. The pursuer was at least two years older than Peter. He had thick hands and little eyes and a bullet head, and his eyes were glowing with wickedness.

For an instant Peter saw the girl's eyes. They were dark pools of flaming fire. Then like a little tigress she was at the other. Her hands struck at his face and for a moment the bully was caught at a disadvantage. He dropped his stick and caught her in his arms. His hands buried themselves in her hair, and Peter saw her blows becoming more and more futile. The pup snarled and darted in at the boy's feet. A kick sent him back howling.

Horror and rage possessed Peter when he saw the girl's head thrust backward, and without a sound he ran out of his cover and caught her assailant by the throat. Then, when the girl was freed, he struck. That was another thing his father had taught him, to fight when it was necessary to fight—*and always for a woman*. His fists struck hard and furiously, and he heard a bellow of alarm and pain from the bully.

The older boy stumbled and fell, and Peter was on him like a cat. He realized this was no time to "play the game fair." They rolled and twisted on the ground, and blood streamed from the bully's nose and mouth. Once Peter saw the girl. She was standing very near, her lips parted, her wonderful eyes shining at him. That glimpse of her was a mighty encouragement. He fought harder, driving his fists home, and kicking. Then they were on their feet again.

It was the bully who renewed the battle. Mauled and bleeding, he had recovered from the surprise attack and his greater bulk and weight began to tell. Exhausted by two days and nights of hunger and flight, Peter felt his strength going. He went down, and the bully flung himself upon him. It was then Peter caught a second glimpse of the girl. She had caught up the stick and was standing over them. He could hear the stick as it struck blow after blow, and his enemy rolled over, half stunned. They were both at the bully then, Peter with his fists and the girl with her stick, and the older boy took to his heels in a wild flight for the safety of the thicket out of which he had come a few minutes before.

Peter wiped his nose and mouth with his sleeve and gasped hard to get his breath. The girl was breathing hard, too, and she was looking at him with such wonder and gladness in her eyes that he wished he was back in the timber again. Then she came to him and began nursing his face with a soft handkerchief, and said things which he could not remember afterward, and Buddy the pup jumped up against him, wagging his knotty tail and licking his hand.

Peter drew back and tried to grin. For a moment he had felt enormously uncomfortable in the presence of this lovely little goddess of the woods, with her soft handkerchief dabbing at his face. Now his old cheer returned. He was glad the fight was over and was strongly conscious that the girl had played no small part in the final victory.

So he said apologetically, "He'd got me if you hadn't come in with the stick."

She stood back and looked at him. She was younger than he, probably not more than thirteen, but to Peter she appeared to be infinitely older in these first minutes of their acquaintance. It bothered him to meet her eyes squarely, they were so big and dark and filled with soft fire, like the velvety, jet-black hair that streamed in dishevelment about her.

"He is twice as big as you," she retorted. "I hate him. He belongs with the tug from Fort William, and every time he comes we have a fight."

JAMES OLIVER CURWOOD

"He's a—a woman-hitter," said Peter.

She accepted his compliment with a dignified nod of her head. Then she stamped her foot and shook her stick in the direction the bully had gone. "If he ever tries to do again what he tried today— I'll—I'll—"

"He won't while I'm around," helped out Peter, swelling with a bit of pugnacious pride. "I wasn't in good shape, and I've been traveling pretty hard, and we didn't have a lot to eat. I can lick him when I'm fed up and rested."

The girl was almost womanly in her swift intuition. Her eyes glowed softly at Peter.

"Who are you?" she asked gently. "I am Mona Guyon, and I live with Josette and Pierre Gourdon at Five Fingers."

"I'm Peter," said the boy. "Peter McRae."

"Where you from?" was her next query.

Peter took time to swallow. His father had not told him how to answer questions. Then he pointed.

"From away off there, miles and miles. My father brought me until we could hear the axes, and then I came on alone. He's coming tonight or tomorrow."

"Is your mother with him?"

"She's dead."

He was not looking at her when she came to him and took his hand, and in all his life he had never felt such a warm, soft little hand clinging to his own as Mona Guyon's.

"My mother is dead, too, Peter," she said. "And so is my father. They were drowned—out there six years ago. It was Pierre Gourdon who brought me in from the rock."

It was an uncomfortable moment, and yet something of joy passed into Peter. His fingers, smoke-stained and soiled, tightened about Mona's hand as they both looked off over the cuttings to the wall of the vast forest that shut out Lake Superior from their view. They could plainly hear the distant murmuring of the surf.

"I'm glad you've come," she said. "I hope you're going to live here. Are you?"

"Maybe," said Peter.

"You're brave, and I like you. If you were that hateful Aleck Curry, who looks like a toad—"

"I wouldn't be him," interrupted Peter.

"No, but if you *were*, and you tried to do what he did, I wouldn't hit you with a stick."

Peter's mind floundered in a futile effort to understand.

"I can lick him tomorrow," he ventured.

With a little laugh she pulled him to the scattered flowers. He helped her pick them up and put them into one big bouquet. Her soft hair touched his hands and he found it easier to look into her eyes. His heart beat fast and he was strangely happy. He forgot his swelling eye and a stiffening lip, but he did think of his father. He would surely beg his father to live at Five Fingers. It would be wonderful there, with someone like Mona to know and fight for.

Then he thought of his message.

"I've got something for Simon McQuarrie," he said. "Dad told me to hurry with it."

"And you're hungry."

She took his hand again, in a possessive and matter-of-fact way. There was something maternal about it, something so sweetly glad and friendly that a great wave of comradeship swept through Peter. He was no longer nervous or afraid. Tonight or tomorrow his father would come, and they would all be happy.

Through a glory of warm sunset they crossed the cut-over opens and came soon to the crest of the green slope that looked down on a little paradise hidden away in the heart of a great wilderness, a paradise of green meadows, of water shimmering like silver in the sun, and of the few log homes wherein lived the people whose paths Pierre Gourdon had blazed through the forests many years before.

"That is Five Fingers," said Mona.

And down the slope she led the way with Peter, still holding him by the hand.

He was speechless as they went. Everywhere he looked the earth was gloriously green, and in this green were the scattered cabins, with little spirals of smoke rising from their chimneys. He could smell this smoke, faintly sweet with the perfume of jack pine pitch and cedar. He saw the big, yellow dunes of sawdust about the mill, and in the mill itself, which had only a roof and no sides, the huge steel saw that was silent for the day blazed like a mirror in the sun. The lowing of cattle came up from the green meadows, and he saw horses grazing, and then his heart gave another jump, for between them and the little plain where the settlement lay were a doe and fawn. His fingers tightened suddenly

JAMES OLIVER CURWOOD

about Mona's hand, and he stopped, an excited wonder escaping in a cry from his lips. The girl laughed softly and freed her hand for a moment to braid back her lustrous hair.

"That is Minna," she said. "We named her after Geertruda Poulin's last baby. Pierre Gourdon allows no killing for miles and miles around here, and the deer feed out of our hands and eat our hay with the cattle in winter. Only—" Her lovely face clouded, and Peter saw a glow of distress in her eyes. "The men kill porcupines because they eat our chairs and doors and windows. But they bury them for me, over there in my porcupine cemetery, and I plant flowers all around them. I love porcupines."

"So do I," said Peter.

She took his hand again, and they continued down the slope. "Uncle Pierre lets me have three of them for pets," she said. "I have a great many pets, hundreds of them. All the birds and deer and bears and wild things for as far as you can see belong to me, and none of them are afraid of me. Uncle Pierre gave them to me, and no one harms them. No one except Aleck Curry," she added with a quick note of fierceness rising in her voice. "He would kill them all if he dared. I hate him!"

"I'll lick him if he doesn't leave them alone," offered Peter. "I can do it when I'm fed up."

She squeezed his hand.

"That's their boat—down there—with the big scow. It comes from Fort William four or five times each spring and summer to take the lumber away. Aleck's father owns it, and I hate him, too. He laughs at Uncle Pierre and wants to bring hunters up."

Peter was silent. A miracle was unfolding itself in his soul and under his eyes. As they came near to the first of the cabins he thought again of his father and his message.

"Where does Simon McQuarrie live?" he asked.

The girl pointed to a little cabin near the mill. "Over there. And that's where I live—in the first of those two big cabins with the rows of white stones around them. Uncle Pierre and Aunt Josette live there, and Marie Antoinette and Joe in the other. Joe is Uncle Pierre's boy, and Marie Antoinette is his wife. You'll love them. Everybody does—except Aleck Curry."

"I smell bacon," suggested Peter.

The girl sniffed.

"It—it's from Simon McQuarrie's cabin," she announced, a little disappointed. "Won't you come down to our place? Please!"

"I've got to see Simon," persisted Peter. "My father told me to see him first."

Simon saw them coming. His hard Scotch face softened as he saw Mona, and he scarcely noticed Peter until they were at his open door. Then Mona said, releasing her proprietary hold on the boy's hand: "This is Peter McRae. His father is out in the woods, and he's coming tonight or tomorrow. Peter wants to see you about something and he's hungry. He just whipped Aleck Curry, and that's why his eye is black and his lip swollen. Good-by, Peter!"

There was something wholly and beautifully satisfying about Mona, and Peter felt himself strangely alone when she left him and he found himself in the cabin with Simon. And then a thing happened which would have amazed all the people in Five Fingers could they have seen it, for Simon McQuarrie, with his honest heart and hard face, had never revealed himself a man of emotion. Yet scarcely had Mona gone when he drew Peter into his arms, and his thin gray face shone with a strange light as he looked over the boy's head into the sunset that flooded the open door.

"Peter—Peter McRae," he said as if speaking to himself. "Helen's boy—and Donald's. It's been a long time since I've seen you, Peter, a long time. And—"

He held him off and looked at him in a way that puzzled Peter. "You look like your mother, boy, when she was a little girl. I knew her then."

Peter was fishing in his pocket.

"My father sent this to you," he said, giving Simon the bottle.

The Scotchman opened it, and Peter watched his face as he read what was on the paper. He saw the lines about Simon's mouth harden and little wrinkles gather about his eyes. Then he turned, crushing the paper tightly in one hand, and added half a dozen slices of bacon to those already in the pan on the stove. After that he read the paper very deliberately a second time, and burned it. He cut more bread, brought out a pie, and while he added finishing touches to a feast that made Peter's eyes shine, he talked—but not about the paper in the bottle. When supper was ready he ate little himself, but watched the boy. Peter was starved. When he was done Simon rose to his feet and passed a big, lean hand over the boy's fair hair. His heart ached. Yet a duty had been imposed upon him, and he did not draw away from it. Words which Donald McRae had heavily underscored in the message he had sent kept repeating themselves in his mind, like a voice which he could not put off or deny.

"Tell him *now*, tonight, as soon as he comes to you," Donald had written. "Before the stars are over me again I want to feel that he knows the truth, and understands, and has forgiven me. It may be I am a coward because I do not tell him myself. But I cannot. I am afraid. I want to think of him always as he has been. I cannot leave him with a heart breaking or his faith dying. God will bless you, Simon. It is for Peter's sake—and Helen's—even more than mine."

They sat down on a bench, facing the last of the sunset, and Simon put his arm about the boy's shoulders. He tried to begin, and something rose in his throat and choked him so he could not speak. He tried again, and said:

"So Mona found you, and you fought Aleck Curry and whipped him?"

"She helped me," confessed Peter. "But I was empty. I can lick him now, when I'm fed up."

Simon's arm tightened. His long fingers touched the boy's cheek gently. "You like Mona?"

"Yes, sir."

Simon waited. Then he said:

"Do you want me to tell you a story, Peter—a story about another girl like Mona, who lived a long, long time ago?"

Peter nodded, wondering whether Simon would then tell him something about the letter that was in the bottle.

The story was short, for Simon McQuarrie was a cold and—most people thought—an emotionless man. But his heart was beating painfully as he began his tale.

"A long time ago there was another girl just like Mona, and just as lovely and sweet, Peter, and there were three boys who grew up near her. But one of these boys was almost a man, much older than the other two, so that when the girl came to young womanhood he was really almost old enough to be her father. And these three all loved her, every one of them, but one of the three was very much like this Aleck Curry you fought and had a heart in him that didn't know what clean love was. Well, of course, she loved just *one* of them, Peter, and he was the best and noblest of the three. Her name was Helen."

"My mother's name," said Peter quickly.

"Yes, and the odd thing about it is the name of the man she married was Donald, just like your father's. That's why I'm telling you the story, Peter. It—it's queer."

Peter was silent.

"The man who was almost old enough to be her father was glad in a way," went on Simon. "No one ever knew just how badly it broke him up, but their happiness in time made him happy, and he was the best friend they ever had. At least, I think he was. But the black-hearted one of the three was different, and one day when Donald and the older man were away he came to her cabin and insulted her, even though she had a little baby in her arms. And just then the other two came back. What would you have done, Peter?"

Peter's body had stiffened.

"If he was like Aleck Curry—I'd—I'd have killed him," he said.

Simon drew in a deep, slow breath.

"And that is just what happened, Peter. Donald killed him. He didn't mean to do it. It was an accident. But it happened. And the other man deserved it. He was better dead than alive. But it made a murderer of Donald, and they hang murderers. So the older man cared for the woman and the baby for three years, while Donald hid himself in the forests. Then—Helen died. And Donald came back and took the boy, and for years after that the law didn't know where he was, and they were happy together, and would always have been happy if the law hadn't found him again, and—"

Simon's voice choked. His arm hugged Peter until it hurt. And then he finished, almost whispering the last words, "Peter, I know it's all true, because the older man's name was Simon McQuarrie—and I'm Simon McQuarrie—and—the boy's name—*was Peter.*"

It was out. He bowed his grizzled cheek to the boy's face and fought hard to choke back the thickening in his throat. It seemed a long time to him that Peter did not move or speak. But he could feel the tremble of the boy's body, and he knew that Peter understood.

"So he won't come back," he said, trying to bring a note of comfort into his strained voice. "At least not for a long time, Peter. And he wants you to live with me. That's what he wrote on the paper you brought in the bottle."

Still Peter did not speak. He was staring through the door, and it was hard for Simon to find more words.

"We'll take good care of you here, Peter."

Then Peter spoke.

"Dad won't come back tonight or tomorrow?"

"No."

"Nor ever?"

"Maybe he'll come, but it will be a long time."

"And they're after him, like they were back there in the woods. They want to—*hang him*?"

"They won't catch him, Peter. That is why he left you here. He can travel faster without you and is safe right now. But we must tell no one else about him. We must keep it all between ourselves—a secret."

Peter slipped out quietly from under Simon's arm. He had no more questions to ask, and Simon made no effort to follow him as he went out into the last glow of the day. Slowly Peter walked past the mill and the yellow sawdust piles toward the timber which axes had not touched at the edge of the clearing. But he no longer took notice of the sunset glow or the twitter of birds or wondered at the molten gleam of the Middle Finger. He entered into the shadowing twilight of the forest and for the first time a sob broke from his dry lips. Then he called his father's name aloud, and the silence that followed emptied his heart of its last hope. He sank down in a huddled heap beside a tree, and his grief found vent in a low sobbing that broke strangely and terribly in the gloomy stillness of the trees. It was in this hour that Peter needed the comfort of a woman's arms. His world was gone. Without his father he wanted to die.

The darkness crept closer about him. And then a little hand, timid, soft, touched his cheek.

"Peter!"

It was Mona. Her beautiful eyes were glowing softly at him in the dusk as he raised his head to look at her through his tears. She knelt down beside him, and he choked back his sobs, struggling to hide his grief and his tears from her. And then Buddy the pup snuggled under his arm and kissed his cheek with his cool tongue. Mona was dabbing at his eyes again with her little handkerchief, and her voice was soft and sweet in its mothering gentleness.

It was then Peter forgot Simon's warning, and there in the deepening gloom of the forest, with Mona close beside him, he told what it was in his heart to tell—all about the police, and the fight and the running away, and now the losing of his father.

"There isn't anyone else but my dad," he half sobbed at the end. "I even lost my dog. I haven't got anything now—an' I wish I was dead!"

"You don't," she reproved, her two hands holding one of his own tightly, "and you *have* got someone. You've got me. I'll take care of you. I will, Peter. I promise. And you can have Buddy, and all my pets—everything

I've got. And—he will come back. Your father, I mean. All we got to do is wait." Her eyes were glowing at him in the dusk. "Why, your father is alive and he *can* come back," she said straight from the heart. "Mine can't. He is dead. And so is my mother."

An emotion new and strange swept over Peter—a flash of dawning manhood stirred to mysterious life by that note of something which had come from Mona's lips, a woman of the future whispering to him, chivalry calling, a boy's soul and a girl's rising for a moment above their years to point out the way to a new tomorrow.

Peter's heart grew warm again. He rose to his feet, and Mona stood beside him. In the darkness they were very close.

"I guess you're right," he said. "Dad won't stay away very long. And I—I'm sorry about your father and mother, Mona. And if Aleck Curry bothers you again, or kicks the dog—"

And so they went back through the dusk to Five Fingers, and this time it was Peter who held firmly to Mona's hand.

VII

His first night in Five Fingers would always remain an unchangeable page in the history of Peter McRae. Time would not dim nor obliterate it but would only mellow the memory of its loneliness and its torture. In the hours when it seemed to him his world had come to an end, years pressed their weight of experience and understanding upon his shoulders, and for a little while pain and the poignancy of fears made him old, and he ceased to be a boy of fourteen.

Simon McQuarrie had left a candle burning in the loft of his cabin. By its light he had made Peter's bed, and had hugged the boy to him for a moment before saying good night; and in going, with his head and shoulders above the trap in the floor, he had paused for a moment to say: "Don't worry, Peter. They won't get your father. And you must sleep, because Mona will be looking for you early in the morning."

Then he had gone.

And now, two hours later, Peter was alone and still awake. The candle had burned out, but the moon was coming up over the eastern forests. It was a splendid spring moon, big and round and full of golden fire, and its glow came in a flood through the open window of the loft.

At the window sat Peter, huddled and quiet. He knew Simon was sound asleep. All of Five Fingers was asleep. From the window he counted six or seven of the dozen log homes which made up the little settlement, and their windows were dark. They were floating in a great, yellow sea of moonlight. He could make out the dark walls of the forest and the silvery sheen of Middle Finger Inlet.

From beyond that sheen came the low murmur of Lake Superior beating against the rocks half a mile away. In springtime there was always this moaning of the big lake at Five Fingers, even on still nights when there was no wind.

And tonight it was so quiet Peter could hear his own heart beating. At times it hurt him. It rose up in him somewhere and choked him. Once or twice, if Simon had been awake, he could have heard the boy sobbing.

But Peter was beyond that now. His pale, thin face looking at the moon over the tree-tops had grown tense and set in its understanding and grief. Out under that moon his father was being hunted. Men were after him—men who would kill him or hang him if they caught him. He was no longer puzzled. His father was gone forever, just as his mother was gone, only she was dead.

He gulped hard, and his fingers clutched at the rough wood of the windowsill. He could not remember his mother except as a beautiful dream. She had come to him sometimes that way, and he had felt the soft warmth of her hands and the sweet breath of her kisses in his sleep. In his brain he treasured a picture of her, but it was only a picture, while his father had been very real. Since the first day he could remember, it was his father who had made up his world, his father who had been pal, comrade and mother to him all his life, and who now—out under the light of the wonderful moon—was being hunted by men with guns, just as they had so often hunted the big white rabbits in the swamps.

Again and again as he sat alone at the window his mind went over the events which had passed so swiftly since the day before yesterday, when his father galloped in from the railroad settlement with the officers of the law at his heels, and together they ran into the safety of the woods, leaving the little cabin in the clearing which had been their home. After that had come the longer flight, two days and nights of exhaustion and hunger, and the final parting when they heard the axes of the men at Five Fingers. It was when he came to that point his heart rose up and choked him, and he wanted to cry out in the stillness of the night. If only his father had put greater faith in his strength and years, and had let him go along! He could run, and hide, and live without anything to eat for a long time, and he could sleep on the naked ground, and swim streams, and he wasn't afraid. But his father had sent him on alone to this strange settlement of Five Fingers, where he had met Mona, and Aleck Curry, and Simon McQuarrie. . .

When his thoughts came to Mona a bit of comfort crept into Peter's soul. It wasn't so bad, with Mona near him. She had come into his life in a most unexpected and beautiful way, and had helped him whip the beast of a boy who had kicked her dog. He could still feel the warm thrill of her little hand as she led him through the woods and slashings into Five Fingers and he could see her eyes glowing at him in the dusk as she said:

"Your father is alive and he *can* come back. But mine can't, Peter. He is dead. And so is my mother."

Peter could almost hear her speaking those words now, whispering them, as if she realized in that instant the sacredness of the trust he had

JAMES OLIVER CURWOOD

put in her. And she was right. His father was alive, and could come back, while hers. . .

The distant murmuring of the lake came to him faintly. It made him shiver. Out there, somewhere, her father and mother had been drowned. He wondered if Mona was awake and was also listening to that sound, so faint at times that it was like a breath of air. It must haunt her, he thought. It was always telling her about what had happened, just as she had told it to him, coming down the slope into Five Fingers, and probably it made her cry when she was alone nights. It was terrible to remember one's father and mother dying like that, both at once, and Peter shuddered.

It made him a little ashamed, too. The sense of manhood which his father had planted and nurtured in him began to rise above his own hopelessness and heartache, and he leaned out of the window to look at the cabin of Pierre and Josette Gourdon, where Mona lived. That was dark, too. But Mona might be awake. He hoped so. Next to his father she was the biggest thing that had ever come into his life, and thought of her, and of her nearness, and of her lying awake thinking about him, sent a warm and comforting feeling through him, just as her gentle hands and soft eyes had brought him a mothering consolation in the earlier darkness of the forest that night.

It seemed to him, now that the reaction had come in his mind, that everything about the night was assuming a new aspect.

It was the kind of night he and his father loved, and its stillness, its shadows and floods of yellow moonlight brought him a new message. *Their* moon, they had always called it.

"You were born on a night with the moon shining like that," his father had told him. "It came in at the window to look at you, and it was mighty pleased."

So the moon had always been a personal thing to Peter, just as it had been to his father. And the Man in the Moon, Peter observed, was in a friendly humor tonight. There was a sly look in his eyes and an odd twist to his mouth, as if he were winking at Peter and telling him how beautifully everything was coming out, both for his father and for himself. Between Mona and the moon the sickness grew less in his heart, and remembering he had not said the prayer which his father had never let him forget, he bowed his face on the windowsill and whispered the words to himself.

When he raised his head a big gray shadow was floating silently in the air just outside his window. It was one of the huge owls which turn snow-white in winter. He could hear the soft flutter of its wings as it twisted and turned and disappeared, more like a ghost than a living thing. And then a swift patter of little feet came on the roof of the cabin. It was another of the night folk, a flying squirrel. A few yards away was the big tree in which it must hide itself during the day. He wondered if the owl and the winged squirrel were among Mona's pets.

His ears began to attune themselves to the different sounds of the night. It wasn't so empty, after all. There was always the murmur of the lake, and he could hear the occasional soft thud of hoofs in the meadow, and the mooing of a cow. A loon sent out its quavering love call from somewhere beyond the dark wall of the forest, and a wolf howled to the north. Now and then, deep in his sleep, Simon McQuarrie gave a snort in the room below. It was as if he were under water and came up at intervals for air, Peter thought.

Then he heard an odd chuckling, and a porcupine came waddling through the moonlight toward the cabin. Peter could see him clearly. He was big and fat and stupidly happy, and chattered like a cooing baby as he approached Simon's woodpile. And at last the tenseness went out of Peter's face, and his eyes brightened in the moonglow, and he pursed up his lips to whistle down softly at Porky. He wanted to warn him of the doom which Mona had said hovered over all porcupines at Five Fingers. But the creature was deaf and dumb and blind. He found the axe which Simon had forgotten, and grunted his satisfaction. Then he humped himself into a comfortable ball and his teeth began working like swiftly beating little hammers upon the helve of the axe, which was salty with the sweat of Simon's hands. Peter whistled.

"Get out, Porky!" he called softly.

He was considering the necessity of going down to save Simon's axe when a second chattering shadow waddled in out of the moonlit open between the cabin and the forest. It was another porcupine, a huge, black fellow who was carrying on an animated debate with himself as he advanced. Peter grinned. He loved to hear the porcupines talk to themselves. But he had never heard one quite like the big black fellow. It was as if a mother pig were coming with a litter of little grunting ones at her heels, and he wondered if Simon would sleep through it all.

The newcomer made straight for the woodpile and the gray possessor of the axe helve turned to meet him. The axe was between them, a sweet morsel for porcupine teeth. Low, throaty sounds floated up to Peter. It

JAMES OLIVER CURWOOD

might have been a meeting of brothers, or of sweethearts, or at least of very good friends if one judged by those sounds.

Then came a swift, flail-like movement of tails, followed by grunts and squeals and blows that sent a thrill of excitement through Peter. It was a glorious fight from the beginning, and somehow the big black fellow made him think of Aleck Curry, and in his eagerness to see the battle he leaned half out of the window.

The fighters rolled directly under him and he heard loose quills flying against the cabin as the tails struck out like clubs.

For a time he could not see who was getting the bad end of it. Then the black, who was more than ever like Aleck Curry, got a swing from the gray's tail that must have filled him with quills wrong-side in, for he let out a wail and began to retreat.

Not until then did Peter hear a sound from the room below him. A door opened. In another moment Simon McQuarrie came round the end of the cabin.

Simon was a tall and ghostly figure in his nightgown, which fell to his knees, and in his hand he carried a club. The club rose and fell and Peter heard a sickening blow. A feeling of horror shot through him.

"Don't kill the white one!" he cried. "Don't kill it!"

Simon McQuarrie, about to make for his second victim, looked up at the window in surprise. Peter saw the gray porcupine ambling back toward the timber, grunting and protesting as he went, and Simon made no effort to overtake him.

"They were having a fine fight," explained Peter. "That black one was Aleck Curry, and the other was licking him. He was smaller, too."

For a space the Scotchman stood silent in the moonlight. Then he asked, "Have you been asleep, Peter?"

Peter shook his head. "No."

"What have you been doing?"

"Just looking at the moon."

Simon turned slowly, with a suspicious upward glance at Peter.

"Better go now," he advised. "If you don't I'll ask you to come down and sleep with me." As he disappeared round the end of the cabin, his scant nightgown flapping above his long and bony legs, Simon muttered under his breath: "Donald was wrong in having me tell the lad. Better to have lied and never let him know. As it is—"

An expression which only Donald McRae would have understood settled in his face, and he paused for a moment at his door to look across the open where Pierre Gourdon's home lay in the radiance of the night. He could see the window of the room in which Mona slept, and the lines about his stern mouth softened.

"Poor little devils, both of them," he said, and went in to his bed.

Peter heard the door close. It seemed easier for him now to lie down upon the blankets. The moonlight streamed in upon him, and Peter could *feel* it. There was always that something warm and comforting about the moon. He closed his eyes, and his thoughts no longer brought a lump into his throat or hurt him. It was as if an older mind were helping him over certain difficult places. It assured him his father was safe. The police would not get him, and it would not be long before he returned. If he failed to do that he would surely write, and Peter could then go to him.

He began to think of Mona. She was, after all, the pleasantest thing he had ever had to think about, in spite of his happiness with his father. He reviewed the fight of that day and grew warm with anticipations of tomorrow and a renewal of hostilities. His hands clenched when he pictured Aleck Curry with his ugly face and big, heavy body, but they relaxed when he visioned Mona as she had taken part in the fight, with her shining black hair streaming about her and flaming eyes so beautiful he had at first been afraid to look at them. In his life in the wilderness he had never had much to do with girls, but here was one who pleased him completely, and all the ideals which his father had built up in him were roused and set on fire. His mother must have been like Mona when she was a little girl, because it seemed to him his father had always pictured her like that.

Then he grew uneasy and shame crept a little upon him. It made him squirm in his blankets to think that Aleck Curry would have whipped him if Mona hadn't joined in those last two or three minutes of the fight. That Aleck was bigger and older than he, and that he had fought under the disadvantages of hunger and exhaustion, did not satisfactorily explain his own failure to Peter. He was glad his father had not seen that fight, even though he had been taken at a great disadvantage. But *Mona* had seen it. She had seen him on the ground in those final moments, with Aleck about to pommel him into disgraceful submission, and she had come in to save him.

There was only one thing to do under the circumstances, and the inspiration of it comforted him. He would go out early in the morning, hunt up Aleck Curry and lick him. He was sure he could do it now, even though he was smaller and lighter than Aleck, for he would be rested and would have a good breakfast to start with.

He fell asleep. The big owl hooted softly from the top of a stub near the mill, and the flying squirrel was joined by its mate in a game of tag on the roof. The moon sailed higher, and under it a buck and a doe crossed within a stone's throw of Peter's window. All this Peter missed in an excitement of his own as his unsettled mind traveled swiftly from one dream to another. First he was fleeing with his father, and they were pursued by a horde of enemies, and all of these enemies were Aleck Currys. After that he dreamed of Aleck and Mona, and he fought so fiercely, with Mona's dark eyes and hair filling his vision, that Simon heard him twisting and groaning and climbed quietly up the ladder from below to look at him.

For a long time the stern Scotchman watched Peter, and in the fainter light of the moon which now filled the room a miracle of change passed over his face and it became as gentle as a woman's. No one, since long years ago, had ever caught that gentleness in Simon McQuarrie's face.

"It seems only yesterday," he whispered softly to himself, in a moment when Peter's pale face lay quietly in the crook of his arm. "Only yesterday, Helen."

Something trembled inside him, and he knew the mother was in that room with Peter, watching over him as he had seen her many times in those years when he had cared for the two, those beautiful but pitiless years when he had hardened his heart against all hope for himself in his devotion and duty to his hunted friend, Donald McRae. Only yesterday! And yet many hard and tedious years had passed since then, and through them he had gone like a piece of iron that is hardened into steel by the alchemy of fire. Tonight had come the mysterious change. He climbed down softly, his heart trembling. He loved Peter. He loved him as he had loved the mother.

VIII

P eter awoke with the dawn, and with that dawn he saw Five Fingers rousing itself into life. All the sweetness of spring was in the air. The delicious morning song of the robins was the first cheering sound that came to him. It was like a beautiful chorus.

"A man cannot be so wicked that the song of a robin will not stir some good in his heart," Donald McRae had taught Peter. "God made that song to begin the day with, and only those buried in the darkness of cities cannot hear or understand the message. Always think kindly of people in the cities, Peter. They are unfortunate."

And Peter thought of that as he looked out of the window on the few log cabins at Five Fingers. He had never seen a real city, but here, with the rose-flush of the rising sun painting the eastern sky beyond the forests, was everything of beauty and glory his mind could conceive. "Here," he seemed to hear his father saying, "is God."

Silvery wreaths of smoke were rising from the stone and clay chimneys of Five Fingers. He heard the gulls and caught the flash of their white wings over the Middle Inlet. Down there, too, was the squat, black tug owned by Aleck Curry's father—the tug which came up from Fort William three or four times a year to carry the lumber away. It was the one ugly thing he could see, and he was glad it did not belong at Five Fingers, and that Aleck Curry did not belong there. Already he was taking a possessive interest in the place, and his heart felt a gloating pride in the fact that he was a part of it, and Aleck Curry wasn't.

He saw men coming up from the bottoms, leading horses. A cheery whistle came to him clearly. The mill, nearly buried in its big yellow piles of sawdust, was only a little distance away, and a man was stoking the boiler with wood. The cloud of smoke that rose out of the tall stack was white and clean, and Peter knew how sweetly it smelled. He sniffed, trying to catch it. And then a wriggling creature came under his window and began making contortions as it looked up at Peter. It was Buddy, the pup. He was just the kind of dog Peter loved, all knots and knobs, with big feet and joints and a head twice too heavy for his body.

"He's growing," thought Peter, as he called down to him. "He's going to be a fine dog."

A few minutes later Poleon Dufresne passed Simon's cabin with a pail of milk and heard the Scotchman whistling. This was unusual, and

JAMES OLIVER CURWOOD

he paused to thrust in a curious face at the door, smiling good morning. Simon was getting breakfast with an almost boyish enthusiasm, and when Poleon saw Peter scrubbing his face his jaws fell apart in amazement.

"Morning, Poleon," greeted Simon. "This is Peter—Peter McRae, and I've adopted him. He's the son of an old friend of mine, and he came last night as a sort of surprise. He's going to bide with me."

This was a lot of information for Simon to give on any one subject at any one time, and Poleon came in with his pail, grinning his appreciation. He laid a hand affectionately on Peter's shoulder and told him how glad the people in Five Fingers would be to have him among them. Peter liked Poleon's round, rosy face with its cheery blue eyes, and when about to go Poleon turned a third of the contents of his pail into an earthenware crock and said to Peter:

"That's for you, boy. Simon here doesn't care for milk, but he must get plenty of it now for you. There's nothing like milk to make you fat and healthy."

It was Saturday. Peter learned that fact half an hour later while he was helping Simon wash the breakfast dishes. It came from a voice behind them, and Peter turned to find Mona standing in the door.

"It's Saturday and there is no school," she announced. "So I have come to get you acquainted with Five Fingers, Peter."

An enormous thrill ran through Peter. She was even lovelier than yesterday as she stood with her slim little figure framed in the doorway. Her beautiful dark eyes were shining, and looking at him, and her wonderful black hair was plaited in a braid that looked like a rope of velvet. Even Simon's undemonstrative face broke into an appreciative smile.

Once he had told Pierre Gourdon it was not good for a child to be as beautiful as Mona. But a new thought came into his mind this morning, a strange and weird thought for a Scotchman of his nature, and he chuckled softly as he told Peter to wipe his hands and go with Mona. Then he went to her, and tilted up her pretty chin, and ran his hand over her smooth hair that was like silk to his work-hardened palm. He had never done that before, and Mona was surprised. She was surprised, too, at the changed look in his face and eyes. He seemed to be a different Simon McQuarrie from the one she had always known.

"So you helped Peter whip that young rascal Aleck Curry, did you?" he asked with a wicked note of exultation in his voice.

She flushed a little and cast a swift glance at Peter.

"Peter had him whipped when I went in," she replied loyally.

"No, I didn't," corrected Peter. "He was just going to mess me up in proper shape when you hit him with the stick. But I can lick him today."

Mona smiled proudly at him. Then she looked sternly at Simon.

"You killed one of my porcupines."

"I had to," explained Simon. "He was eating my axe. Peter will take him over to the cemetery for you."

He returned to his work and Peter and Mona went to the dead porcupine. Buddy was sniffing suspiciously at the corpse, and at sight of the red stains on the earth Mona shivered.

"He didn't need to kill it," she said. "I heard you call to him to let the white one go. He could have let this one go, too."

"You heard me?"

She nodded. "I saw the candle in your room until it went out. Then I sat at the window in the moonlight. I didn't feel like sleeping."

"Neither did I," said Peter, his heart beating strangely. "I—I was wondering if you were awake. Did you hear the lake?"

"I always hear it."

He picked up the dead porcupine, feeling that he had said something wrong. Mona took the other foot and together they carried their burden beyond the farthest cabin to a high little meadow at the foot of a green knoll. Here, Peter observed, were many scores of green little mounds, and many others over which the grass had not grown, and still others very fresh. And everywhere among them flowers were growing. Mona pointed out a spade, and he dug a hole. When the porcupine was buried, Mona said:

"That is the twenty-seventh this spring. I wonder why porcupines like cabin doors and windowsills and axes and table legs when there are so many nice things to eat in the woods?"

"It's the salt," explained Peter. "They like to eat anything somebody has handled. Once, when we were away, they ate our windows until all the glass fell out."

"I put salt in the woods, lots of it," said Mona. "The deer like it too, and the rabbits, and the mice, and almost everything alive except the birds. Uncle Pierre has the tug bring me a barrel of salt every time it comes. Last time that beast of an Aleck Curry stole pepper from the tug's kitchen and put it in my salt."

"I'm going to lick him today," he assured her.

In her possessive little way she took his hand as they walked back. "I don't want you to fight him, not unless you have to, Peter. He isn't worth it. You have nice eyes, and they don't look good swollen half shut. I wish mine were blue."

"I don't," declared Peter with a suddenness that startled him. "They're—they're—"

"What?" she insisted.

"They're—awfully pretty," finished Peter bravely. "I never seen—I mean I never *saw* such pretty eyes."

He felt like wriggling down into his collar, and looked away from her. Mona blushed, and if Peter had observed he would have seen her eyes sparkling.

"And I wish I had light hair, too—like yours," she added.

"I *don't*," he fought manfully. "Your hair is—prettier than your eyes. When I first saw you, there in the sun, I thought—"

"What did you think?" she asked with interest.

"I dunno. I dunno what I thought."

He was tremendously uncomfortable, and was glad the musical droning of the sawmill began just then. That was another thrill, the clean, high-pitched cutting of steel through wood. There is something chummy and companionable about the sound of a sawmill at work in the heart of a forest country. It is friendly even to a stranger and makes one feel at home, and when Mona and Peter came to the mill the half-dozen men there were going about their duties as if they were a pleasure instead of work. They were a happy lot. Peter could see that with his boyish eyes, and his heart responded quickly to the gladdening pulse of it.

Then Mona ran up quickly behind a man who was twisting a log with a long cant hook and tried to cover his eyes with her hands. In a moment the man had turned and had her up off the ground, tight in his arms. Mona kissed him, and Peter thought he had never seen the face of any man filled with a happiness like that which he saw in Pierre Gourdon's. And Mona, holding out her hand to Peter, said:

"This is my Uncle Pierre. Come and kiss him, Peter."

And there, with both the young folk in his arms, and the big, steel saw laughing and wailing in their ears, Pierre Gourdon, into whose heart God had put a passionate love for all children, kissed Peter. In thus welcoming the boy he drew him so close that for an instant Peter's face touched Mona's soft cheek, and so warm and sweet was it that through all the years that followed Peter never forgot that wonderful moment.

Then Pierre Gourdon said, holding Peter off at arm's length, and looking at his eye which was still dark, and his lip which was swollen: "So you are the young man who whipped Aleck Curry for annoying Mona? Why, Aleck is half again as big as you—"

"And I didn't whip him," interrupted Peter. "Not alone. I was tired and empty as a drum. He was licking me when Mona jumped in. She helped a lot."

Laughter filled Pierre's eyes, and then a shadow followed it. The gentleness in his face gave way to a stern resolution.

"Aleck is not a good boy," he said. "I will not have him troubling you, Mona. If he does it again you must tell me."

"She needn't do that," protested Peter quickly. "I'll take care of her. I'm going to lick Aleck Curry today."

Pierre Gourdon looked at the boy, and the sternness left his face. "Peter, you're a man. I love boys like you." He ran his hand over Mona's silken hair, just as Simon McQuarrie had done. "I guess I won't worry over you and Aleck any more, *Ange*. I think Peter is going to do what he says."

"I won't have him fight Aleck," declared Mona. "If he does, I'll fight, too!"

When they had left Pierre and were going toward the Gourdon cabin, Peter asked, "What did he mean when he called you *Ange*?"

"It's a name he gave me the day he brought me out of the water when my mother and father were drowned," explained Mona softly. "It means something much nicer than I am."

"I don't believe it," said Peter. "What does it mean?"

"Angel."

"Oh!" Peter was silent for several moments. Then he said: "I like it. I guess that was what I must have been thinking when I saw you first yesterday, there in the sun, with your hair all down and the flowers around you. First off you sort of scared me."

"I *must* have looked ugly enough to scare anyone," agreed Mona depreciatively. "But I like my hair down when I'm alone in the woods."

"So do I," said Peter. "And you wasn't ugly. What's that building down there, with the box-like thing on top of it? Looks like a church."

"It is—and our school. Uncle Joe's wife, Marie Antoinette, teaches us. She's beautiful, Peter. Uncle Pierre says she is as lovely as Aunt

JAMES OLIVER CURWOOD

Josette was when she was young. Aunt Josette is beautiful, too. You've been to school a lot, haven't you?"

"Not so much."

"But you talk well."

"My father taught me. Every day I studied, and he heard my lessons, even when we were on the trail. My dad was—" He stopped, the odd thickening coming in his throat again.

"I love your father," said Mona gently. "Last night I prayed he'd come back, and he will. Uncle Pierre says it was prayer that brought me to him. He says prayer is always answered, if you believe hard enough."

"My dad says that, too."

"And I'm going to pray every night, Peter. I'm going to pray for your father to come back. *And he will.* "

The little doubt which had planted itself like a seed in Peter's mind was growing in spite of Mona and the beauty at Five Fingers. "If he comes back they may catch him," he said. "And if they do that—" She saw a queer, twisted look like a shadow in his face, and her fingers tightened. "They'll kill him," he finished. "That's what Simon McQuarrie says."

After a moment Mona said: "I wish we could tell Uncle Pierre. He always brings things out right. And this is coming out right, too, Peter. I know it."

Without logic, she was sweetly comforting. Her gentle assurance was a buoy to which Peter's courage and hope clung tenaciously, and he stole a hungry look at her when her eyes were turned away, and his heart beat fast. In a vague and unanalytical way the thought was in his mind that God could not help answering Mona's prayers. If He did not, there could be no God. And he was sure there was one—just as sure as he was of the trees and flowers and birds and blue sky all about them. Donald McRae had planted that faith deeply in his boy.

"Did you ever have many prayers answered?" he asked her.

"Yes, when I prayed *hard*," she replied. "I'm praying for something to happen to Aleck Curry, too. And it's going to happen, Peter. I know it's going to happen."

"What?"

"Anything—almost. I wish the crows would pull his hair out!"

Suddenly she stopped herself with a jerk. "There he is now—down there on the Finger. He is throwing stones at my gulls!"

"I'll stop him," said Peter, starting off.

She caught him by the arm. "I won't like you if you fight. Aunt Josette and Marie Antoinette are waiting for us, and they won't like you either."

She took possession of him again, and Peter gave himself up, though he could hear a challenging shout coming faintly from Aleck. And then out of the door of one of the cabins came a tall, slim woman with a face so sweet in its smile of welcome that Peter smiled back shyly, even before Mona had said, "This is my Aunt Josette."

For an hour after that he was meeting people at Five Fingers. First there was Marie Antoinette, who was younger than Aunt Josette, but only a little prettier, Peter thought, and who said she would have a place for him in school next Monday morning. From one cabin to another Mona made him go with her, until he had met the Poulins and Dufresnes and Croissets and Clamarts and children and babies until he began to have trouble in remembering their names.

Then they came to the last cabin of all, and this cabin looked like a doll's house to Peter. And the person they found in it was like a doll, too. At first Peter thought she was a playmate of Mona's, for she was only a little taller, with blue eyes and red lips and gold-brown curls tied back with a ribbon. Mona introduced her proudly.

"This is Adette Clamart, Peter—Jame Clamart's wife, and she *graduated* from the school of Ste. Anne de la Perade before Jame brought her to Five Fingers! And the baby—" She dragged him to the side of a crib and Peter looked down upon the round, cheerful face of young Telesphore Clamart, eight months old. Telesphore eyed Peter speculatively for a moment and then his countenance broke into a smile and he held up a pair of chubby arms. Mona uttered a gasp of delight. "He likes you, Peter! Put your head down. He wants to hug you."

Peter felt himself growing red and hot as he bowed his head to young Telesphore. The baby dug his fingers in his hair and squealed in triumph. It was the first baby he had ever touched, and suddenly he forgot the two girls and his embarrassment as he felt a soft little mouth touching his cheek. He laughed back at Telesphore, and when the baby freed his hair and he stood up straight again he thought Adette's eyes, bright with the glory of motherhood, were almost as beautiful as Mona's. He fumbled in his pockets to find something for Telesphore and produced his jack-knife.

"You can have that," he said, speaking directly at Telesphore.

When they were about to go Adette put her hand affectionately on his shoulder. "Mona told us what happened yesterday in the woods, Peter, and Jame and I love you for giving Aleck Curry that beating. It was splendid of you to fight for Mona like that!"

In the clearing Peter said to Mona: "It isn't true. I didn't lick Aleck Curry. Why do you tell them that?"

"It is true," retorted Mona with an obstinate little toss of her head.

"I was getting the worst of it when you came in with the stick."

"No, you weren't. He was almost choking for breath. I couldn't help hitting him with the stick—that's all." And then she added: "Why is it you don't want me to think you whipped him? I've told everybody you *did*!"

Her question and a quick flash in her eyes sent a little thrill through Peter. Was it possible Mona really believed he was getting the best of the fight when she began pommeling Aleck Curry with the stick? He flushed as he thought of his position at that moment, flat on his back with his legs in the air and his arms helpless under Aleck's weight, and Aleck himself just on the point of annihilating him! Surely Mona could not have been blind in those moments. She must have seen his peril, even if Aleck was panting for breath. Peter looked at her, trying to measure the truth of the matter. But Mona's eyes were innocent. If she was lying to him, she was doing it beautifully.

In a vague sort of way the problem weighed itself in Peter's mind, and he saw even more clearly that it was necessary for him to whip Aleck Curry that day. The responsibility had now become a grim and insistent one, for if Mona really *thought* he had whipped Aleck, he must do it in fact to save his own self-respect; and if she was shielding him from embarrassment and shame, as he partly believed, by spreading a false report of the combat, then it was doubly necessary for him to retrieve himself and prove his prowess by whipping the tug master's bullying son.

From the corners of his eyes he began questing for Aleck, who had disappeared from the strip of sand below them, though he did this in such a way that Mona did not guess his intention. She showed him her pets, and it was then Peter saw something which he had never seen before, though he loved all wild things. At Mona's soft little calls the big-eyed moose birds which Peter called whisky jacks fluttered about her and ate crumbs out of her hands. Down on the white sand of the Middle Finger the gulls gathered close about them, like a flock of chickens, begging in soft, throaty notes for the tidbits which she had brought from the cabin. She sat down in the sand and they climbed over her lap. One huge white fellow pecked at her shining braid.

"That's Bobo," she explained. "He always wants to eat my hair!" A one-legged gull hopped on her lap and began eating greedily the handful of bread-crumbs which she offered him. "And this is Dominique. I call him that to tease Dominique Beauvais, who is so fat and round. I don't know how he lost his leg, but I believe Aleck Curry must have shot it off a year ago. I wish Aleck's father would never bring him here again!"

IX

It was almost noon when Peter left Mona and returned to Simon McQuarrie's cabin. His head was in a whirl and his heart stirred uneasily between joy and grief. Not for many minutes at a time had his thoughts been away from his father. Even when Mona's dark eyes were smiling at him and her sweet voice was talking to him, his father's white and hunted face was a vision that never quite faded out of his momentary flashes of happiness. Deep down in his heart was an emptiness which even Mona could not fill, an aching pain which her beauty and her gentleness softened but could not quite drive away.

And Mona tried. In her heart, which was sometimes a woman's heart in a child's breast, she knew that Peter was grieving and fighting to hide his grief. The tragedy in her own life, and a sorrow which had been deeper and more pitiless than Peter's, made her understand and feel what even Adette in her young motherhood might not have sensed so clearly.

It seemed only yesterday to Mona that her mother had laughed and played with her under the big, white sails of the ship, with her father watching them, and only yesterday that the terrible thing had happened in the sea. No one, not even Pierre Gourdon, knew how vividly those hours and days came back to her at times. The forest and the wild things shared her secret, but no others. Over the two graves in the little cemetery at Five Fingers she had said quietly to Peter that morning, "My father and mother, Peter"—and that was all.

Something in her voice held Peter from asking for the story of that frightful hour in the maelstroms of the Pit, where Pierre Gourdon had saved her and her father and mother had died. But he felt it. It crept into him and became a part of him, and even Pierre Gourdon would have found it difficult to explain what was born in their hearts in those moments when Peter looked at the big stone into which had been roughly cut the words, "Paul and Mona Guyon, Died Sept. 27, 1900"— and then said gently to the girl who stood fighting bravely at his side, "I'm sorry, Mona." For to Pierre they were children.

But there was something in Peter's soul that was struggling beyond childhood as he returned to Simon's cabin. Three days, and this day most of all, had shown him his first dim vision of the bridge which spans the illusive way between boy and man. He had lost his father. But his father was not dead, while Mona's was gone forever. Out of the chaos in his mind these facts kept repeating themselves, and with them came ever more insistently the desire to do something for Mona. And one possible achievement loomed big—the whipping of Aleck Curry!

Thought of it made his blood tingle. He did not ask himself what it was that Aleck had done to incur Mona's displeasure. It was sufficient for him to know that she was praying for calamity to fall upon his head. She wanted the crows to pull his hair out. She had prayed for that last night—when she had prayed for his father. And she was sure that God answered prayer.

But it was his own feud with Aleck that fired both his chivalry and his hatred—memory of that moment in which the tug master's son had thrust Mona's head back brutally in the edge of the forest, with his big, coarse hands fastened in her hair. In his first encounter with Aleck he had saved Mona but had failed to avenge the outrage. He was sure he could do it now.

Simon took him among the men after dinner and he became acquainted with them all. They went back into the cuttings, and it was three o'clock before Peter found himself alone. Then, instead of going back to Mona, he circled in the edge of the timber until he came to the end of the finger of evergreens that reached almost to the inlet. His heart gave a jump when he saw Aleck on the tug shooting at the flying gulls with a slung-shot. Peter had made up his mind to challenge his enemy calmly and without excitement, as his father would undoubtedly have challenged a man in a similar situation. But his plan changed suddenly. He picked up a stone and hurled it with such accuracy that Aleck, seeing the missile, dodged. Then he jumped ashore.

Peter waited for him. He was not afraid, but his heart was beating fast. Aleck seemed to have grown considerably overnight, Peter thought. He was almost as big as Jame Clamart, and his face was red with an exultant passion as he advanced, stuffing the slung-shot into one of his pockets. There was no doubt this was just the opportunity Aleck was looking for, and Peter retreated with caution into the balsams and cedars.

Aleck began to run—and Peter ran. He was light as a rabbit on his feet, and as he hopped over logs and underbrush he heard Aleck crashing like a big animal behind him. Twice he allowed his enemy to come almost within reach of him, and then spurted ahead. At last, in the edge of a little cut-over clearing, Aleck stopped. He was puffing and blowing and his fat face was covered with sweat.

JAMES OLIVER CURWOOD

"Runny-cat!" he choked derisively. "Runny-cat—runny-cat—"

He caught himself in amazement as Peter turned and advanced toward him. "Always smile when you're in a tight place," Peter's father had taught him, and Peter tried bravely to live up to the rule. A fixed grin was on his face. "I'm going to lick you," he announced cheerfully. "You're nothing but a girl-beater and a windbag, an' your wind's all gone. I wasn't running *away* from you, Fatty—I was leadin' you *on*!"

Aleck stood aghast, gulping hard to get his breath. It seemed impossible that a boy so much smaller than himself would dare face him with such monumental nerve. The bully in him was maddened by Peter's next insult. "You're nothing but a girl-fighter—a hair-puller—a big tub of fat," Peter informed him, "an' you'll be yelling for help when I get half done with you!"

And then Peter jumped in. He was quick. His fists were small but hard. His wind was good. And the suddenness of his attack took Aleck off his guard. The first blow was what Peter called a stomacher, and Aleck let out a huge grunt. He bellowed anathema as he began to swing his heavy arms. Peter reached his nose and one eye and his mouth. He was like a hornet. His two small fists were swiftly moving hammers, and Aleck had never experienced anything like the hail of their blows. They took away from him what breath he had left; his nose began to bleed, his lip was cut, and then Peter gave him another stomacher. Could he have lasted for five minutes at the speed he was going, Aleck would have been a wreck.

But Peter was delivering all his metal in one smashing broadside. Aleck floundered and puffed. One eye closed quickly. Blood smeared his face and shirt. His big mouth began to swell. He was not fighting muscle and brawn—but *nerves*. Every nerve in Peter's body was at its breaking point, and he was like a thing gone mad. But he was beating against mass of dull and stupid flesh that had but few nerves to be shocked into submission. His blows began to carry less force, and he was compelled to breathe with his mouth open. He gave Aleck one last slashing cut in the mouth and then his strength seemed to break. His enemy's arms tightened around him and they went down together. Peter was under, just as in that other tragic moment when Mona had saved him. But there was no Mona to save him now, not even Buddy to nip at Aleck's legs and heels. His one consolation was a final look at Aleck's face close above him. He had done a pretty good job, anyway. In another minute or two the bully would have quit.

Both rested, gaining their breath. Then Aleck began to pommel, weighting Peter down with his entire bulk.

"I got you now," he managed to gasp. "I got you!"

Peter saved his breath. He realized the futility of struggling against that weight with what little strength was in him and concentrated all his effort in shielding his face. Aleck was like a porpoise, and every half-minute or so was compelled to cease his jabbing to get a new supply of breath, a large amount of which he wasted in verbal laceration of Peter's feelings as he pommeled with his fists.

"I'm a tub of fat, am I?" he demanded at the beginning of each fresh attack. "I'm a windbag, eh? A girl-beater, am I? Take that, an' that, an' *that*! An' yell for your girl, Petey, yell for your girl to come an' help you!"

Then he would pause again to gather lung momentum for another attack. Each assault left Peter a little bit more helpless than before. He could feel himself swelling. One eye, he knew was entirely shut. The other he saved by shielding it against his arm. His thoughts were growing a little hazy, too, but all his mental and physical discomfort was dissipated by the threat of a new horror which came in a sudden inspiration of triumph from Aleck's swollen lips.

"I'm goin' to yell for Mona," he said. "I'm goin' to have her come and see what I've done to you! A tub of *fat*, am I? Take that—an' that—"

And he did yell when he got his wind again. In reality his challenge for Mona to come and see her Petey licked was husky and not far-reaching, but it seemed to Peter the whole world must hear it. "An' when she comes I'm going to make you say you're licked or I'll beat your head off," Aleck told him. And then he sat up straight, his heavy bulk astride Peter's slim body, and called Mona's name again. Peter's brain went hot. Was this to be the answer to Mona's prayer? Had Mona really prayed, or had she fooled him? Faith rode over his doubt. Mona wouldn't lie. She had prayed, and the trouble right now was with him—and not with Mona's prayer.

Aleck's swollen face was growing purple in its vociferous calling for Mona. In a moment of safety Peter took a look at it with his one good eye. A thrill shot through him when he found the weakness had left his arms. He was breathing easily, too, in spite of Aleck's weight. If he could only get up—if he could have just one more chance at that fat, swollen face—

It was something quicker than Peter himself that moved him, an intuitive flash, a lightning-swift call of his brain upon hidden forces

JAMES OLIVER CURWOOD

of self-preservation within him—a twist, a convulsion of his body, a squirming upheaval so sudden and unexpected that Aleck lost his balance with Mona's name half out of his mouth, and the other half never came. He fell sprawling, and Peter was upon him again like a cat. Aleck's face was his target, and he beat it—fast, furious and hard. He was amazed at the return of his strength. It exhilarated and inspired him, and in his mad enthusiasm he bit one of Aleck's ears. A roar of pain came from the bully. Peter's fist lodged squarely in Aleck's eye, and a second howl followed the first.

At heart the tug-master's boy was a coward, like every bully, and in another minute he was crying for quarter. But Peter's momentum was too great to be stopped on such short notice. He continued, until in the end Aleck Curry was a blubbering, wind-broken, thoroughly whipped rascal, hiding his face in the earth.

Not until then did Peter stand up, seeing the world dimly with one eye. And then—in that glorious moment of triumph and answered prayer—his heart stopped dead in his body for a single moment. Not ten feet away from him stood Mona! Even with his fading vision he saw the wild flush in her face and the joy in her eyes. The truth they betrayed turned his darkening world suddenly into a paradise. *She had seen him whip Aleck Curry!*

He turned to Aleck. "Get up!" he said. "Get up or I'll kick in your ribs!"

Aleck dragged himself to his knees, then slouched to his feet. He was a pitiable sight. His eyes were little slits. His face was swollen until it looked as though he had the mumps. He was blubbering and gasping for his breath, and for a moment he did not see Mona.

"Are you licked?" demanded Peter, coming close to him.

Aleck drew back and put up a shielding hand. "I guess I got enough," he conceded.

"If you ain't sure—I mean if you *aren't* sure—I'll finish it," said Peter.

"I got enough."

"Then gimme the slung-shot."

Aleck surrendered the weapon. In that moment he caught a dim vision of Mona. He gulped and swallowed a lump in his throat.

"Now promise Mona you won't bother her any more. Promise—or I'll lick you again!"

"I promise."

"An' you won't throw stones at her gulls?"

"No."

"All right, Fatty. Now go on back to the tug. *And stay there!*"

He watched Aleck until he had disappeared among the cedars. Then, his business done, he turned toward Mona. A little shyly, with shining eyes, she came to him. He wiped his eye. He could just see her.

"Oh, Peter!" she whispered softly. He could feel her soft little handkerchief at his face, just as he had felt it that first day in the edge of the forest. And she was saying, "Peter—you're glorious!"

And then something happened that sent a tremble through the world on which Peter stood. Raising herself on tiptoe, Mona kissed him softly and sweetly on his swollen lips.

"There, that is what Aleck Curry has wanted all the time, and I'm *giving* it to you. Say thank you, Peter!"

"Thank you," said Peter.

X

Peter was conscious of the fact that he had lived a long time in the last three days and four nights. His adventures during that brief period of time had run the entire gamut of human emotions, with the possible exception of a desire to laugh, and his fourteen years of life seemed entirely out of fact. This philosophy did not strike Peter, but it did work into the troubled soul of Simon McQuarrie as he told Pierre Gourdon why it was that Peter's father was a hunted man, fleeing for his life, and how it had come about that Peter was now in Five Fingers seeking refuge with him.

"And I'm going to keep him," he said. "I love the boy."

What Simon had to say struck deep into Pierre Gourdon's heart, for it recalled the day of years ago when he had made his great fight in the sea to save a strange woman and her little girl, and had succeeded in bringing only the child, Mona, ashore. And Mona had grown to be a part of his soul. So when Simon had finished, Pierre nodded his head thoughtfully and said:

"Mona brought Peter to me today. He has the making of a man in him. And he has promised to whip Aleck Curry if he troubles Mona again." He chuckled and shrugged his shoulders. "Aleck is almost twice as big as Peter," he added. "But the boy has courage. It may happen. And—we will make this a home for him, Simon."

"And if that round-headed young blackguard of an Aleck sets upon Peter again," said Simon slowly, "I'll make his father take it out of his hide or never sell him another foot of lumber!"

The gentle smile did not leave Pierre's eyes. A forest man, and son of many generations of wilderness people, a warm thrill of superstition and an immeasurable faith in the God that had made his beautiful world lay deep in his soul. Simon guessed what was in his mind when he saw him looking at a green patch of flower-strewn slope where lay the graves of Mona's father and mother.

The smile faded slowly from Pierre's face, and a little of anxiety, of dread almost, replaced it.

"The years have been kind to us," he said, speaking more to himself than to Simon. "It has been a long time since Dominique Beauvais and I brought our wives through these forests for the first time, and now there are more than fifty of us here—all our own people and friends.

There has been little of tragedy and much of happiness. The plot up there is empty—except for Mona's people. Sometimes—I am afraid."

"Peace and comfort have been with us," agreed the Scotchman. Behind them were the yellow piles of sawdust and the droning of the big steel saw in Simon's little mill as it cut its way through the hearts of timber. Simon loved the mill as Pierre loved the cabins he had helped to build, for the mill had brought prosperity to the wilderness people. It had also made necessary the ugly black tug which lay down in Middle Finger Inlet. The creases grew deeper in Simon's hard face as his eyes rested on the tug. "I wish some other man than Izaak Curry was taking our lumber," he said. "Maybe I'd like him if it wasn't for his boy. If that ugly lad ever puts his hands on Peter again, or on Mona—" He hunched his gaunt shoulders with a suggestive grunt.

Pierre was looking off toward the timbered line behind which Lake Superior was hidden, half a mile away. For a moment after Simon's threatening words he remained silent. His face was thoughtful.

"It is strange," he said, giving voice to what was in his mind. "Through children has come most of our happiness at Five Fingers, Simon—and all of our tragedy. It was seven years ago that the strange ship went to pieces out there and I saved Mona from the sea. She is one of us now, and if she should be taken away our hearts would break. And now comes Peter, whose mother is dead, and whose father is worse than dead—for Peter—because he is an outlaw. It makes me think of a long time ago when a boy came into Ste. Anne de Beaupré, away down on the St. Lawrence, just as Peter came to Five Fingers three days ago. His father and mother were dead of the plague back in the forest, and he was ragged and starved, and the first person he met was a little girl, just as Peter met Mona, and afterward he fought for her, and married her when he grew old enough, and—she is Josette, my wife. It is almost as if Peter was *me*. And I am wondering—"

He did not finish. But Simon nodded understandingly.

"Things happen like that," he said.

OUT OF THE EDGE OF the evergreen timber which ran down to the white sands of Middle Finger Inlet Mona was leading Peter. One of his eyes was entirely closed. His lips were swollen and his face was grimy and red with the marks of battle. He was a little dizzy. There was a ringing in his ears, and with his one good eye he could see the world but dimly. The green forests were a blur. The sunlight was a mellow

JAMES OLIVER CURWOOD

glow. Mona's face, flaming with pride and joy, was an ethereal vision of loveliness which he saw as if through a number of gossamer veils. But in spite of his wrecked appearance his heart was beating with a swift and glorious exultation. He had kept his promise to Mona, to Simon McQuarrie and to Pierre Gourdon, for he had met and whipped Aleck Curry. The tug-master's son had begged for mercy, and the riotous thrill of it all was that Mona had looked upon that splendid battle and the ignominious defeat of the overgrown bully upon whose head she had earnestly prayed calamity might fall.

Peter was fighting hard to maintain a calm and dignified mental balance as they came out of the forest. Mona's fingers clung to his hand. Her face was flushed and her eyes were shining like lovely stars. But it was the kiss he felt most of all—that warm and sweet and amazingly unexpected tribute she had placed on his lips in the moment of his triumph.

It was a new thing to Peter. Since his mother had died he had never experienced anything like it and he could only faintly remember his mother. Through the years since then his father had kissed him every night before he went to sleep. But Mona's kiss was different. It remained with him in a strange and embarrassingly persistent way.

"I knew you could do it," Mona was saying, a tremble of pleasure in her voice. "I just knew it, Peter! Does your eye hurt?"

"Not much."

"Can you see?"

"Pretty good."

She drew in a breath of deep and sincere appreciation.

"I got there just in time to see you bite Aleck's ear," she said. "Oh, how he did howl!"

Peter's conscience smote him.

"It ain't—I mean, it *isn't* fair to bite another fellow's ear," he explained, "but he stuck it in my mouth and I couldn't help it."

"I wish you'd bit off his nose," said Mona. "If I were a boy and had hold of his ear with teeth like yours, I wouldn't let go."

A generous impulse filled Peter's breast. "I'll lick him again tomorrow if you want me to," he offered.

They went up the green slope from the inlet. Peter could hear better than he could see. He could hear the soft croaking of the gulls and the singing of the birds and the steely music of the saw in the mill. His bad eye was toward Mona, so that unless he gave his head a full turn he could not see her at all. A sweaty discomfort possessed him whenever he believed she was making a fresh survey of the disfigurements Aleck had fastened upon him. With his triumph rode the humiliating conviction that his face was out of joint and not pleasant to look at.

"It'll be better tomorrow," he said.

"What will?" she asked.

"My face. It must look sort of funny."

"Not half as funny as Aleck Curry's," she comforted him. "And if anyone dares to laugh at you—after what happened out there—"

Peter caught the flash in her dark eyes. In spite of his protest she pulled him through the open door of Jame Clamart's cabin. Adette was bending over the crib of young Telesphore. Her big blue eyes widened and she gave a little gasp when she saw Peter, his hand still held in Mona's.

And then, to his horror, she giggled.

In an instant Mona was at her side.

"Adette Clamart, don't you dare laugh!" she cried. "If you had seen it! If you had seen him whip Aleck Curry—"

"But his eye!" exclaimed Adette chokingly. "I mean *that* eye, Mona—the one that's open! It looks so—so funny!"

"He's better-looking right now than Jame Clamart will ever be," retorted Mona with fierce dignity. "He hasn't got a snub nose, anyway—and that's what your baby is going to have when he grows up!"

"But his *eye*!" persisted Adette, the giggling choking her. "Why is it so round and glassy, Mona? It's just like the end of my new glass salt shaker! Oh, oh, *oh*—"

"Adette Clamart!"

Peter, stunned and speechless, watched Mona drag Adette into the kitchen. As if drawn by an irresistible magnet, his one eye followed them, and Adette—looking back—gave a final little screech of laughter before the door closed behind her.

Peter heard the tittering beyond that door, and Mona's protesting voice rising above it. He felt as if warm water had been poured down his back. He was clammy, and his heart had sunk down into his middle. He must be a terrible sight!

Then he saw young Telesphore looking at him over the edge of the crib. In one of his fat fists the baby clutched the knife which Peter had given him earlier in the day. Peter went nearer and grinned at his young friend. The effort hurt him. Telesphore's mouth fell slowly ajar as he

JAMES OLIVER CURWOOD

stared at Peter. He gave no sign of recognition. The jovial comradeship of a few hours ago was gone and his gaze was steady and perplexed. And then, as if desirous of possessing another strange article of interest, he dropped his knife and reached for Peter's one eye.

Peter drew back. Adette was still laughing at him and Telesphore did not recognize him! He remembered a little mirror hanging on the wall and hurried to it. He was shocked. The thrill of triumph left him. His pride sank—and he sneaked through the open door as quickly as he could and trotted toward the big yellow piles of sawdust, hoping he might reach them before Mona discovered his flight. Screened by the piles, he came up behind Simon McQuarrie's cabin and almost bumped into a little man with a great head of shaggy gray hair, a round face with rosy cheeks, and eyes that were at first amazed and then twinkled merrily as they looked at Peter. He was a stranger. But swiftly and instinctively Peter liked him. Something in the way he rubbed his hands together and chuckled built up a confidence and comradeship between them immediately. Peter attempted a grin.

"I been in a fight," he acknowledged cheerfully, for there was an attitude and quality about this little man that demanded some kind of explanation. "I been in a fight with Aleck Curry."

"And he worsted you," guessed the merry stranger.

"No, sir. I beat him up. I made him howl, and he promised never to bother Mona or her pets again. Mona knows. She saw it."

The little man placed a hand on his shoulder. It was a gentle hand. Its touch comforted Peter.

"Come in and let me fix you up, Peter. That is your name, isn't it—Peter McRae?"

"Yes, sir."

They went into the cabin. The little man seemed at home in Simon's place, for he found the medicine cupboard immediately, and was soon busy poulticing and bandaging Peter's tortured face.

"Aleck is a troublesome boy," he said. "I hope you punished him well. But he is so much larger than you! Aren't you afraid of what may happen next time?"

Peter shook his head. "I know how to do it now. I run away from him until he's winded, then beat him up. I'm going to lick him again tomorrow if Mona wants me to."

"Good!" smiled the little man. His face grew rosier and a light was in his eyes that pleased Peter. "But I wouldn't try it on Sunday," he advised.

"It's bad luck to fight on the Lord's Day. If you'll wait until Monday, I will take you out into the woods and show you a few tricks that may help you! And if it can be quietly arranged, Peter, I would like to see the next fight you have with Aleck Curry.

"You like fights?" asked Peter.

"In a good cause—yes."

Peter was thoughtful as his cheerful and comforting companion fastened a bandage over his closed eye.

"Sunday isn't such a bad day for a fight," he argued. "You could get Aleck Curry out in the woods somewhere, tell 'im you wanted to show him something, an' I could sneak up—an' we could have it right there. I ain't—I mean I'm *not* afraid of Sunday!"

"I'm not thinking so much of you as I am of myself," said the little man, laughing softly. "I mustn't let pleasure come before duty—on Sunday. You see, I have to preach tomorrow."

"You have to—*what*?"

"Preach. Down there in the little church. I'm Father Albanel, Peter."

For the second time in the last half-hour Peter's earth seemed slipping unevenly under his feet. *Father Albanel!* Mona had told him about the wonderful forest missioner who had no church and no set religion, but who wandered through hundreds of miles of wilderness, preaching the faith of God wherever he went, and who came every few weeks to Five Fingers. "All the forest people love him, and he is so good I think God must love him most of all," she had said. "He buried my father and mother." And this was Father Albanel—this little man with the jolly face and twinkling eyes, and he—Peter McRae—had invited him to witness a fight on Sunday! He squirmed uneasily. He could feel the hot blood rising up through his neck into his face. He wet his swollen lips and tried to save himself.

"I didn't know you was the preacher," he said. "I guess mebbe it isn't right to fight on Sunday."

Father Albanel's hands pressed gently upon the boy's thin shoulders. "It's right to fight any time, Peter—when you have a just fight to make. God loves a peacemaker but He also has no use for a coward—and no one but a coward would refuse to fight for Mona. Will you come and hear me tomorrow?"

"I'll come," promised Peter.

When Father Albanel had gone he climbed up the ladder to his bed of blankets close under the sweet-smelling cedar roof and undressed. The sun was low in the west and the afternoon song of the mill had ceased. The robins were chirping their evening notes. It was supper time, and Simon McQuarrie was late. Half an hour passed before Peter heard him enter the cabin. He came directly to the ladder and climbed up. In the twilight he bent over Peter.

"Feeling sick, Peter?"

"No, sir."

Simon knelt upon the edge of the blankets.

"I've heard about the fight," he said, in a voice which trembled a little in its unaccustomed softness. "Mona told me, and then Adette, and after that I went down to the tug to have it out with Izaak Curry—and his boy. But—Peter—lad, when I saw Aleck I had no heart to speak harshly to his father. I'm proud of you!"

In the silence he bent his face nearer to Peter's.

"Want something to eat, lad?"

"I can't eat," explained Peter huskily. "My mouth is swollen shut."

It was then Simon McQuarrie's hard lips touched Peter's cheek— the first kiss he had given in many years.

"Good night," he whispered. "You're Donald McRae's son—every inch of you!" And Peter listened to his heavy feet as he slowly descended the ladder.

XI

T he moon did not come up that night. Darkness shut in the earth, and with it came a warm and sullen stillness, broken only by low intonations of distant thunder, advancing over the roofs of the forest. A long time after Simon had gone Peter went to the window and sat staring out into the gloom. The air was drowsily heavy and bore with it the cooling breath of rain. After a little a swift whispering ran through the forest and the first gentle patter of raindrops fell on the cabin roof. The thunder crashed nearer and vivid flashes of lightning cut like flaming knives through the blackness. In a moment, it seemed to Peter, the storm broke in a deluge that set the log walls atremble. It beat straight down, and did not come in at the window. Peter did not stir. As long ago as he could remember his father had taught him to be unafraid of the awesomeness and beauty of thunder and lightning, and many times they had watched a storm together until the boy was thrilled by the significance and the mystery of it.

It was his father he missed tonight, the immeasurable thrill of his voice, his presence and his love. Without reason his eyes strained questingly in those brief moments when the lightning flashes filled the world with a white radiance. In that light he could see the mill, stark and vivid, like a skeleton illumined by fire, the trees, the cabins, the stub in which the flying squirrels lived, and the edge of the forest. He did not miss that half of his vision which he had lost in his fight with Aleck Curry; he had forgotten the fight, and even Mona Guyon. For a time his thoughts were alone with his father, and with his yearning and his loneliness an unreasonable hope filled his soul—the hope that his father would keep his promise and that out in the glare of the lightning he would see him coming from the forest into the clearing. His heart ached for that. He did not know it, but under his breath he was sobbing a little.

It was the truth, forcing itself upon him, the sullen, terrible truth, driving him back from the window and sending him creeping to his blankets, where he lay huddled and still. He had never hated anyone, not even Aleck Curry. But he was beginning to hate somebody— something—now. He hated the men who were after his father, and he was beginning vaguely to hate that controlling force which both his father and Simon McQuarrie had told him was the law. If his father

JAMES OLIVER CURWOOD

had only taken him! If they were only together now, away out there in the forest, under a log or snuggled in the shelter of an overturned root—anywhere—just so they were together!

Why had his father lied to him, promising him he would come back in a day or two? Why had he sent him on alone to Five Fingers? Peter choked back the sob in his throat. *He knew.* It was because his father loved him—because he knew that he could never return, and wanted him to have a home with Simon McQuarrie.

Burying his face in his arm, Peter gave up to his grief. It was a silent, choking grief that ate into his heart but brought no cry to his lips.

The thunder and lightning passed and the rain settled into a steady patter on the roof. It was like hundreds of gentle fingers tapping within a few feet of Peter's head. It comforted him in his aloneness and his grief. Mona was listening to that same friendly patter on the cedar shingles. Tomorrow he would see her again, and his heart grew warm. A part of her seemed to come into the darkness of his room, and he could see her eyes shining and feel the touch of her hand—and the kiss. And afterward he fell asleep, stirred by the strange and comforting sensation that Mona was near him.

But in sleep he lost her. He dreamed that he was trying to steal away from Five Fingers to go in search of his father, but again and again Simon McQuarrie caught him and brought him back. At last success came. It was night, and he was crawling out through his window into the moonlight, with a pack on his back. He jumped to the ground and made for the woods. And then a strange thing happened. Where his father had left him he found footprints on the earth. They were very clear, and shining, as if made of bright silver, and they reached a long distance ahead of him through the forest. It puzzled him that his own feet left no trail at all while his father's trail was so clear.

Days and nights seemed to pass as he followed persistently this silvery trail. Then he came to a wonderful forest where the trees were so tall their tops seemed lost against the sky. He walked on flowers. Great masses of purple violets crushed under his feet, roses filled the air with sweetness, wild geraniums nodded and bowed to him, and crimson splashes of fire-flowers carpeted long aisles and broad chambers of this mysterious paradise.

He came at last to a waterfall. It did not roar, like waterfalls he had known, but fell with a rippling song. Near the waterfall was a cabin, and straight to the door of the cabin led the silvery trail! Peter followed it. He opened the door and went in and his father was there. He turned to greet Peter and did not seem surprised. His face was smiling and happy, and tender with the old cheer and the old love.

"I thought you would come soon, Peter," he said. *"I've been waiting for you."*

It was then Peter awakened. The patter of rain on the roof had ceased. The night had cleared and was filled with stars, and a sweet warmth came in through the open window. His dream had been overwhelmingly real, and it left him with his heart beating strangely. He did not sleep again but lay awake until the stars began to fade in the gray light of dawn. Then he dressed himself, making no sound that might disturb Simon. When he looked down from his window he almost expected to see the marks he had made in his dream-leap. And it could be done—that jump! He crept out backward, lowered himself full length from the windowsill and dropped easily to the rain-softened earth.

He went toward the stream which came down from the timbered hills and ridges. The birds were beginning to sing, the robins first, twittering their sweetest of all songs, with eyes half closed. It grew gently, each soft note increasing in strength until the invisible chorus filled the clearing with its welcome to the day. A thrush joined in. Bright-winged bluebirds flew ahead of him, and sweet-voiced brush sparrows cheeped and fluttered in their coverts, waiting for the sun. Even the water dripping from the trees held in its sound the cadence of whispered song.

And as if this melody held a spell which they were powerless to combat, or which inspired them to silence, the raucous jays were still and aloof, the whisky jacks waited in fluffy brown balls, a cock-of-the-wood clung to the side of a tree, his plumed head and powerful bill making no sound upon the wood, and ahead of Peter a gray owl retreated to a deeper and darker hiding-place.

The forest was a cathedral, and its symphony seized upon Peter's soul and lifted it on a great wave of anticipation and hope.

His father was listening to the birds, too. He was waiting for the sunrise. And a stirring thought came to Peter. If his father did not return, he would do what he had done in his dream—go in search of him. He was sure he could find him.

He undressed at the edge of a pool in which the water was warm enough for a swim, and came out of it a little later shivering—but still thinking. The early rays of the sun were breaking over the tree-tops

JAMES OLIVER CURWOOD

when he returned to the clearing. His bad eye was half open and most of the swelling was gone from his lips. Simon was getting breakfast and was surprised that Peter should come through the door instead of down the ladder.

During the next hour his shrewd eyes saw a change in the boy. Peter was restless and asked questions. Where would his father be likely to go? Had he said anything about it in his letter to Simon?

The Scotchman shook his head, guessing a little of what was in Peter's mind. He explained the vastness of the forests. They reached a thousand miles north and twice that far east and west, and one might lose himself in them all his life. Their bigness did not discourage Peter.

"I think I can find my father," he said. "If he doesn't come back I'm going to try."

The thought gripped him more tenaciously as the early hours of the morning passed. Simon brushed and mended him, and said he should have new clothes as quickly as they could be brought from the settlement on the railroad, and he talked of Aleck's defeat, and of Mona, and of the wonderful beaver colony two miles away, but the new thrill in Peter's blood swept over all other things that might have interested him.

He would not tell Simon, but he was going in search of his father— soon. It might be that night, or the next, if he could get things together for a pack.

The sun was well up when he saw Mona come out of the Gourdon cabin, and he went across the clearing to meet her. He was a little upset, for he would have to apologize for running away from her in such a boorish fashion yesterday. Mona's appearance this morning set his heart aflutter. She seemed almost as old as Adette Clamart, and not at all like the little fighting comrade who had helped him whip Aleck Curry at their first meeting. She was dressed in spotless white, and her long hair rippled and shone in the sun, and her dark eyes were so beautiful that for a moment or two Peter could find nothing to say as she looked at him.

Mona was not entirely unconscious of her disconcerting loveliness, and her eyes shone and the color grew prettier in her cheeks when she saw its effect on Peter.

"This is my Sunday dress," she said, helping him out of his embarrassment. "Do you like it?"

Peter shifted, and thought quickly. "You look like a snowbird, one of the kind with a black topknot," he complimented her. "What do you think of *me*?" And he turned so that she could see where Simon had mended his rusty clothes.

The sparkle died out of Mona's eyes, and in the moment when his back was toward her Peter did not see the look of pity and tenderness that took its place, and with it a shadow of something else, as if he had hurt her.

"I put on this dress for you. That's what I think of you, Peter."

"I got better clothes," he explained, "but we came away so fast we didn't have time to bring them."

"I'm glad you didn't. I like you the way you are. Do you like me, Peter—really?"

"A lot."

"How much?"

Peter turned over various terms of measurement in his mind. "Next to my father," he said.

"Then why did you run away from me when I was in the kitchen with Adette Clamart?" she asked.

Peter flushed. "I dunno. Guess I didn't like to be laughed at. And the baby—he didn't know who I was."

The soft notes of a bell tolled over the clearing, and Peter drew himself erect and breathed a little tensely as he listened to it. "I used to hear a church bell like that, a long time ago," he said, softly. "I can just remember it."

She touched his arm as they listened. "I was coming to take you to church. Father Albanel says you promised."

She started down the slope, walking slowly, with Peter at her side. He thought it was interesting how the sound of the bell suddenly opened the doors of Five Fingers.

Pierre Gourdon came out of his cabin with his wife, and Josette was dressed in white, like Mona; and Marie Antoinette, waiting with Joe and their two children to greet them, looked like a slim white angel to Peter. Even Geertruda Poulin, who was almost as wide as she was high, wore a dress as white as the gull's wings down in Middle Finger Inlet.

The children were prim and starched and the men were in clothes which Peter had not seen them wear before, their faces shining with the effect of lather and sharp razors.

And loveliest of all the girls and women, Peter thought, was Mona— lovelier even than Adette Clamart, who came hurrying to them with laughing eyes and red lips and rebellious curls dancing about her

JAMES OLIVER CURWOOD

pink cheeks to beg Peter's pardon for laughing at him the preceding afternoon.

To Peter's infinite dismay Adette seized his head between her two small hands and kissed him squarely on the eye which had looked so funny to her yesterday.

"There, I'm sorry, Peter," she said. "But you did look so funny."

She was gone like one of the dainty, golden canaries that nested in the clearing, running to catch up with Jame, her husband, who had Telesphore in his arms.

Fire leaped into Mona's cheeks.

"I won't have Adette Clamart doing that," she protested indignantly. "If your eye needs kissing—"

Peter was wiping it with the back of his hand.

"That's right, wipe it away," she encouraged spitefully. "I hate her!"

Peter said nothing. But he saw Mona's lovely eyes flash in Adette's direction when they were seated on one of the wooden benches in the little church. Adette smiled mischievously and nodded her head, but Mona made no response except to tilt her pretty chin a little higher in the air and look straight ahead of her to the platform where Father Albanel was ready to begin the service.

The little missioner's face was even rosier and jollier than yesterday, it seemed to Peter, and he was smiling and nodding and rubbing his hands as if this particular hour was the happiest of his life.

Peter, looking secretly about him, was impressed by the fact that this was unlike any other Sunday meeting he had ever attended. He missed the serious and almost awesome solemnity of the other similar occasions he could remember. Here everyone was free and easy and refreshingly happy. Even Simon McQuarrie's emotionless face was more gentle, and he smiled when he saw Peter, and a ripple of laughter ran easily through the gathering when young Telesphore crowed delightedly and waved his arms in an embracing greeting to all about him. Then came the tinkle of a bell, and suddenly the room was very quiet.

What happened after that was like a dream to Peter, and it seemed constantly to be awakening something new and happier within him. He had never heard singing like that which filled the little church. Mona's voice was clear and soft as the crested warbler's song which he loved; and when she looked at him and whispered, "Sing, Peter," his courage came to him, and a little at a time he lifted his voice until his boyish tenor rose clearly at her side. When they sat down she was nearer to him, so near that her wonderful white dress crumpled close against him and a tress of her shining hair fell upon his hand.

"I love your singing, Peter," she whispered to him again.

His heart beat fast and his hand twitched nervously under the silken caress of her hair. Until now—this hour when they sat so close together in the church—he had not felt the deeper stir of that emotion which was growing in him. Surreptitiously his fingers closed about the soft tress of hair. Mona did not know it, no one knew it but himself, and he looked straight ahead while his heart beat still faster and the warm thrill of his secret sent the blood into his face.

Father Albanel was talking. And in a trance Peter listened. What struck him, and what he remembered so clearly afterward, was the way in which the little missioner talked about all living things, as if the flowers and trees had hearts and souls, and God loved the forests and all wild things just as much as He loved people. Peter had heard his father say many of those same things, only in a different way—for Father Albanel's voice was like deep music that reached down into the soul, and there was no whisper or stir among those who listened to him.

He seemed to be looking straight at Peter when he talked about Faith, and what faith meant in the lives of men and women and children; and to make this clear to the children of Five Fingers he told the legend of Nepise, the beautiful Indian maiden, who was known as the Torch-Bearer. It seemed to Peter the missioner was describing Mona, for Nepise was the loveliest girl among all her people, with eyes that were pools of beauty and hair that fell about her like a shining black garment. The story became a tragic and living thing to him; he saw the plague-stricken Indian people, and when Nepise died the effect upon him was like a shock. But she had made her dying people a promise—a wonderful promise!—to come back in spirit, bearing with her the Torch of Life, and with this flaming torch she would go from tepee to tepee and from village to village, and all who had faith in her would see her and to them would come health and happiness. And Nepise kept her promise, and forever after that, and up to this very day, the Indian maiden was known throughout the wilderness as the Torch-Bearer.

When Father Albanel had finished Peter looked at Mona. Her red lips were parted, her eyes were aglow, and in her white throat a little heart seemed beating. And when they stood up again to sing his fingers

JAMES OLIVER CURWOOD

still held the soft tress of hair, and this time Mona saw it, and smiled at him, and Peter was no longer afraid of his secret.

After Father Albanel's benediction Mona led Peter a little hurriedly from the meeting-house, but without losing her prim dignity so long as she thought Adette Clamart's eyes might be upon her.

"I shan't speak to her all day!" she confided in Peter.

They passed near the tug and saw Aleck Curry fishing from the stern, and Mona told him that neither Aleck nor his father ever came to church. Then they came to a narrow foot trail that was new to Peter and for half an hour walked slowly out on a green-timbered point of land until they reached the big lake. It was the finest view Peter had ever had of Superior. The great sea seemed to engulf the world, and away out there were three white dots which were ships under canvas. It was warm and calm, and he was puzzled by a sullen, booming roar until Mona led the way down a break in the cliff and showed him the Pit, where the surf and undertows boiled and rumbled even in fair weather. And in storm—

She tried to tell him what it was then, when the great rocks were like so many monsters, grinding things to pieces, and when nothing that lived could exist for more than a minute or two in what Pierre Gourdon called the maelstroms. They found a clean white rock, worn smooth by the water, and sat down, and Peter wondered at the change which came into Mona's face.

"Can you remember your mother, Peter?" she asked softly.

He was silent for a moment, and then said, "I've seen her a good many times when I was asleep."

"Do you still see her?"

"I did two nights ago."

"Is she pretty?"

"Yes."

"So is mine." She folded her hands in her lap and added quietly: "Out there is where my mother and father were drowned. Uncle Pierre tied me to his back and brought me ashore."

Then she told him the story of the wreck of the sailing ship, and how Aunt Josette and Marie Antoinette and Father Albanel and all the people of Five Fingers said it was a miracle that even one should come ashore alive. And she was that one.

"Father Albanel sometimes comes down here with me," she said. "I love him. He always tells me about Nepise. Isn't that a pretty name,

Peter? It means Willow Bud. But after she died and her spirit came back with the torch they called her Suskuwao, which means the Torch-Bearer. I love her, too. Do you?"

Peter nodded. "I was thinking of you," he said desperately, trying to get the choking thought out of him. "Father Albanel was looking at you when he told about the Indian girl. That's what you've been to me since I come—a—a sort of torch-bearer, like he said she was. I dunno what I'd have done if it hadn't been for you."

It was out, and for a moment or two the suffocating realization of what he had said made it difficult for him to breathe easily. Mona did not look at him. Her shining eyes were fixed steadily upon the vastness of the lake.

"Was that why you touched my hair, Peter?"

"I guess so."

"You like me—*like that*?"

He nodded again, finding the moment too tremendous for words. And this time Mona was looking at him. There was an earnestness in her face which made her seem older to Peter. Her eyes were a woman's eyes, calm and steady in their gaze, as they studied him for a moment.

"And I like you, Peter," she said then, "I like you so much—that I never want you to go away from Five Fingers."

"And I never want to go," he said. "Not if my father comes back."

"He will come!"

Her voice was quick and sure and filled with a vibrant ring that sent a little tremble through him. She was sitting very straight, and a gust of wind stirred her hair so that it rippled and floated about her, and Peter—looking at her with wide eyes and swiftly beating heart— thought of Father Albanel, and of Nepise the Torch-Bearer, and the beautiful faith the little missioner had visioned entered into him and he believed. And the strange and thrilling impulse came to him to put his hand to that soft cloud of Mona's hair and tell her that he believed. But he did not move, nor did he speak. For a space Mona seemed to be far away from him, gazing at something which he could not see out beyond the turmoil of the Pit. Her fingers were interlocked in her lap, and not until the voice of Jame Clamart hallooed down from the top of the cliff was the spell of silence broken.

Mona started but did not look up. She knew Adette was there, smiling down at them and ready to wave her hand. Quite calmly she said to Peter:

JAMES OLIVER CURWOOD

"It's that Adette Clamart. Will you promise never to let her kiss you again?"

"Sure—I promise," said Peter.

"As long as you live?"

"As long as I live."

"Cross your heart, Peter!"

Devoutly Peter took the solemn oath.

"I'm glad," said Mona. "I don't like kissing—but if it has to be done I'll do it!" And a fiery little note in her voice was so combatively possessive that Peter suddenly felt himself a helpless but willing slave in chains.

And in the days and weeks that followed his first Sunday in the settlement this bondage was stronger than the hungering loneliness for his father which pulled him at times toward the big forests of the north. Mona's world became his world. He began to fit into its play, its duties, and the family communism of its environment. He went to school. At odd hours he worked about the mill and helped in the spring planting, and later in the tilling of the soil.

In the passing of the summer Mona and Peter spent much of their time together in the cool depths of the forests. On these adventurings they were inseparable, and their favorite haunt, specially on Sunday afternoons, was a beaver colony a mile and a half up the shore of the lake and a little back in the rough ridges and hills. The beaver settlement was Mona's own property, and it was one of the laws of Five Fingers that no one should despoil it with trap or gun. It was five years ago, Mona told Peter, that four old beavers emigrated from some one of the colonies back in the hills and she and Pierre discovered them building a dam at this place. There were now over thirty of them. A long time ago they had ceased to be afraid of her, and some of them were so friendly she could touch them with her hand. But they were alarmed when Peter came with her and for days scarcely a head would show when he was about. Very slowly and with extreme caution they began to accept him as a part of Mona, and the first cool breath of autumn was in the nights before they would openly disclose themselves or play on their slides or proceed with the varied duties of their lives when he was watching the big dark pool in which they had built their homes.

XII

In September a sinister and foreboding gloom seemed to creep out of the wilderness surrounding Five Fingers.

The golden autumn, with its soft Indian summer and its radiance of color, died almost before it was born. The birch leaves did not turn yellow and gold but stopped at a rusty brown; the poplar leaves curled up and began to fall from their stems before the first frost; mountain ash berries were pink instead of red, and heavy fogs settled like wet blankets between the ridges, while in the swamps the rabbits were dying in hundreds and thousands of the mysterious "seven years' sickness."

The men at Five Fingers, and especially Pierre Gourdon and Dominique Beauvais, who read the wilderness as if it were a book, regarded these matters with anxious eyes. It was Pierre who called attention to the going of the bluebirds a month before their time, and noted first that the red squirrels were gathering great stores of cones, and that the robins were restless and uneasy and were assembling in the flocks which presaged sudden flight.

Then, one sunset, a great flock of wild geese went honking south. They were high and flying very fast.

Pierre Gourdon pointed up. "When the wild geese race like that in September—it means a bad winter. Only twice have I seen it. The last time was two years before we came to Five Fingers—a year of starvation and plague; and the other time—" He shuddered, and shrugged his shoulders, for that other time was in boyhood, when his mother and father had died back in the forests, and he had dragged himself starving and nearly dead to Ste. Anne de Beaupré.

Colder nights came, filled with moaning winds, and the days were darkened by ash-gray skies through which the sun seldom shone warmly, and more and more frequently came the honk of geese racing south. Peter could hear them at night, in darkness and when the stars were shining, coming from the north, crying down their solemn notes of passage from the high trails of the air.

And these same nights he heard the wolves howl back in the hollows and ridges and deeper hunting grounds of the forests, and Pierre Gourdon listened uneasily to the cold, hard note in their voices, and said to Dominique:

"The wolves will run lean this winter, and when hunger trails the wolves, famine is not far behind."

But it was the dying of the rabbits more than the crying of the wolves that worried them at first. The plague-stricken animals were lying everywhere, even up to the steps of the cabins, and one day Peter counted so many in a corner of the swamp that Simon McQuarrie's eyes widened a little with doubt when he told his story. Once every seven or nine years had the rabbit plague swept on its devastating way through the wilderness, but never had Pierre or Dominique or Simon seen it so destructive as this year, and the nearer howling of the wolves and the strange, clammy nights with their deathlike fogs roused in Pierre Gourdon's heart the ghosts of old superstitions and old fears put there in tragic days when he was a boy.

And then came a night when the world seemed filled with wet smoke, and on that night the gray Canada geese came down from the north in a multitude so great that they filled the sky over Five Fingers with a winged deluge, and thousands of them dropped into the inlet and the clearing to rest. Their honking was a bedlam which made sleep impossible, and with the dawn Peter could see them darkening the fields and the water of Middle Finger Inlet. When the various companies and regiments began taking wing the sound they made was a steady thunder that sent a weird and thrilling shudder through earth and air. There were ten thousand pair of wings in that southward moving host, Pierre Gourdon said. Peter had never thought there were so many wild geese in the world and it puzzled him that not one of them was killed by the men at Five Fingers.

"A wild goose mates but once," Pierre explained. "If his mate dies, he does not take another, but lives alone for the rest of his life. Memory and loyalty like that men do not have, and so it is a crime to kill them." Then he added, looking up thoughtfully at one of the winged triangles racing through the sky, "And the gray goose lives a hundred years!"

In October what were left of the big snowshoe rabbits began to turn white, and the wind kept steadily in the north. Snow fell early. All through November the big lake was lashed by fierce gales; the Pit roared and whipped itself into furies, and the gulls were gone entirely from Middle Finger Inlet. In a single night, it seemed to Peter, winter came. And from the beginning it was a black, ominous winter. For days at a time there was no sun. The sky was shut in by a gray canopy of cloud. When snow fell it was hard and biting, and riding with the wind, it stung the flesh like fine shot.

In December came a change. The winds died, the skies cleared a little, and day and night it snowed until the wilderness was smothered and the evergreen forests bent to the snapping point under their burden. Trails were closed and the hollows between ridges were filled. One day Poleon Dufresne snowshoed in from the railroad settlement, half dead from exhaustion and bearing the news that all the world was shut out by snow, and that it lay twenty feet deep in the open places. And quietly he gave other news to Pierre Gourdon and Dominique and Simon McQuarrie. The dreaded plague of the wilderness—the smallpox—had already begun to stalk through the northland.

Following the deep snows came a cold so intense that the men no longer ran the hazard of frosted lungs by working in the woods, and all wild life seemed to have become extinct. Between the lake and the settlements along the line of steel one could scarcely have found the trail of a cloven hoof, for the deer and moose were yarded deep and struggled breast-high against snow for the bush-browsing that kept them alive, while the caribou, milling against wind and storm, had left the snow-smothered country for feeding grounds farther north. It was a winter that began—first of all—with starvation. The icy coating of the trees left no budding for the grouse; small creatures smothered in thousands under the hardening snow crust which could soon bear the weight of a man; foxes and ermine gnawed bark in their hunger; with the rabbits gone, owls died of a sickness which ravages them in times of forest famine—and the empty stomachs of wolves brought them nearer and nearer to the clearing until frightened horses broke halters in their stalls and cattle bellowed in their terror.

Peter had never heard wolves as they cried out now. Sometimes their wail of hunger was almost a sobbing in the night, and again it was bitter and vengeful as hoof and horn beat them back from some yarded stronghold of moose and deer.

Each day and week Peter came to understand more of the tragedy through which he was passing. It was one of the "black years." Father Albanel came to the settlement early in January; he was thin and haggard, his eyes deep-set, the rosy color gone from his face. In the little church he asked the people of Five Fingers to offer up prayer for the thousands who were sick and the hundreds who were dying through all the great wilderness from Hudson Bay to the Athabasca and from Big Lake to the Barren Lands. Over all that country the plague was raging, sweeping like a forest fire from tepee to cabin, until in certain

JAMES OLIVER CURWOOD

far places the great Hudson Bay Company could no longer bury its dead, and masterless dogs ran with the wild things in the forests. Pierre Gourdon's face was almost as haggard as Father Albanel's, and Mona called Peter's attention to it, with a tense and strange look in her eyes.

"I overheard Uncle Pierre and Aunt Josette when they were talking last night and they said they weren't afraid for themselves but that they were afraid for me," she said. "Why should they be, Peter? I don't get sick easily."

"You're a girl, that's why," he explained.

"But if I should get sick—what would you do? Would you dare to come and see me?"

"I'd come."

"Even if it was the plague?"

"I'd still come."

"I'd like to have you, Peter. If I was sick and you didn't come, I think it would make me feel so badly I wouldn't get well."

And that night, with the wolves wailing at its doors, the blighting hand of the red plague fell upon Five Fingers!

It touched Geertruda Poulin first, and Jeremie, her husband, nailed a red cloth over his cabin door to keep the children at a distance, and that rag, fluttering in the winds, soon filled their hearts with a greater terror than if they had seen a *loup-garou* haunting the edge of the forest or the grim hunters of the *Chasse-galerie* riding through the gloomy sky, for they were told that to go near it meant death. And then, three days later, little Tobina fell ill, and with a pale, brave face and eyes in which there was no sign of fear Marie Antoinette went into the plague-stricken cabin to nurse them. After that Joe Gourdon's face was like a mask carven out of stone until the night when Jame Clamart pounded at his door and cried out the terrible news that Adette was down with the fever. And that midnight Josette calmly kissed Pierre and Mona good-by and went to her. Until she was gone Pierre held back the sob in his throat—then it escaped him, and he held Mona close, so close that it hurt her. It was on a Sunday morning, bitterly cold and filled with gusty winds, that Jeremie Poulin staggered out from his door and flung up his arms to the sky, and the word passed from cabin to cabin that Geertruda was dead.

Alone, barring all others from their company, Simon McQuarrie and Father Albanel dug with picks and grub-hoes the first new grave in the little cemetery. Chunk by chunk they broke out the frozen earth, and when it was dark—so dark no eyes could see them—they helped Jeremie Poulin carry his dead over the clearing and upon their knees prayed with him at the grave-side. After that they lived in one of the barns, visiting only the sick and the dead, and each morning and evening Simon would shout to Peter through the megaphone of his hands, asking him if he felt pain or dizziness or fever, and warning him to stay in the cabin. Then Sara Dufresne and two of her three children were stricken and Jean Croisset died so suddenly that the shock of it stopped every heart in Five Fingers. Pounding of hammers came from the barn, and the next morning there was another mound of brown and frozen earth in the cemetery. A day later Dominique Beauvais, with his house full of children, nailed up the red badge of sickness over his cabin door.

Each day Peter saw Mona. They spent their hours together, and Pierre Gourdon watched them as a hawk watches its young. At night they sat at their windows, for after Jean's death the skies cleared and a glorious moon filled the world with light. And one night Peter heard the hammers pounding again, and in the gray of dawn—still sleepless and wide-eyed—he saw Father Albanel and Simon and Jeremie Poulin come from Dominique Beauvais's cabin bearing a long, grim thing among them; and when they had reached the burial slope he saw them turn back, and enter the cabin again, and come forth once more with their shoulders bent under a burden. Peter's heart choked him. He sobbed and clutched his hands at his breast. It was Félipe and Dominique, the two youngest of the Beauvais children, whom he had seen carried to the burial plot.

Sobbing, he ran toward Mona's home. The door opened and Pierre Gourdon came out. Peter stopped a few paces away, for there was something in Pierre's face that frightened him. At first he thought it must be the madness of the fever; then his ears caught words, strange, hard words that froze his blood and that seemed to come with a mighty effort from Pierre's ghastly face. Mona was sick! She was in bed— and he must return to Simon McQuarrie's cabin and not come again within breathing distance of the house! Peter moved closer to the door, powerless to speak, and Pierre thrust him back so roughly that he fell to the ground.

"Go away!" he commanded, raising a hand as if to strike the boy.

Through the open door Peter had a glimpse of Josette's face looking out at him, so white and haggard that for a moment he thought it was an old woman's face. He cried out to her but in the same moment she was gone and there came no answer.

Then he spoke half defiantly to Pierre.

"I want to see Mona," he said. "I promised her I'd come if she was sick."

"Go!" said Pierre again, pointing sternly toward Simon McQuarrie's cabin. "You can come halfway to learn how Mona is, but if you come this near again I shall have you taken from Five Fingers!"

Peter drew slowly away, staring in horror at Pierre and the cabin behind him. He slumped down on the doorstep at Simon's place and did not feel the bitter cold. He saw Pierre enter the cabin, and then he watched the gray figures in the distant cemetery as they moved slowly about, piling the last of the frozen clods upon the burdens they had carried through the dawn a few minutes before. And Mona was down with that same sickness—which meant death!

In his torment he picked and twisted at his clothes until his thin fingers were blue with the cold. Pierre came out again and put up the red cloth, and then he went to intercept the three men who were on their way from the cemetery to their quarters in the barn. Father Albanel and Simon McQuarrie returned with Pierre and entered the cabin where Mona was sick. In a few minutes Simon came out and seeing Peter huddled on the doorstep, approached as near to him as he dared. He asked the same questions, and gave the same warnings, and assured Peter that Mona was only slightly ill, and that she would get over it very quickly. But there was in his face the same look that had been in Pierre's, and Peter knew he was lying.

"She is going to die," his heart kept crying, and he dragged himself into the cabin and flung himself upon Simon's bed, and when Joe Gourdon came in he was crying, his head buried in his arms. With his beloved Marie Antoinette keeping guard in Jeremie Poulin's house of death, Joe was making a courageous fight. "Tobina Poulin is past all danger, and if things go well Aunt Marie Antoinette will come home in a few days, and then you can come to us," he comforted Peter. "Meanwhile I'm going to stay with you."

But Joe's cheerfulness was mostly forced. News came early in the day that Adette Clamart was very close to death, and that Jame and Father Albanel were constantly at her bedside.

That night sheer exhaustion brought sleep to Peter. He was awakened by a pounding at the door. Joe's voice called out below and another answered it from outside. It was Jame Clamart, going from cabin to cabin in a madness of joy, telling the people of Five Fingers that the crisis was over and Adette would live.

Peter could hear the running crunch of Jame's boots in the hard snow as he hurried on to the next neighbor and for a long time after that he lay awake in the cold darkness of his room, thinking of Mona. Fear of death had not gripped him so terribly before. In the tragedy of others he had felt shock; its suddenness and horror had stunned him and filled him with dread, but the physical grief of it had not touched him deeply until now. He was sick, but the sickness was in his heart, as if something had been cut out of it, leaving in its place an emptiness which made breath come to his lips in smothered sobs. And that something which had been taken away from him was Mona.

When he closed his eyes he could see her clearly on her white bed, her long hair streaming about the pillow, her face pinched and thin, and all the time she was wondering *why he did not come*. She was going to die; he could think of nothing but that, and after a little one thing persisted in traveling through his brain so frequently and so terribly that he called aloud for Joe. The maddening picture was that of Father Albanel and Simon and Jeremie Poulin marching through the gray dawn to the burial plot with the bodies of Félipe and Dominique Beauvais.

Joe came up, and for the rest of that night Peter lay in the shelter of his arm and fell asleep again.

The next day came with good omen. A bright sun rose over the forests, clearer and warmer than it had been for many weeks. Herman Vogelaar, whose laughter had gone with the death of his daughter, Geertruda, came at breakfast time with the word that Adette was entirely out of her fever, and that Poleon Dufresne's wife and three children were much better than yesterday. Father Albanel, he said, had spent the last half of the night with Mona. Mona was very sick. She was worse than Adette had been, or even Geertruda, in the same length of time. He was afraid—But Joe gave him such a fierce scowl he did not finish. Peter saw the scowl and the nervous twisting of Herman's fingers at the lapels of his coat as he tried to think of something with which to cover his blunder. He wanted to ask Herman to speak what had been on his lips, but instead he put on his coat and cap and heavy mittens and went out into the day, hoping that somewhere he would see Father Albanel.

As if his hope were a prayer quickly answered, Father Albanel came from the Gourdon cabin. The little missioner advanced, keeping the wind well in his face, and when he was fifty paces from Peter he stopped and called to the boy to stand where he was. Peter tried to speak bravely when he asked if Mona was going to die.

"She is very sick," said the missioner. "We must pray for her, and believe with all our might that she is going to get well. I think God will let her live."

"I promised I'd come if she was sick. I got to keep my word. I'm not afraid."

Father Albanel shook his head.

"It is impossible, Peter. There are too many of us down now."

"I won't get sick," said Peter doggedly.

Father Albanel spoke sharply. "Keep to your cabin, my boy, and be as brave as Jame Clamart has been. If Mona grows worse, I will tell you."

Each morning after this he brought news of Mona to Peter. For a week there seemed to be no change. On the eighth day she was worse; on the tenth Pierre and Josette and Father Albanel were fighting desperately to save her life.

The tenth night came. It was past midnight when Peter crept softly to his window and opened it. With as little sound as he could make he drew himself through and dropped to the ground. He ran away quickly, the brilliance of the stars sending his shadow along with him. He did not stop until he reached the Gourdon cabin, and there he hugged closely against the log wall, his heart beating wildly as he waited. Above him a light glowed feebly against the curtain in Mona's room. He wanted to call to her; he puckered his lips and almost gave the whistling signal which she knew. Then he heard a sound, a movement of some kind, and stealthily he approached a lower window. He could see Josette very clearly. She was seated in a chair with her face bowed in her hands, and Pierre was standing at her side, gently stroking her hair. Father Albanel was behind them, his face white and torn with grief. Then Peter saw that Josette was crying.

A terrible fear gripped him as he drew away from the window. What he had seen could mean only one thing. Mona—*was gone*. He looked up at the dim light above him again, and in that moment his soul cried out against all those who had kept him away from her. He went to the kitchen door, opened it, and entered. This time he would scream and fight if they tried to keep him back. But no one heard him. Father Albanel's voice came to him faintly. He was praying.

Peter reached the stair and went up quietly. The door of Mona's room was open. A lamp, turned low, was burning on the table.

He approached the bed, scarcely knowing that he was moving toward it. His heart was crushed, his world crumbled and gone, for Mona must be dead or they would not leave her like this, and Josette would not be crying down below. Even his father could not have helped him now. Nothing could help him, with Mona *gone*. He stumbled to his knees beside her and his cold fingers twined themselves about the soft braid of hair that fell over the side of her bed.

A stifled, despairing sob broke from him then as he stared at the thin face that lay so still and lifeless in the pale light of the room. He had a great desire to touch it but a moment of dread made him hesitate. Then his hand crept slowly over the coverlet until it rested against Mona's cheek, and the sobbing in his throat was choked back, for the flesh he touched was hot. His heart thumped until the sound of it seemed to fill the room. Mona's eyes were opening! They were looking at him! And then—

Two thin, white arms reached up and encircled Peter's neck, and very faintly he heard his name whispered. He pressed his face down close to Mona's.

"I'd have come sooner," he apologized, "but they wouldn't let me in!"

And somehow, in that great moment of their lives Peter's lips touched Mona's, and as the girl's flagging spirit came at last in triumph back from the edge of death Father Albanel entered the room; and when he saw what had happened he spoke no word, but in silence made the sign of the cross upon his breast and stood with his gray head bowed in voiceless prayer.

JAMES OLIVER CURWOOD

XIII

It was many minutes before Peter looked up and saw Father Albanel standing at his side. The little missioner made no movement except to place a hand gently on the boy's head. Mona's eyes were wide open and in them was a light of almost unearthly happiness as she looked at Peter. In the pale lamp-glow it seemed as though death had already possessed her, except for those great, shining eyes out of which Father Albanel saw all fever had gone.

In a voice that was low and choking he said, "You must come away now, Peter—for a little while."

Mona's hands rose in weak protest to Peter's shoulders, and he bent to meet them, pressing his face down again without shame or embarrassment so that her soft cheek lay close against his own.

Joy and gentleness fought with a gathering fear in Father Albanel's face, and a little at a time, but firmly, he drew Peter away, while between the words he was speaking he breathed a prayer to Sainte Anne and the Mother Mary asking that the boy might be spared the curse of the deadly malady with which he had come in contact.

At the door Peter turned, and Mona's eyes were so strangely and darkly beautiful that he reached back his arms to her with a little cry. "I'll come again, Mona! I will! I'll come *soon!*"

They went down into the room where he had seen Josette and Pierre, with his hand held tightly in the little missioner's. He had never seen a face more terribly white than Josette's, and Pierre was like a haggard old man. He looked up at Father Albanel. The missioner's face was streaming with tears, and through the tears he was smiling. Then he began to speak. He told how Peter had stolen into the house and had gone to Mona.

"God sent him," he said. "He has done more than all the physicians and medicines in the world could have done, for he has brought Mona back from the very gates of death. *She will live!*"

The last three words drowned all others for Peter. His breath came in little jerks. Then he found himself crying—in Josette's arms.

Josette pressed Peter to her and covered his pale, cold face with kisses. Her great eyes seemed to drown him with their nearness, and then she too was sobbing, with his face hugged close to hers. It all passed in a very few moments, it seemed to Peter, and Josette went with

Father Albanel to Mona's room. She came back in a little while. Her eyes were shining and the whiteness was gone from her face.

"It is true—God has been good to us again," she said, looking into Pierre's wildly questioning eyes.

"The fever is broken. Her skin is soft and moist. And—she—*wants Peter*!"

Josette and Pierre understood the look that came into Father Albanel's face. They waited for him to speak.

"Please let me go," begged Peter. "I won't make a noise. I'll sit quiet."

Father Albanel swallowed a lump in his throat.

"And mebby—if I ask her—she'll go to sleep," urged Peter.

The missioner nodded his gray head. "That's it," he said, looking first at Pierre and then at Josette. "I think if Peter were there, she would sleep. The boy has already been exposed. It cannot be worse. It is God's will. Let him go and sit beside her."

A joyous thrill went through Peter. Father Albanel turned to him and put his hands on the boy's shoulders.

"You must tell her you can stay only if she will try very hard to go to sleep. After that you mustn't talk to her. And just as soon as she is asleep you must slip away quietly and come back to us here."

"I promise," said Peter.

Josette helped him off with his coat. Then she kissed him, and Peter went softly up the stair.

Though he came with scarcely more sound than a shadow to her door Mona heard him. Her eyes were watching for him, so big and shining in her thin white face that to Peter she seemed all eyes. He did not trouble with a stool or chair but knelt beside her bed. Mona's hands went up to his face and their gentle touch drew him down until she kissed him on the lips. There was no hesitation in her act. It was as if she had always kissed him.

"Please kiss me, Peter," she said.

He kissed her.

"I was dreaming that over and over," she smiled at him faintly, "and you didn't come. Now it's true. And—I'm—so—glad—"

"You mustn't talk," he warned, remembering his duty. "They said if *you* said anything after I told you this I'd have to go downstairs. They want you to sleep.

"An' I want you to *sleep*," he added courageously. "You mustn't say another word—not one!"

Mona started to speak, then put a finger to her lips, and her eyes glowed at Peter until he felt creeping through him an overwhelming desire to kiss her again. She tucked her hand in his, and he settled down, sitting on the floor. Mona closed her eyes and gave a deep sigh. Her fingers squeezed Peter's, and Peter's fingers squeezed back.

Half an hour later Josette tiptoed up the stair. Quietly she came through the dim light to the bedside. Mona was asleep. She was breathing evenly for the first time in many days. Peter had leaned over so that his cheek was resting on the thick, soft braid of her hair. Mona's hand was still clasped in his. And he too was asleep.

Josette drew back as quietly as she had entered and returned to Pierre and Father Albanel.

Hours later Peter awoke. He thought he was dreaming at first. Then he found his fingers buried in Mona's braid, and saw her pale face against the pillow. Everything returned to him in a moment, and he moved his cramped legs an inch at a time, and very quietly got on his feet. Mona was asleep. He bent over and listened to her breathing. Then he looked at the little clock that was ticking on a shelf above her table. It was four o'clock. Almost time for the gloomy dawn to come. He must have slept a long time! And Mona had slept too. His heart beat joyously as he backed slowly toward the door, careful not to make the slightest sound.

In the room below he found Father Albanel sitting with his gray head bowed over a book which had fallen into his lap. But Josette heard him, still as he had been, and came out of her room. She was in a white nightgown with soft arms bare to her elbows and her hair in two long, loosely plaited braids.

To Peter she was more than ever like an angel.

"Sh-h-h-h!" she whispered, putting a finger to her lips. "Everyone is asleep, Peter—except you and me!"

She took his hand and led him into the spare room which had once been Joe's, and sat down with him for a few moments on the edge of the bed.

"You are going to stay with us for a while," she said in a voice so low and sweet that it was like music to Peter. "Will you like that?"

He shook his head affirmatively. "I wanted to come all the time. I promised Mona I would—if she was ever sick."

Josette drew his head gently against her breast. He could hear her heart beating.

"I am Mona's mother. After this—how would you like me to be *your* mother?" she asked softly.

"I—I'd like it. But I gotta live with Simon. Dad told me to—until he comes back."

The arm about his shoulders tightened a little.

"Yes, you must live with Simon. I wouldn't take you from him. But I'm going to be your mother, Peter—just the same. From now on, all the time, you belong to me just as Mona does."

"I guess that's why Mona likes me—because I haven't got a mother," he tried to explain. "But my dad's coming back. He'll love you too. Nobody can help loving you, can they?"

"I don't know, Peter."

"Simon says they can't. My mother was just like you. I've dreamed of her lots of times."

"Does she look like me—in your dreams, Peter?"

"Last time I thought she *was* you. We were out in the woods picking flowers, an' Mona was there. Then she faded away. She always fades away, just sort of melts until you can't see her—my mother, I mean." Suddenly he asked, "Did you ever see Mona's mother?"

"Yes, Peter."

"Was she pretty?"

"All mothers are pretty, Peter."

Peter pondered for a moment. "I guess mebby they are," he said, and then added a little dubiously, "except now and then. I'll bet Aleck Curry's mother isn't pretty!"

"To Aleck—she is beautiful," whispered Josette, and drew herself gently away from him. "You must undress and go to bed now, Peter. Good night!"

For a while after she was gone he sat on the edge of his bed wondering what she had meant in saying that thing about Aleck Curry and his mother. A beast like Aleck *couldn't* have a pretty mother. But her words troubled him even after he was undressed and in bed. If by any chance Aleck *did* have a pretty mother—why—it wasn't right for Mona and him to hate Aleck as they did, that was all!

He didn't sleep much between then and morning, and when he came out of his room, just as the first cold light of the winter sun was falling in the clearing, happier faces greeted him. Mona was better. In the reaction of joy that had swept over the household there was once more laughter in the kitchen. Josette went up the stair singing. And when at last she called down for Peter he found Mona bolstered up in her bed, and Josette was brushing her hair, which streamed about her in long, beautiful cascades of silken softness. Mona's eyes and face were different this morning. She was more like the Mona he had known, only thinner and whiter, and she smiled at him when he came through the door.

With Josette so near, Peter was a little self-conscious and clumsy in his greeting. But Mona held out her arms, just as she had done last night, and pulled him down to her, and kissed him.

From that day the great fact in the lives of the two children was accepted in Five Fingers. Mona and Peter belonged to each other. And so sure was Father Albanel of God's intention in the matter that he felt no worry about Peter, in spite of the fact that the boy had come in fearfully close contact with the deadly malady.

"He will not catch the sickness," he said confidently. "God didn't send him for that."

And as day after day passed, and only good news continued to come from the Gourdon cabin, those who had at first doubted also came to believe; for Mona's coming back from death, and Peter's escaping the plague, were miracles like those which happened at the precious shrine of Ste. Anne de Beaupré, and only God could have brought them about.

In two weeks Mona was out of bed and on her feet. And from that day, Peter noticed, she did not hold out her arms to him again, or ask him to kiss her. But her eyes were always soft and full of happiness when he was near her.

The last of winter passed, and spring came. May followed April, and flowers sprang up in the clearing. The birds returned, work began in the fields, and in the sweetness and promise of life Five Fingers rose out of the grimness of its tragedy.

One warm day when they had gone to the big beaver pond, just a week after Mona's fourteenth birthday, Peter said something that he was *thinking*, and didn't mean to say at all. He had been thinking it off and on for a long time, and the words slipped out of him before he knew it.

"You never ask me to kiss you any more," he said.

"Girls don't ask boys to kiss them—not unless they're sick," replied Mona, looking at him with eyes so bright that Peter felt every drop of blood in his body rushing to his face.

"Then I—I sometimes wish you was sick again!" blundered Peter.

"Peter!"

"Yes, I do," he affirmed stubbornly.

Mona's cheeks were flushing until they were the color of a rose.

Suddenly her eyes flashed and she stamped a little foot.

"You don't want to kiss me *or you'd ask for it*!" she cried. "I always had to make you!"

It was a new thought for Peter to ponder upon. Half an hour later, when they were almost home, he came to a decision.

"I do!" he exclaimed suddenly.

"You do *what*?" asked Mona, who had been livelier than ever in hunting for flowers.

"You know."

"I don't."

"You can guess."

"I'm not going to guess."

"I'll give you three chances," offered Peter.

"I don't want them."

Peter was desperate. "You didn't mean what you said, then?"

"What did I say?"

"You said I didn't want to kiss you or I'd ask for it."

"Well—you haven't asked."

"I did. I just asked."

Mona's lovely eyes opened wide.

"Did you, Peter? I didn't hear it. Please ask again!"

Peter gulped.

"Will you?" he asked.

"Will I *what*?"

"Let me kiss you?"

For what seemed at least an hour to Peter she stood looking at him.

"If I do—will you promise never to kiss any other girl?"

"I promise."

"And never let any other girl kiss you? I mean Adette Clamart, too!"

"Sure I do."

"As long as you live?"

"As long as I live."

With a little gesture of gladness and satisfaction Mona Guyon held up the prettiest mouth in all Five Fingers, and Peter kissed it.

JAMES OLIVER CURWOOD

XIV

In the weeks and months following the plague at Five Fingers Father Albanel did not forget his promise to Peter, and back in the shelter of the woods, where their secret was safe between them, he taught the boy "how to fight like a gentleman—if he had to fight at all." It was then Peter learned there was something more helpful than brute strength, and as his skill increased and he mastered one after another what the little missioner called "the tricks of the fighting game," his enthusiasm rose to a point where he could scarcely keep his secret from Mona. Their boxing-gloves, which Father Albanel had smuggled from the settlement, they kept securely hidden, and not until years later did Peter know that the holy man who was teaching him had at one time been regarded by fighting men as the handiest man with his fists between Fort William and Hudson Bay.

What he had learned he did not fully realize until early in June, when Aleck Curry and his father and the hateful black tug returned to the settlement. Using the influence of a brother who had been successful in politics, Izaak Curry had obtained timber concessions in several directions about Five Fingers, and now built himself a cabin near the shore, but hidden back in the spruce. This he tenanted with a third brother and his wife, and with them Aleck lived while the tug was making its trips between Five Fingers and Fort William.

Aleck had grown still bigger, and in spite of Peter's resolution to make friends with him he would have none of it. His hatred for Peter was like some deadly thing that had poisoned every drop of blood in his veins, and Mona's growing beauty, and her quite open affection for his rival, stirred something that was more than hatred—more than brooding vindictiveness—in Aleck's heart. His father was rich, and he knew what that meant back in town; and his uncle was a power in politics, and had recently become Commissioner of Provincial Police. It enraged him that these facts carried no weight in Five Fingers. His own importance as the son of a rich man and the nephew of a Commissioner was utterly unrecognized here, while in town it had given him a position of first rank in spite of his bullying nature. This lack of appreciation, as he thought of it, he laid entirely at Peter's door, for it was Peter who had robbed him of his chances with Mona in the first place, and it was Peter who was keeping her away from him now.

So it was not long after Aleck's arrival before the climax came. It happened well out of sight of everybody, where Aleck had schemed that it should be, for he wanted no interference in his "beating up" of Peter. In the end both boys returned to the settlement with bleeding noses and black eyes. Neither was whipped. Aleck was dumbfounded. That his size and weight and all the training he had given himself during the winter had failed to beat Peter was unbelievable.

For two weeks after the fight there was not a day, excepting Sundays, when Father Albanel and Peter did not "take a walk" in the woods together. And along with these secret sessions Peter took advantage of every opportunity to run and swim that he might add to his wind. Almost daily he accepted insults from Aleck in order to avoid a fight, and never a day passed that Father Albanel did not repeat his warning to Peter to postpone further combat as long as possible. But the time came when Aleck once more followed up insult with physical action, with the result that he suffered a defeat so completely decisive that in August he returned to Fort William, fairly laughed out of Five Fingers.

Mona now made up Peter's world, and in his heart she kept constantly burning the faith that his father would return. But when winter came again, and another spring, and there was still no word from Donald McRae, Peter came at times to believe that his father was gone out of his life forever.

Aleck Curry again returned to Five Fingers in this third summer of Peter's life there. He was nineteen now, and was commissioned by his father to take an interest in his lumber business along the coast. A year had made a big change in him, and his hatred for Peter and his passion for Mona he kept more to himself. His father told Simon that in another year Aleck was going to join the provincial police, and would soon hold a commission in it. . .

Early in September, when Mona was in her sixteenth year, the event against which Peter had been steeling his heart for many months became a fact. Pierre and Josette had long planned that after Marie Antoinette's teaching in the little settlement school Mona should spend a year, and possibly two, under the tutelage of the Sisters in the Ursuline Convent in the city of Quebec. On the day Mona left, accompanied by Joe's wife, who went to see her safely settled in the distant city, Peter's world went as black as on that other day when his father disappeared out of his life.

The winter that followed was an endless one for Peter. Once each week, as surely as the weeks came round, he received a long letter from

JAMES OLIVER CURWOOD

Mona, and five times during the winter he made the trip to the railroad settlement alone that he might not miss the love and cheer which came from her. And he was at the train to meet her, with Pierre and Josette and Marie Antoinette and Joe, when she came from the school in June.

At first he was dazed by the change in her, she had grown so much taller, and more beautiful, and he stood as if turned into wood while she greeted and kissed all the others. Then she turned to him, and her face was flooded with a color which he had never seen in it before. And after that—he could never remember how it happened—their arms were around each other, and Mona was crying—crying until tears blinded her—and he was kissing her, and she was kissing him, and then ran away from him to hug all the others again.

This summer in Five Fingers decided the lives of Peter and Mona. She was almost seventeen. She would go to school one more year, because that was the desire of Josette and Marie Antoinette. She would be nearly eighteen then. And when she was nineteen—on her nineteenth birthday, if Peter liked it that way—she would marry him.

During the second year of her absence Peter devoted every energy of soul and body toward making himself worthy of her. He worked and planned and studied hard under Marie Antoinette and Father Albanel. During this year several changes came to Five Fingers. Simon McQuarrie ended his dealings with Izaak Curry, and to rid their paradise of a bad memory Adette Clamart deliberately set fire to the Curry shack after he had gone, so that nothing remained but a square of ash and charred timbers. "And the wild phlox will cover that next summer," said Adette with a grim little shrug of her pretty shoulders.

Aleck Curry joined the police. In a day and a night, it seemed, he sprang into a great bulk of a man, heavy-faced, huge-shouldered, a giant in strength and physique, and with a hatred for Peter in his heart that had grown more merciless with the passing of years. He saw Mona each summer, and when she returned from her second year at school her beauty stirred in him a passion which submerged all other instincts and desires. He became a watchful, waiting beast, hiding the flame that was consuming him, preparing himself for the opportunity which he was determined should some day come his way.

As each week brought nearer the day of their own supreme happiness Mona and Peter no longer sensed this menace, or even thought of it, and because Aleck was so utterly outside all the possibilities of her life the deeper sentiment of womanhood growing in Mona compelled her to treat him more kindly. Even Simon's suspicions were dulled, for during the winter preceding her nineteenth birthday Aleck visited the settlement only twice. Another spring and summer followed. The twelfth of the coming October was Mona's birthday. On that day she would become Peter's wife. It was planned that they should live with Pierre and Josette until the good logging snows came, when all of Five Fingers would join in building their home.

It was on a day in August that Mona set out alone for the beaver pond, carrying a basket in which was her own and Peter's supper. Peter, returning from a trip up the shore, had promised to meet her before sundown in their old trysting-place, where two winters before he had built her a little "play-house" cabin.

And on this same afternoon, as Mona left the settlement, a stranger was making his way toward it.

An attitude of unusual caution and a haunted way of looking about him were the two things one would have noticed first as he came out of a swamp into an open forest of white pine. He drew in a deep breath of the freer air, and with a gesture of relief wiped his face with a hand that was rough and twisted and scratched by contact with briers. He was oddly disheveled and smeared with swamp oil. His gray head with its grizzled and uncut hair wore no hat, his shirt was in rags at the throat and sleeves and his trousers were tucked into high boots which bore evidence of having gone through mud and water to their tops. Upon his shoulders he carried a pack, and though the tenuity of its folds emphasized its lightness in weight, the man freed himself from his burden with an audible gasp of relief.

Then he leaned against a pine and looked back at the swamp from which he had come, listening with singular intentness for any sound which might strike with warning or unusual import upon the languorous stillness of the afternoon. His face was pallid under its stubble of beard even after the heat and exertion he had passed through; his cheeks were sunken as if by sickness or hunger, and his lips were drawn and thin. In his eyes seemed to lie all the strength that remained in the man. They were furtive and questing as they watched, missing no shadow that moved.

The sweetness of ripened summer, its lazy whisperings and the stillness which comes in a deep wood when the sun is overhead lay about him or trembled softly in the air. For hours he had been in an oven of swamp heat and winged pests; here it was cool. In the pine tops a hundred and fifty feet above his head was a faint stir of the breeze that came from Lake Superior. It reached down and touched his hot cheeks. He could taste the invigorating freshness of it, and there came slowly a change in his restless eyes, a softening of the tense lines about his mouth, a lighting up of his face where before it had held only suspense and watchful uncertainty. He picked up his shoulder pack, carrying it in his hand as he turned away from the swamp.

The transformation in the man's face was strangely at odds with the painful physical effort which accompanied his tedious progress. He no longer looked behind him but kept his eyes ahead, as if anticipating at any moment the appearance of something of vital importance toward which he was struggling with the last bit of strength that remained in his body. When at last he came to a little brook, gurgling between the pine roots, he fell rather than knelt beside it, and drank like one dying of thirst. Then again and again he plunged his face into hands filled with cold water and wet his head until his gray hair was dripping.

He followed the brook. Several times he stumbled and fell in the rougher places and once his toe caught a root and he plunged into the stream itself. At the end of an hour he had traveled a mile. Then he came to a knoll of hardwoods, crossed it and made his way down through a lacework of yellow birch until he arrived at the edge of a deep, still pond that began in sunlight and lost itself in the almost cavernous coolness and shadow of a spruce and cedar forest. Instinctively the man knew it was a beaver pond, and almost instantly he had proof it was alive. A warning tail lashed the water with the sound of a paddle struck sideways, and across the pool, a short stone's throw away, an object moved through the water.

Dizzily the man sat down. His vision was clouded so that it was difficult for him to see even the moving object. He fell upon his side and stretched himself out on a couch of thick green grass. In another moment he was lying with his eyes closed but with ears keenly alert. During the next half-hour he heard every sound about him; then his pale eyelids closed heavily and a weariness of brain and body which he could no longer combat dulled his senses to a physical and mental inertness which was almost sleep.

In this state of somnolence he had lain for possibly a quarter of an hour when a sound reached his ears which first opened his eyes and then brought him in a quick and defensive movement to a posture that was half sitting and half crouching.

The sound came again, and amazement replaced the alarm in his face. What he heard was a feminine voice, strangely soft and subdued in this place of coolness and shadow and mysterious stillness. It was a note of laughter, almost birdlike in its sweetness, and the man's fingers clutched at the breast of his ragged shirt as he listened. Then he began to crawl slowly in the direction of the sound, making his way through a green thicket of willows, careful that no twig snapped under his weight to give warning of his approach. Suddenly he came upon a scene whose unexpectedness was almost a shock to him.

He had reached the farther edge of the willows, and before him was a little meadow not more than half an acre in extent, green and filled with wild flowers. Almost within reach of his hands was a mountain ash weighted with ripening fruit, and under this tree, close to the edge of the pool, a girl was seated on the grass, partly facing him. His first glimpse of her was of a bowed head crowned by a wealth of coiled hair; then, as she looked up, he saw her face. Her cheeks were flushed, her dark eyes shone, and as she laughed again she snuggled her face close down over a furry thing scrambling about in her lap. The man saw there were two of these creatures—baby beavers. His eyes wandered a little. At the edge of the pond, half out of the water, was a full-grown beaver. And this older inhabitant of the place was conscious of his presence in the willow thicket!

The girl was talking and laughing with the little ones, calling them by name. One was Telesphore and the other Peterkin—and the man drew in his breath with a gasp. He watched her tease them with a carrot. One scrambled up and tangled a foot in her hair.

"Peterkin!" she cried. "Peterkin—you little ruffian!"

The old beaver remained stolid and motionless, watching the menace in the willows. A companion swam lazily past, scented the danger and struck the water a blow with his tail before he dived.

The girl looked up quickly and spoke to the old beaver. "What is the matter, Peter?" she cried. "Don't be foolish. Come and get your carrot!"

It was then she heard a little cry behind her, and turned and saw the man's face in the willows.

JAMES OLIVER CURWOOD

XV

Mona Guyon was not afraid. She was startled, and thrilled by an instant intuitive sensing of the unusual and the significant in the man's unexpected appearance. Yet the color did not leave her cheeks nor did a cry come to her lips. She thrust the baby beavers from her lap and rose unexcitedly to her feet, tall, slim and amazingly beautiful.

She was looking steadily at the man, and as she looked her heart beat a little faster, for the wilderness had taught her a quick and definite understanding of the story she saw written in the wild face among the willows. Its tragedy flashed upon her before her parted lips had found words—hunger, sickness, the emaciation and weakness of a man who found less discomfort upon his hands and knees than upon his feet.

As she looked at him a change came into his face that the man himself could feel as there swept over him a slow and inundating sense of shame. Every instinct of chivalry in him revolted at the ridiculous and alarming figure he must be making of himself. But even in this moment of surprise and distress he did not entirely lose his sense of humor. He tried to smile. The effort was nothing short of pathos.

"I beg your pardon," he said as he rose a little unsteadily to his feet and came out of the willows. His raggedness and the coarse stubble on his face could not conceal the consciousness of pride with which he straightened himself and bowed to her. "I have come upon you like a wolf, and I know I look like a wolf. But I assure you I am as harmless as a sheep, and if you don't mind dividing your carrots with me—" He nodded toward the little yellow pile of carrots she had brought for her beaver pets.

His voice was pleasant. It made her think of Father Albanel, and as he spoke a smile was in his eyes and on his pale lips. She went quickly to his side and put a hand on his arm. Its firm young touch seemed to steady him.

"What has happened?" she asked. "You look—"

"Sick—and a little mad," he finished for her, when she hesitated. "But I'm mostly hungry, and if I may have the carrots—"

She helped him to the foot of the tree and he dropped down beside it with a weakness that made him hunch his shoulders in disgust.

"I have something better than carrots," she said. "Please sit here and I will get it."

She hurried across the little meadow to a deeper shade of thick-growing jack pines on the farther side, and the man turned his head to follow her movements with his eyes. Her beauty was twisting at something in his heart. A long time ago he had known someone like her. The slim figure, walking swiftly across the open, took him back twenty years, and he could almost hear a sweet voice calling his name, and in a place very much like this, with the coolness of the wilderness all about and the sun shining through the trees. His hand touched the scrub of beard on his face and he shivered. The thought came to him that the girl was afraid of him and was running away. As she disappeared among the banksians he reached for one of the raw carrots and began to eat it.

Mona returned so quietly that he did not hear her until she was at his side. She brought a basket and a small pail of cold spring-water. She spread a napkin on his lap and loaded it with the contents of the basket. He was sensitively conscious of her eyes upon him and he tried not to appear ravenous as he began with meat and bread.

"I'm spoiling your picnic, child," he said, speaking to her feebly like a man who was very old. "I'm sorry."

"You're not spoiling it," she cried, leaning toward him with a gesture full of sweet tenderness. "Oh, I have been so happy today—God has made me happier by bringing me here in time to help you!"

"Happy," he whispered, as if to himself. "It is wonderful to be happy. I have known—what it is."

It was her struggle to appear natural now as he ate. She had never been so intimately close to starvation and pathos and weakness in man.

"Were you lost?" she asked.

He caught quickly at her suggestion. "Yes, lost—in the woods and the swamps between the railroad and here. I was trying to find a place called Five Fingers."

She gave a little exclamation. "I'm from Five Fingers. It is not far. Uncle Pierre calls it a mile and a half."

Mona wondered at the strange silence which came over the man, and the suddenness with which his hunger seemed to be satisfied.

"You have been an angel to me," he said, when he had finished. "And—things love you. Even the wild creatures." He was looking at the baby beavers, humped into furry balls at the edge of the pond. "You called one of them Peterkin, and the old beaver Peter. I wonder—why?"

"And there is a bear cub I call Pete," she added. "It is because—"

JAMES OLIVER CURWOOD

"Yes—"

Her eyes were shining.

"Because I am going to marry a man whose name is Peter."

It did not seem strange to her that she should be confessing the secret of her happiness to a man she had never seen before.

There was something in his eyes which made her want him to know, a mysterious gentleness that seemed to plead for her confidence and her friendship. It gave her a pleasurable thrill to tell someone that she loved Peter and was going to be his wife. And this man was unlike any other who had ever come from the outside world into the wilderness isolation of Five Fingers.

In his rags and misfortune and his whitening hair and pale, thin face, she saw something which stirred more than her pity. And it was more than faith.

Just what it was, in that moment, she did not know. She was puzzled by the tremor which ran through his body coincident with her mention of Peter.

"And this Peter—" he began feverishly. The words seemed to choke in his throat, and he passed a hand over his eyes as if to wipe away a mist. Then he said: "He is a lucky lad. Is his name Peter McRae?"

"Yes. How did you know?"

"And—you love him?"

She nodded. "I was only thirteen then, but I loved him the first day he came to Five Fingers and fought Aleck Curry for me. Aleck was a bully and was pulling my hair."

The mysterious stranger bent his gray head so that she could not see his face. "That was six years ago last May, in the afternoon. And—Peter—did he ever tell you about—his father?"

"Yes, that same night. It was in the edge of the forest, and it was growing dark. He had brought a letter from his father to Simon McQuarrie, and Simon had told him the truth. He said his father had killed a man—accidentally—a long time ago, but that the police wouldn't believe it was an accident and were after him, and would hang him if he was caught. And ever since then—"

She was at his side, staring at him as he slowly raised his head, the color gone from her face and her white throat beating with the sudden mad pounding in her breast. "Ever since that night—that very hour— we have prayed together for Peter's father to come back. And you— *you*—"

He could not escape the wild questioning in her eyes and their demand to be answered.

"Would you have *me* Peter's father?" he asked uncertainly. "This way—an outlaw—ragged—dirty—a beggar—"

There was an almost tragic note of hopefulness in his voice.

"Yes," she cried, her voice breaking in excited entreaty from her lips. "If you are Peter's father, tell me. We have waited. And I have told him you would come. Oh, I have *promised* him that, and have asked God every night to make it come true. Are you—" Her hands were reaching out to him.

"Yes, I am Peter's father."

There was no flash of joy or pride in his acknowledgment of the truth. His head sank upon his breast as if a sudden weariness had overcome him, and a moan of protest was in his voice. And then a thing happened which swept the bitterness and grief from Donald McRae's heart. He caught a glimpse of Mona's face, gloriously flushed in this moment of her answered prayer; and then her arms were about him, her soft cheek against his rough stubble of beard, and for an instant he felt the swift pressure of her lips against his.

He raised his hand and touched her hair. "Child," he cried brokenly, "dear child—"

She sprang up from him, half laughing and half sobbing, and ran out from under the mountain ash tree and stood in the edge of the clearing. With her hands in the form of a megaphone she called: "Peter! Peter! *Oh, Peter!*"

With a protesting cry he climbed to his feet and went to her. She saw the white, almost frightened look in his face and eyes. "Don't do that!" he exclaimed. "For God's sake—don't! Peter must not know I am here."

In her amazement her hands fell slowly from her face to her side. "Why?" she demanded.

"Because—" He stopped, listening to a voice that came faintly from out of the forest.

"That is Peter," said Mona. "We are going to eat our picnic supper here—at the pool."

"It is Peter—*coming*—"

"Yes."

He tried to breathe steadily, tried to speak calmly as he took her hand and stroked it with nervous gentleness. "What is your name?"

JAMES OLIVER CURWOOD

"Mona Guyon."

"Mona—Guyon. It is a pretty name. And you are sweet and good and beautiful. Peter's mother was like you. And—I am glad you love my boy." A new strength seemed to possess him.

The voice came again out of the forest, a little nearer this time, and Donald McRae held the girl's hand closer, and a tremor went through him as he smiled at her in the way he used to smile at his boy in the old days of their comradeship and happiness.

"That is my call," he said evenly. "Peter's mother and I used it twenty years ago, and afterward I taught it to Peter. It carries a long distance in the woods."

It was not his poverty and his weakness that affected Mona most. Something more than pity overwhelmed her—his forced calmness, the strange light in his eyes, the almost superhuman fight he was making to rise up out of his rags and his misery in the most tragic hours that could have come into his life. His words and his appearance set her heart pounding fiercely. She was a little frightened and wanted to put her arms about him again and hold him until Peter came. What did he mean?

"Why mustn't Peter know you are here?" she demanded. "*Why?*"

He led her back in the willows. In a moment they were hidden.

"Are you brave enough to hear? And do you love Peter enough to help—me?" he asked her.

"Yes, yes, I will help you."

He stood so that he could look out of the willows and across the meadow through which Peter would come. A moment of despair and hopelessness twisted the muscles of his face.

"He must not see me," he said in a voice that was hardly more than a strained whisper. "Child, you must understand—you most of all. Don't you know why I ran away from Peter that day near Five Fingers, and sent him on to Simon McQuarrie? It was so Peter might have a chance in life that he never could have with me, even if I escaped the law. I, too, have prayed—every day and every night through the years that have been more than eternities for me; prayed that good and happiness might come to him, and that in time even the memory of his father would wear away. But never for an instant have I been able to forget my boy. He has been a part of my soul and body, walking with me, sleeping with me, sitting with me beside my hidden camp-fires at night, until at times the desire to see him once more was so strong in me that it almost drove me mad. And all this time I was hunted, running from place to place, living in swamps and hidden depths of the forests, avoiding men and places of habitation—but with Peter always at my side, just as he looked that last terrible day at the edge of Five Fingers when he pleaded with me to take him along—"

His lips trembled and a shiver ran through his body.

"And through those years Peter *was* with you—Peter and I," replied the girl. "Summer nights we used to ask the moon where you were, and when it was cold and stormy we—we prayed. And on Christmas—Peter always got a present—for *you*."

A joyous light passed over his haggard face. "You thought of me—on Christmas?"

"Yes, always. And Peter asked me to keep the presents carefully in my cedar chest, for we knew you would come back some day. And now—"

It was Peter's voice that came to them again, much nearer. Donald's arms fell away from the girl, but she raised her face quickly and kissed him. Her eyes were filled with tears.

"Peter is wondering why I do not answer. Please—please—"

In his indecision he bowed his face in his hands. It was with an effort that he shook himself free of temptation.

"I must tell you quickly, and you must understand," he said desperately. "The police are close after me again. That is why I was in the great swamp to the north—to get away from them. If I come back into Peter's life now it can only be for a few hours, and you know what it will mean—a fresh tragedy for him, a new grief, pain, disgrace, a black cloud of unhappiness over the paradise which you have made and can make for him. I have come back to see him, to look at him, to carry away a new picture of him in my heart. But he must not know. And if you love Peter—if you care a little for what is in the heart of his father—you will make it possible for me to look upon my boy. I will hide here, in the willows; and you two, there under the ash tree—"

"It is wrong," broke in Mona. "Oh, it is terribly wrong!"

"No, it is right," he persisted. "It will make me happy—to see him so near to me, hear his voice and know that life and God and *you* have been good to him. If I see Peter, child, if his hands touch me, if we are together again—it may cost me my life. For those things would hold me; I could not go away again after that, and the police are near, very near, and if they should catch me—"

JAMES OLIVER CURWOOD

The sag that came into his shoulders gave eloquence to the thing which he did not finish, and Mona's eyes burned with a fire which dried up her tears. "If I bring Peter down there, under the tree, will you promise not to go away until I have seen you again?" she asked.

"Yes, I promise that."

"Even if it is tomorrow, or the next day?"

"I will wait."

It was hard for him to lie, looking into the beautiful eyes that were fixed upon him so steadily. But he did it splendidly; so well that Mona did not guess the falsehood back of his last great fight.

She turned from him swiftly with her face toward the meadow.

"I will bring Peter—down there," she said.

She ran to the mountain ash tree and in a few breathless seconds rearranged the luncheon basket and tossed half eaten bits of food into the pond. Then she hurried across the meadow. Peter's call came to her again, and this time she answered it. In the deep shade on the farther side of the meadow she stopped and pressed her hands to her face. Her cheeks were hot. She was fighting against a sense of overwhelming guilt, for in this hour, this very minute, she knew she was not only betraying Peter, but committing the sacrilege of repudiating answered prayer. And Peter must not know!

He could not fail to see her excitement, unless—she laughed softly as the old, sweet thought came to her. Peter loved her hair. He loved to see it down, as on that first day six years ago when he came upon her in the edge of the forest near Five Fingers. She paused again, and her fingers worked swiftly among its lustrous coils until they fell about her. Peter would guess nothing now—when she came to him like this, in a way that shut his eyes to all the rest of the world.

She could hear him coming through the brush. He was running, and she guessed at the alarm which was urging him because she had failed to answer his calls until that last time, when she knew her voice had not sent forth the old cry in just the way it should have greeted Peter.

She stood very still, so that when Peter leaped over a fallen tree not twenty paces away from her he did not see her. He stopped, his head thrown back, breathing quickly, and listening; and in this moment Mona recalled the other day of years ago when he came into the cutting near Five Fingers and found her struggling with Aleck Curry, the bully of the settlement.

He was the same Peter, only now he was a man. His hair had not darkened and his eyes were the same blue. He was the clean-cut, fearless, sensitive Peter who had gone into battle for her against a boy nearly twice his weight and years older. The years had given a splendid change to his body. He was still slim, like the old Peter, and there was a litheness and alertness in him which filled her with pride. She held her breath, watching him, and exulted when she saw the anxiety in his face. Then he called again, and in the moment of silence which followed she suddenly clapped her hands and laughed.

Peter turned in amazement, and when he saw her standing as she was, with her long hair streaming about her, he drew in a deep breath, and the blood surged into his tense face as he came to her. The happiness which swept his anxiety away brought a responsive glow of joy into her eyes, and as she held out her arms to him she forgot for a moment the man hidden among the willows near the mountain ash tree. For a little while Peter held her so close she could feel the thumping of his heart, and not until he had kissed her hair and her lips did he seem to have breath to ask why she had not answered his calls.

"To punish you for making me wait so long at the pond," she said. "But"—she raised a soft tress to his lips—"I was sorry, at the last moment, and did *this* for you, Peter. Will you forgive me?"

She was thinking of Donald McRae again, and slipping her hand into Peter's, she led him toward the pond. And Peter, in the sweetness and joy of her presence, guessed nothing because her fingers tightened in his hand or because her breath came more quickly than usual.

They drew nearer to the ash tree and the willows. She knew that Donald McRae was now looking upon the face of his boy; she could see the clump of twisted bushes behind which he was hidden, and caught a movement in their tops, as if an animal or a breath of wind had disturbed them.

They were under the ash tree when she flung back her hair, no longer making an effort to hide from Peter the distress in her face. He was shocked, even a little terrified at her appearance. Involuntarily her glance went beyond him to the thicket which concealed Donald McRae. It was only a few steps away, and she knew Peter's father could distinctly hear what they said. Then she looked at Peter again, and smiled gently at his suspense as she raised one of his hands to her lips in the soft caress that always wiped away his troubles. And in that same moment she drew him a step nearer to the willows.

JAMES OLIVER CURWOOD

"Something happened before you came," she said, speaking so that Donald McRae would not lose a word of what she was saying. "I think I must have had a—a—dream—and it was terrible!" She shuddered, and listened to the breaking of a twig in the willows. "I am foolish to let it frighten me."

His arms were about her, his fingers smoothing back her shining hair as relief leaped into his face.

"You were asleep, *Ange*—with me bursting my throat to make you hear from the forest?"

She did not answer his question. Instead, she said: "Peter, you have not lied to me? You believe in prayer?"

He bent his lips to her white forehead. "Yes, *Ange*, and yours most of all. God has answered you, and always will."

"And we have prayed a long time for your father to come back?"

He nodded wonderingly. "Yes, a long time."

She spoke slowly then, and her words were for Donald McRae and not for Peter.

"And if your father does not come, if you never see him again, your faith in the God we have prayed to for so long will be a little broken, will it not, Peter?"

She waited, holding her breath for fear even that sound might come between Peter's answer and the man in the bushes.

"He will come—some day—Mona."

"That was what he promised you—the day he sent you on alone to Five Fingers, and ran away from you? And you have always told me that next to your faith in God you believed in your father. You have never thought that he lied to you that day in the edge of the forest?"

He stared at her, speechless, and in that moment she faced the willows with a glow of triumph in her eyes.

"Down in the little church at Five Fingers Father Albanel has always taught us not to lie and to be true to our promise," she said, speaking directly at the willows. "Peter, if your father should break his faith, or I should break mine, it would be terrible. And that is what happened—in my vision—and it has frightened me." She rested her cheek against his arm so he could not see her face. "I was here—under the tree—when in this vision your father came. He was ragged and tired and sick—and so hungry he ate carrots I brought for the beavers. He had come just to look at you, Peter, but not to let you know. He said it would make you unhappy; that it was best for you that he should never come into your life again—and he made me promise not to tell you that he was here.

"And I promised. I did—I promised him I would be a traitor to you, after all the years we have waited for him, and prayed for him, and *believed* in him."

Her arms crept up to his shoulders. "If I should do a thing like that God would never forgive me, and you—if some day you found out what I had done—would never have faith in me again. Would you?"

She hid her face against his shoulder, her heart beating wildly, her body trembling. For she had seen another movement in the willows and she was afraid that Donald McRae was going away.

"It was only a dream," Peter was saying, holding his arms closely about her. "You are not afraid of dreams, Mona?"

And then from behind them came a voice.

"God forgive me my weakness!" it cried. *"Peter—Peter—"*

Donald McRae stood out in the open at the edge of the willow thicket. He had forgotten the rags and mud that covered him, and was no longer a fugitive with the lines of a hunted man in his face. The present was for a space obliterated—the present with its menace of the law, its exhaustion and its poverty; and he was standing once more in the warm glow of that day of six years ago when he had said good-by to Peter. In those seconds, when Peter stood shocked into deathlike stillness by the sound of the voice behind him, Mona could see Donald McRae with his outreaching arms; but as Peter turned slowly, facing his father, the strain broke in a hot flood of tears that blinded her vision.

And then—

"Dad!"

It was the strangest cry she had ever heard from Peter's lips, and with an answer to that cry in her own choking breast she turned away as the two men came into each other's arms. She passed out of sight along the edge of the pond, scarcely seeing the path ahead of her, and unconsciously she kept repeating Peter's name in a whisper, as if—even though she had prayed so long for this hour to come—she had never quite expected its fulfilment.

JAMES OLIVER CURWOOD

XVI

U nder the ash tree, for a few moments Peter was the boy again; the boy of yesterday, of years ago, when the world had held nothing for him but his father; and there was no change in the touch of the hands that had always given him comfort and courage and a love that was almost like a woman's in its gentleness. Not until Donald McRae held his boy off, with a hand on each shoulder, did something besides the madness of joy at his father's homecoming begin to thrust itself upon Peter. Then he saw the change—the naked breast, the half-bared arms, the mud and the rags, and the face and hair in which years had stamped their heels unpityingly. He tried to choke back his horror, to keep it out of his face, and to do this he laughed—laughed through the tears and sobbing breath—and pointed to a white birch tree in which a blue jay was screaming.

"The blue jay, dad!" he cried. "Remember that day—behind the log—with the blue jay in the tree-top, and the sapsucker pecking at our elbows, and the violets between my knees—"

The hands on his shoulders were relaxing.

"I've never seen a blue jay but what I've thought—of you," said Donald McRae. "And the river—behind us—and how we got away from the police—and the rabbits we roasted—and—and—" The world was twisting and turning round again. He tried to smile, and reached out gropingly for Peter. "The swamp was hot, Peter. And I am tired—tired—"

Peter's arms caught him as he swayed. His thin face was whiter, and his eyes closed as he still tried to smile at his boy.

Mona, braiding her hair as she waited beyond the willows, heard Peter's frightened call. When she came running to him he was kneeling beside his father, cooling his face with water from the pond. Donald McRae lay upon the grass. He was scarcely breathing, and under the scrub of beard his emaciated face was like wax. An agony of fear and grief had driven the happiness out of Peter's face, and he tried to speak as he looked up at Mona.

She saw what had happened as she knelt beside him and took Donald McRae's head tenderly in her arms. Excitement and his last great effort to fight down his weakness had given a semblance of strength to this shell of a man. But it was gone now, and the full measure of its tragedy struck like a charge of lead to Peter's heart.

Mona, feeling Peter's grief, and guessing swiftly the thought that had made his wordless lips white and trembling, said to comfort him: "He hasn't been this way long, Peter. It was the swamp. He told me the police were after him, and he hid himself there. The heat—bad water—"

She tried futilely to explain away the horror of the thing—to make Peter believe this wreck of a man was not the product of months and years of hardship and suffering, but had reached his condition because of a passing torment that had covered only a few days in the swamp. But she knew she was failing, and she stopped before she had finished, with her head bowed before Peter's eyes. She heard his tense lips whisper "the police" as if the words choked him as they came out, and then he went down again to the edge of the pool for water. She wet her handkerchief when he returned and held it over Donald's eyes, and Peter unlaced the worn-out, muddy boots—and suddenly a sound came from him, a little cry of unutterable understanding as his hand found in the trampled grass the half-eaten carrot which his father had dropped.

She had never seen Peter's face so white, and never before had she seen a look in his blue eyes so unlike the Peter she had grown up with, and played with, and loved.

"He is breathing easier," she said. "It was the excitement, the shock—"

He nodded, and replied in a dead, even voice: "I know what it was, *Ange*. I know." He took one of his father's hands and held it between his own, looking at the face in Mona's arms into which life was beginning to return and breath to come more evenly. "It has been a long time, dad. Six years—six years like those three days when the police were hunting us in the forest, and you caught rabbits for me to eat. But it is ended now."

Mona's heart throbbed. "We will keep him with us, Peter—always! We will hide him—somewhere—never let him go away again! Oh, it will be easy for us to do that, and Father Albanel—and Simon—will help us—"

A deeper breath trembled on Donald McRae's lips, but it was not that breath, or the faint moan that came with it, that stopped her before she had finished. Peter was looking over her head at something beyond her. He dropped his father's hand, and what she saw in his face drew a gasping cry from her even before she knew its cause. She turned and looked. And then, in an instant, she was on her feet with Peter.

So quietly that no sound of footfall or breaking twig had given warning of his approach, a man had stolen upon them. He stood not a dozen feet away, dressed in the field service uniform of the Provincial Police. That was the first terrible fact which telegraphed itself to her brain; the man was an officer, he was after Donald McRae, and he had caught them! But this first alarm gave place to a greater shock as her eyes saw the face above the uniform. It was a large, coarse face streaming with sweat; the lips were heavy, the nose big, and the eyes were small and too close together for one who bulked so large. It was a face filled with triumph—an exultation which the man made dramatically poignant as he stood with his heavy hands on his hips, looking from one to the other with a smile that was deadly in its promise twisting the corners of his mouth.

He did not speak, did not even move, but waited while his presence crushed like a weight of horror upon the two who were staring at him. His eyes rested on Mona, and the wicked gleam in them—the thought which they could not hide, merciless, sure, almost gloating—drew his name from her lips in a cry that was filled with fear, with half disbelief, with a note that almost called for pity.

"Aleck—Curry!"

The man's heavy head nodded, but he did not speak. It was still too great a moment of triumph to be broken by voice. He looked at Peter, and then, slowly, significantly, at the unconscious form of Peter's father. God could not have given him a greater hour than this! For if it had not been for that man and for Peter, he might have had the girl. It was Peter who had come in his way from that first day when they had fought over Mona in the edge of the clearing; it was Peter who had whipped him, Peter whom he had grown to hate above all other things on earth—and it was Peter's heart and soul and happiness, almost his very life, that he now held in the hollow of his hand!

And he would make him pay.

"Yes, *it is ended now*," he said, repeating Peter's words of a few moments before. "And I'm rather glad. The swamp was hot and filled with mosquitoes."

Something clinked as he fumbled at his belt and the sound sent a chill of horror through Mona. He held out the manacle irons so that she could see them.

"I've got to do it," he said, a mocking apology in his voice. "Distasteful, but necessary." He faced Peter. "Your father knew we were close behind him, and it won't do him any good to play dead. He's slippery, and I'm going to put these on him. I guess—" He swung his heavy head toward Mona again. "I guess Father Albanel and old Simon can't help him very much from now on. It was nice of you to think of it, though, Mona. You were always so tender-hearted—when it came to Peter!"

He was still the old bully and his voice trembled with the suppression of his triumph. This was his master stroke. It was not capture of the man whom the law would condemn to hang that thrilled him most; it was the twisted beauty in Mona's face, the shock and terror in her eyes, and the helplessness and despair he saw in Peter's. He did not hurry, did not call for an instant upon the dignity of the law, but twisted the knife of his vengeance slowly.

When Mona's eyes turned from him to Peter her heart stood still. He was gray. There was no blood in his lips. He was looking down upon the still, upturned face of his father, and his hands were clenched. When he raised his head she saw that his eyes were no longer Peter's eyes. He advanced slowly toward Aleck Curry, and the manacles rattled as Aleck dropped them to his belt and shifted a hand to his pistol holster.

Peter did not hear the click of steel or sense the menace of the shifting hand. One thought pounded maddeningly in his brain; his father had come back to him, he was *home*, and in the first hour of his return this beast had come into their lives again to break down every hope and prayer they had built up during the years. In Aleck Curry he saw not only that merciless law which had run his father like a rat from hole to hole, but a monster of vicious hate, a lustful, bullying boy grown into a still more vicious giant—and Peter's desire was to kill him.

Mona saw the deadly intent in his slow advance even as Aleck Curry saw it. She saw more—the hand on the pistol, the tightening fingers, the dangerous gleam that flashed in Aleck's eyes—and Peter with only his naked hands! A cry of warning came to her lips—of a terror which robbed her of the power to move. The cry ended in a scream, for as Peter leaped in, Aleck raised the pistol and fired. A terrible sickness came over her, a sickness which for an instant swept away her strength.

Peter felt the hot breath of the pistol in his face and the explosion was so near it fell like a blow against his eardrums. It was not a shot intended only to frighten him, for death had missed him by less than the width of his hand. Aleck released the trigger of his automatic and crooked his finger again, but even quicker than that movement was Peter, who flung himself with all his weight under his enemy's arm as the second shot was fired. He did not strike, but with both hands clutched Aleck's wrist, and at the same time tripped his foe so that they went to the earth together, with Aleck on his back.

In this instant there came upon Peter a crushing realization of the almost deadly odds against him. Into every nerve of his body flashed the truth—that he was fighting a man who wanted to kill him, who in reality had the right to kill him, and whom the law would not only vindicate but would commend for killing him. He was an outlaw, fighting against the almighty omniscience of that law, and what the world would regard as justice. And his survival now, like that of his father, depended upon beating it. He must break his enemy's wrist. Get the gun. Kill or be killed.

Every ounce of his strength he exerted upon the wrist as Aleck flung his free arm in a powerful and throttling embrace about his neck. He drew the wrist in, twisted it, and tried with a sudden effort to give it the final breaking snap, but it was like a piece of steel that would not break. The thick fingers did not loosen their hold on the pistol, and in spite of his desperate effort Peter's staring eyes saw the black muzzle of the weapon forcing itself a fraction of an inch at a time toward his body.

Now, when it was too late, he knew that in this close embrace he was not a match for Aleck. His quickness and his tirelessness counted for nothing. Aleck, slow, heavy, with not a quarter of his endurance, but with the brute strength of three men in his coarse body, could crush the life out of him in close quarters. Yet these first few thrilling instants Peter knew this thought was not in the other's mind. All of his enemy's great strength was being exerted in an effort to point the pistol at his body.

Those two or three minutes in which he knew he was fighting to save his life seemed like an eternity to Peter. He saw Aleck's face, twisted in a leering grin, its bloodshot eyes laughing at him, its thick mouth mocking him as the powerful arm and wrist broke down with a slow, torturing sureness all the force he was putting against it. The gun was already at right angles to his body, and suddenly Peter realized why Aleck Curry had not used the choking force of his other arm before this. He had waited for the right moment—and that moment had come. The arm tightened. It was like a half-ring of steel, crushing Peter's neck and twisting his head so that his widening eyes left the pistol and stared into the lower branches of the ash tree.

In that moment he saw Mona. She was staggering up from the edge of the pond with something in her hands which looked like a chunk of mud. Her face passed over him, desperately white, and then she had fallen on her knees and he could hear the *beat, beat, eat* of that something in her hands close to his ears. A terrible cry came from Aleck Curry, and the throttling arm about Peter's neck relaxed until he could turn his head again, and he saw Mona pounding his foe's pistol hand with the stone that had looked like a chunk of mud. He saw the hand redden with blood saw the thick fingers loosen their grip on the pistol, and then swift as a flash Mona had snatched the big automatic and was backing away with it in her hand.

With a mighty, upward heave of his body Peter freed himself, and with that movement came a wild cry out of him, a joyous approval of what Mona had done. Aleck lunged after him. They came to their feet. Peter's fist shot out to the other's jaw, and as Aleck staggered backward, almost falling under the force of the blow, Peter turned to take the pistol from Mona. She was halfway to the pond, and even as he cried out in warning and dismay the weapon left her hand, circled through the air and disappeared with a splash in the water. At his cry she faced him and ran back and thrust the mud-covered rock in his hand. Then he saw the terror in her eyes—the agony of fear that had made her throw away the weapon that had almost taken his life.

He let the rock slip from his fingers and fall to the ground in spite of the exclamation of protest which came from her white lips. He did not see her stoop quickly and pick it up as he advanced to meet Aleck Curry. His foe was hunched forward, like a gorilla, his head lowered, his huge fists clenched, his face distorted by the shock of Peter's blow and a rage which gave him a terrible aspect.

Then he rushed in, his arms apart, his great hands reaching for the man he hated. With the quickness of a cat Peter met his attack, avoiding the arms and the huge hands, leaping in, striking and darting back. He drove blow after blow, and one of them, catching Aleck again on the jaw, had behind it all the weight and force of his body. But even that scarcely more than rocked the brutish head on its thick neck. He advanced slowly and steadily, taking the blows as he moved like a juggernaut upon Peter, driving him an inch at a time toward the edge of the pool.

Suddenly Mona ran in from behind, and with both hands she raised her stone and beat it between Aleck's shoulders. She raised it again, trying to strike his neck or his head, when with a bellow Aleck flung himself around, his great arm flying out like a beam. The blow caught

Mona with all its force and sent her in a crumpled heap to the earth. Not a cry came from her lips, but a yell of fury burst from Peter's. He rushed in, and a hurricane of blows smashed into Aleck's face, cutting his lips, blinding him and choking the breath in his throat. But in that blindness and pain his hand reached out and caught Peter as their feet sank in the mud at the edge of the pond. A cry of triumph came from his bleeding mouth. At last his moment had come.

As Peter felt himself dragged into the deadly embrace his mind worked swiftly. His one chance now lay in the depths of the pool, and unless he could get his enemy there he was lost. Thrusting up his hands, he clenched them in Aleck's hair and put all his weight in dragging the head downward. The movement had its effect, and a step was gained toward the edge of the muddy shelf that terminated abruptly in eight feet of water. Unconscious of the trap, Aleck bent himself forward, putting all the crushing strength of his arms in the grip about Peter's body, and as Peter flung the weight of his head and shoulders in the same direction their balance was upset and they plunged into the pond.

As they struck the water Peter drew a great breath into his lungs, and in the same moment his foe relaxed his grip and began to flounder wildly in an element in which, even in the days of their boyhood, he had never been at home. His face rose above the surface for an instant, and Mona saw it as she staggered to the edge of the pond. It was then a deadly weight attached itself to one of his kicking legs, and not until Peter had dragged his burden to the muddy bottom of the beaver stronghold did he release his hold. He shot up for air, and scarcely had Aleck's body struggled to the surface when he dived again, and a second time bore his victim under. This time he expelled most of the air in his lungs, and for a few seconds hung on like an anchor.

A third and a fourth time, Aleck rose, fighting for his life, but the fifth time it was Peter who buoyed him up and brought him nearly unconscious to the shore. He noticed the livid mark made by Aleck's hand on Mona's forehead as she helped him drag the heavy body out of the water. In another half-minute he had the manacles intended for his father about Curry's wrists, and with his belt he securely lashed his prisoner's legs together. Then he faced Mona.

The same question was in their eyes. In Mona's it was a wordless terror. Peter looked at his father. He was stirring. A hand rose weakly from the grass. He had seen nothing of the struggle, heard nothing, and thought of him was first to leap into Peter's mind.

"He doesn't know what has happened!" he panted. "We must get him away, Mona. If anything would kill him now, it would be knowledge of this—that the law has found him—and that I—in helping him—have become an outlaw myself."

She came to him quickly and put her hands to his face, just as she had done on that other day years ago when he had fought his great battle with Aleck. "They can't blame you alone, Peter. I helped." She held up her lips, but instead of kissing them he pressed his own to the reddening mark on her forehead. "There is the little cabin," she whispered. "We can take your father there. And—I love you, Peter!"

She stood back from him, her eyes shining with sudden inspiration.

Aleck Curry had coughed the water out of his lungs and was twisting in his bonds. His voice called loudly as Peter bent over his father. Donald's eyes were opening.

"We must hurry!" urged Mona. "We must get away—where he is safe—where he cannot be found!"

Peter raised his father in his arms. The weight of the emaciated body sent a stab of pain through him. It was as if he had picked up the limp form of a boy.

Mona, close at his side, smiled into the grief-filled eyes he turned toward her. Together they hurried across the meadow. And then Mona ran on ahead, following a scarcely worn path through deep timber until in a few moments she came to another little meadow; here, under a clump of hardwoods, was a tiny cabin of logs—the "play-house" Peter had built for her two winters ago as a refuge and rest place for her when she came to visit her beaver pets. Inside a screened porch was a couch of saplings, and on this she had spread blankets and cushions by the time Peter arrived.

Donald's eyes were wide open, and he was smiling up wanly at Peter. "Never thought the day would come when you'd be lugging your dad around like this, did you, Peter?" he asked, and tried to laugh. But the moment his head touched the soft cushions his eyes closed again. Peter drew Mona away. "There is a boat down on the shore of the lake," he said, his voice steady again. "I'm going to force Aleck Curry into it and take him out to that little rock island two miles from the mainland. No one ever goes near it, and we can keep him there a prisoner until dad gets well, and then—" An angry yell came from the beaver pond. "Aleck is getting nervous," he finished. "You stay with dad, Mona. Tell him I've gone to Five Fingers for things he needs. I'll come back that way, and will get here before dark. Good-by, *Ange*!"

JAMES OLIVER CURWOOD

He kissed her. For a moment Mona clung to his hand.

"When you are down by the big stub—and if everything is all right—send me back the call," she entreated.

She watched him until he disappeared. Then she sat down close beside Donald McRae and held one of his limp hands. After what seemed to be a long time there came back to her clearly Peter's signal-cry, telling her that all was well, and that he was on his way to the prison island with Aleck Curry.

Over the forest fell a deep and quieting silence. Never had it seemed so intense to Mona, as she sat with Donald McRae's hand held closely in her own. The man's fingers were intertwined with hers as if he was afraid she would leave him; and his breath, coming more evenly and yet as faintly as the breath of a child, told her that complete exhaustion had at last overcome him with a sleep that was almost like death.

Twilight dusk began to fill the aisles of the woods, and with this dusk the last red glow died out of the west, and with it came the hour Mona loved more than all others—when darkness began to close in a velvety mantle over the world. The stillness, the soft whisperings of the forest and the peace that always came with night gave her courage and strengthened her faith. And at last, from beyond the beaver pond, she heard again Peter's cry. He was returning.

And as if he, too, had heard that cry, Donald McRae stirred softly and whispered Peter's name.

XVII

Quietly Mona went out to meet Peter. "He is sleeping," she said, as Peter's arm closed about her in the thickening darkness. "If he can only pass the night that way he will be strong and well again in the morning." Yet her voice trembled as she tried to bring him comfort. "Aleck is safe?" she whispered. "He is on the island?"

"Yes, he is safe for tonight—and maybe for a number of days. After that—"

He stopped, not knowing how to finish, and Mona's soft hand caressed his cheek. "We will tell Simon, and Uncle Pierre, and Father Albanel," she suggested. "Surely they will know how to help us!"

"I've been thinking about that," he said slowly, with his lips against her hair. "You must promise me not to tell them, Mona. I think it is necessary. At least they must not know until tomorrow or the next day. Will you remember that?"

"You are sure it is best?"

"I believe so."

"Then I will remember."

They drew near to the door of the cabin and listened. Faintly they could hear Donald McRae's breath as he slept.

"I must take you home," he whispered.

They hurried through the gloom, hand in hand. In half an hour they had reached the cliff trail that led to Five Fingers, and here Mona insisted that Peter turn back, while she went on alone. She was glad Pierre and Josette were at Joe's house when she came to the settlement. She called good night to them through the open door, and went to her room, with the excuse that she was tired.

She sat down at her window, and watched the moon come up. Later she heard Pierre and Josette when they returned. And after that, one after another, the lights went out in Five Fingers until the cabins lay like great shadows in the slumbering stillness. In this stillness she heard the clock in her bedroom tick off every second of the hours.

Until now she had never believed that answered prayer could bring with it a grimness and torture of tragedy like that which had descended upon her life and Peter's. Passionately she sobbed out her hatred for Aleck Curry, the monster who at last had descended upon them with his vengeance.

As the hours dragged on she found herself fighting more and more desperately against the desire to steal quietly from her room, tiptoe down the stairs and go to Simon McQuarrie's cabin that she might confide in him all that had happened that afternoon. Only Peter's warning to keep their secret locked tightly in her own breast held her back. Yet in Simon rested her last hope, for from the first day Peter had come into the old Scotchman's life he had found home—and a protection and love which in Mona's thoughts made him almost of Simon's flesh and blood. The impulse to go to him—to be false to Peter for the first time in her life—was a torment in her brain, and where one little voice had urged her at first, a hundred added to their insistence now. Slowly the revolt became a conviction that it was right and reasonable she should go to Simon, in spite of her promise to Peter.

Quietly she opened the door to her room and went down the stairs, making no sound to disturb Pierre and Josette Gourdon. A slim, pale figure, she crossed the clearing and paused in the shadow of the cabin where the Scotchman lived. Instinctively she looked up at Peter's window even though she knew he was in the forest with his father. Then she knocked on the door. Her heart throbbed as she listened for a response inside. It seemed to beat loudly, as if crying out against her faithlessness in breaking a promise to Peter. She knocked again, and in a moment she could hear McQuarrie moving. She counted his slow footsteps as they came across the floor. Then the door opened, and his tall, gaunt figure stood above her, swathed in a nightgown that fell to the toes of his feet. At any other time Mona would have laughed at the grotesqueness of his appearance as he stared down into her white face, with a nightcap on the back of his head.

He reached out a hand. *"Ange!"* he gasped. *"You!* What is the matter?"

She slipped past him and closed the door.

"Please light a lamp," she said. "Please—"

Simon struck a match. The flare of it illumined his face, tense and set in its amazement. When the lamp was lighted he took down a coat from a peg in the wall and put it on. Then he turned to Mona again. She stood before him with her hands clasped at her breast, and in her dark eyes was a look that alarmed him. And he could see in her bare throat the little heart-beating throb that always came when she was stirred by deep emotion.

With a desperate little cry she caught his hand. "Something terrible has happened," she whispered. "Something—you should know. But I promised Peter. I promised him I would tell no one—not even you. But I've got to turn that promise into a lie. If I don't—" The words broke on her lips. And then: "Peter's father has come back. He is with Peter now in the cabin near the beaver pond!"

Simon McQuarrie stood back from her, his hands dropping slowly and limply to his sides. Then he raised one of them as if to brush a shadow from his forehead, and his nightcap fell to the floor. "Donald McRae—has come back!" he repeated, and the deep lines in his face softened as Mona looked at him, and joy trembled in his voice when he spoke. "Thank God, *Ange*! Why do you think it is so terrible? We have waited and hoped for a long time—" He stopped. What he saw in her face and eyes swept a sudden change into his own, and he caught her arm as the gladness died on his lips. "Has anything happened?" he demanded. "Has anything happened—to Peter—or to Donald McRae?"

She began telling him in a low voice, while Simon stared at her with his big hands reaching out as if to grip at something in the space between them.

"I was at the beaver pond when Peter's father staggered out of the willows and almost fell at my feet. I didn't know who the man was, but he was sick and tired and starving—so hungry he ate carrots I had meant for the beavers. I gave him our lunch, and while he was eating I learned he was Peter's father. It made me happy. Peter was coming to join me, and I told Donald McRae. He begged me not to let Peter know he was there. He wanted to hide in the bushes, and look at him without being seen, and then go away again. He said that was why he had come back—just to get a look at his boy. He told me the police were after him again, that they were driving him like a rat from hole to hole, and that his presence could only bring unhappiness and tragedy to Peter. So he hid in the willows, and Peter came."

"And then?"

"In the end Peter's father staggered out of the bushes, and I left them together. Peter called me a little later and I ran back. Donald McRae was on the ground and at first I thought he was dead. Not until then did I realize how terribly sick and weak he was. We were on our knees beside him when he looked up, and there—there—grinning down at us—was the man Peter's father had been running away from. Oh, he was terrible—big and sweaty and leering down at us, almost laughing in his triumph, and—Simon—Simon—it was *Aleck Curry*!"

Her despair broke in a sobbing cry, and now the bones of Simon's great hands made a snapping sound as he clenched them, and his thin, hard face was gray in the glow of the lamp. "What happened then, Mona?"

"When Aleck went to put the manacles on Peter's father there was a fight—a terrible fight—and Aleck tried to kill Peter with a gun. He shot twice. I helped with a stone, and at last Peter got him into the pond, and almost drowned him. His father was still unconscious when we carried him to the cabin. Then Peter took Aleck down to his boat and to the little rock island two miles out from the shore. He is there now—a prisoner. And—what will happen to Peter? What can the law do to him?"

Simon paced slowly back and forth across the floor. His face was a mask of iron. His long nightgown flapped about his feet, and again his big, hard hands hung limp and straight at his sides.

"If Aleck escapes from the island and arrests Peter, or reports the affair to headquarters, it means the penitentiary," he said as if speaking to himself rather than to Mona. "And that is what will happen—if Curry has his way. He hates Peter. He would like to see Donald McRae hung, and Peter in prison, and *you*—" A tigerish gleam was in his eyes as he faced her. "Why didn't Peter kill him when he had the chance?" he cried, as for a single moment his self-control broke its leash. "As a boy he was a brute and a bully, and as a man his soul is that of a monster—even though now he is a part of the law. He wanted you—always. I know it and could see it even when you were children. And for what he wants he would wreck the world. Why didn't Peter kill him? Why—with these two hands—" He reached out his long arms and his fingers closed like talons of steel. Then he checked his passion. His arms dropped again. "But it is best he didn't," he finished. "It is best—even though a snake has a better right to live than Aleck Curry!"

He continued his pacing across the floor, and with each step his stern face grew harder until at last it seemed to have no emotion at all—the hard, set, fighting face which Simon McQuarrie always turned upon his enemies. For a few moments he seemed to forget Mona. Then he asked: "What is Peter going to do? What does he *plan* to do?"

The question was so sharp it sent a little shiver through her, and Simon's eyes were looking at her with the steely coldness of ice.

"I don't know. Peter doesn't know—except that he means to keep Aleck Curry on the island until his father is well and can get safely away."

Simon grunted. "You mean the rock with nothing on it—two miles straight out from the beaver pond?"

"Yes."

The fingers of Simon's hands were twisting again.

"Constable Carter dropped in on us late this afternoon," he said shortly. "He told Pierre and Dominique he was on his way into the Georgian Bay country and would rest here for a few days. He lied. He's working with Aleck Curry, and if Aleck doesn't show up soon—if he starts smoke signals going out on the island, and Carter sees them—"

"Aleck hasn't any matches," Mona interrupted him quickly. "Peter took them away from him."

Simon's face was lightened for an instant by a flash of exultation. "Peter is improving," he conceded. "If he had only used as good judgment at the beaver pond, when he could have rid us of this snake forever—"

Mona's cry of horror stopped him. In a moment he was at her side, and his long arms were about her tenderly. "I didn't mean that, Ange!" he cried, trying to laugh as he saw the agony of fear in her eyes. "It's a bad situation, so bad that I don't see a way out for Peter just now—but we won't kill Aleck, and we'll get Peter out of it somehow. He was right in making you promise not to tell anyone, and I'll keep it all to myself—even from Peter and my old friend Donald McRae—until Carter leaves the settlement. I'll manage to get him away in a day or two. And meanwhile you and Peter must keep Curry on the island, and watch every step you take so that Carter won't get suspicious. And above everything else—*most important of all*—don't tell Peter you have confided in me. Let me know everything that happens, but don't tell Peter that I know. Do you understand, Mona?"

She felt the suppression of something in his voice that was unlike Simon McQuarrie, something that thrilled and frightened her, yet she nodded her head and said: "Yes, I understand. I won't let Peter know. And I'll tell you—everything."

His arms drew her a little closer, and in him above all other men she had faith in that moment. She did not see his face above her, a face which for a single instant darkened with a look so pitiless and menacing that even Simon sensed the danger of its betrayal, and held her for a moment longer. Then with the gentleness which love for Mona and Peter had bred into his stern nature, he led her to the door.

"You must go home now, and to bed," he said. "It is your fight as well as Peter's, and you mustn't let anyone see that you are worried tomorrow—especially Carter." He opened the door. "Good night, *Ange!*"

"Good night!" she whispered as she slipped out.

He closed the door and listened for a moment to her retreating footsteps. When he faced the lamp and looked up at Peter's room, a new and strange light was in his eyes, and he spoke softly, as if to the spirit of someone who was waiting and listening up there.

"It's my turn now, and I'll care for Peter," he said. "A long time ago Donald McRae killed the man who insulted his mother, and it is no more than right and just that Simon McQuarrie should kill the man who would destroy her boy."

Then, slowly, he began to dress.

For a little while Mona hesitated in the shadow of the tall spruce tree that grew not far from Simon's door. She could hear her heart beating as she looked back at the light in the cabin. She was glad it was over, glad she had told Simon the truth, even as she thought of her promise to Peter.

Yet one thing she had kept to herself, and for a moment she felt the urge to go back and confide in the iron-willed Scotchman her own personal fear of Aleck Curry. Never until this night had she been afraid of him. She had defied and hated him as a young girl, and as she grew older had loathed and repulsed him for the persistence of his passion. To fear him had never entered her head, even in the days when once or twice she had used her hands in defending herself against, his unwelcome attentions.

But now she knew that Aleck's hour had come. Even though he was temporarily a prisoner on the island, he held her happiness and Peter's fate in the hollow of his hand. That fact, its significance, its terrible import for her, she had seen in Aleck's exultant face and eyes at the pool. In that hour his joy and triumph was not that he had run down Peter's father, but that *she* at last had come within the reach of his desires. And the fight had added to his mastery, for it had outlawed Peter and had given to the man she hated the final power to wreck her world. And she, of all that world, was the only one who knew what Aleck's price for the freedom of those she loved would be.

The thought was a monstrous thing in her brain. She had fought it, had beaten it back with the strength of her will, and she struggled with it again as she turned away from the light in Simon's window. Her hands clenched and a bit of savagery leaped through her blood as she went again through the moonlight. She had seen the deadly fire in the Scotchman's eyes, and that fire was now in her own. Over and over she told herself that she was still unafraid of Aleck Curry. Her lips whispered the words. But in her heart, fixed and implacable, remained the fear.

She had almost reached the shadow of Pierre Gourdon's cabin when a figure stepped out to meet her. It was Peter. His startled face questioned her in the moonlight.

"I thought you were asleep," he said in a low voice. "And so—I was passing under your window. I wanted to be near you for a few moments."

He put his arms about her and looked anxiously into her face, and then he laid his lips against her soft hair.

"It was impossible." She shivered against him. "I undressed, as you told me to do, and I went to bed. But I had to get up. I kept thinking, thinking—until I felt like screaming, or jumping out of my window and running to you."

"You are a little frightened, *Ange*—after what happened at the pool. But it will all come out right. Aleck is safe. He can't harm us—"

She looked up quickly, and saw in his eyes the same look that had been in Simon's. Her arms tightened about him.

"Peter, you don't need to hide anything from me," she protested. "We're both thinking the same thing—afraid of the same thing. It's Aleck Curry—and what he will do when he gets off the island. We can keep him there until your father is well, and safe. But after that—what will happen to you?"

Peter tried to laugh. "They can't do anything worse than send me to prison, and if they do that—would you mind waiting for me, *Ange*?"

She knew the effort he was making to speak lightly, almost playfully, and her heart throbbed with the eager quickness of her answer. "I would wait for you all my life, Peter."

With a sudden movement he drew her into the shadow of the cabin. His eyes were searching the farther edge of the clearing.

"Look!" he said.

Her eyes pierced the moon glow. And then, dimly, she saw a moving shadow. It came nearer, and turned toward Simon's cabin. Instinctively she guessed who it was, but waited for Peter to speak.

"I found him nosing around when I returned to the settlement," he said. "A little while ago he was here, looking up at your window; then he went to Simon's, and afterward sneaked off into the edge of the forest. I don't know who he is, but I was within ten feet of him and he wears a uniform like Aleck's. He is watching for dad. He is also suspicious and is wondering why Aleck doesn't show up."

"His name is Carter," said Mona. "He came to Five Fingers this afternoon."

XVIII

For a long time they stood in the shadow of the cabin, and the sleepy stillness of the night with its soft chirping of crickets and gentle murmuring of the lake surf brought a soothing peace to Mona. With Peter's arms about her she was no longer afraid. He told her what had happened since she left his father. Twice Donald McRae had awakened from his sleep of exhaustion and had asked for her. A thrill of pleasure was in Peter's voice as he told her this; it made him happy to know that his father loved her, and that he even whispered her name in his feverish slumber. Some day the whole of their prayer would be answered; things would turn out right; and they would all be happy.

Not until he had gone, and she was alone in her room, did Mona note how swiftly the time had passed. The hour hand of the little clock was at three. She did not undress, but sat down at her window, with her face turned toward the coming of the dawn. And now that Peter's love and the unbreakable strength of his optimism were no longer at her side, her thoughts began pressing upon her again, dispelling the comfort he had given her and weakening once more her faith and hope in what the day would bring. She was glad she confided in Simon, for he was the rock to which she clung in these hours of her own helplessness. And yet—what could Simon do? Wherein was he less helpless than herself—or Peter? She shivered as she recalled the grim and terrible look that had last rested in his face. And that same look had been in Peter's—a flash which he had tried to hide from her! Her heart jumped and for an instant her fingers clutched at the sill of her window. Would one of them—Simon or Peter—*kill Aleck Curry*?

It seemed to her that a terrible truth rushed upon her all at once and caught like a living thing at her throat until it was difficult for her to breathe. There was no hope for Peter as long as Aleck lived! The words almost came from her lips. Unless Peter ran away, wandering and hiding like his father, no power could keep him from going to prison. But if Aleck should never leave the little island—if he died there—and no one knew of the fight at the pool—

She bowed her face in her arms. It would be so easy of accomplishment—so terribly and frighteningly easy! Peter might do it! And Simon—the look in his face—his eyes—what he said—

"No, no, no," she whispered to herself. "Anything—anything but that!"

She raised her head to meet the first rose-flush of the dawn. But this morning there was no responsive thrill in Mona's breast. A question was repeating itself in her brain. Would she be able to go through the day without giving herself away? Could she meet Pierre and Josette Gourdon, and Marie Antoinette, and Father Albanel, and Adette and Jame Clamart—and not let them see her torture? Would it show in her face when she met Carter, of the Provincial Police?

Until the first white spirals of smoke began rising from the cabin chimneys she sat at her window. Then she rose, and her beautiful face was almost stern in its resolution. She let the sunlight stream into her room, and in its radiance she unbraided her hair and brushed it until it lay about her in the rippling glory that made Peter the happiest and proudest of all men. She dressed it carefully, and tried to sing as she made herself ready to help Josette with the breakfast—for she always sang in this first hour of the day. But the notes seemed to stifle her this morning.

It was then, looking out from her window, that she saw a grayish haze rising between her and the face of the sun, and the smell of it came to her faintly. It was smoke.

When she went below it was Pierre she met first. He kissed her. But anxiety was in his face.

"It is happening again this year," he said. "The forests to the north and west are afire. It will not come near Five Fingers, but it makes my heart ache to know that a world is being turned dead and black because of someone's carelessness!"

So it was the fire which gave Mona an excuse for what was lacking in her eyes when she went to help Josette with the breakfast. And it was this same fire, with its thickening gloom of smoke, which helped her through the day. For to Mona a living tree had life and soul, and to see trees destroyed in countless thousands was a tragedy in her life only a little less terrible than the plague of smallpox which had once cast its shadow upon Five Fingers.

She went to Simon's cabin as soon after breakfast as she could make an excuse, and there she met Carter. Her first glimpse of him filled her with uneasiness and dislike. He was a hawk-nosed, shifty-eyed man in whom nature seemed to have sacrificed every softening quality to an uncompromising sense of duty, and his eyes rested upon her face so intently as Simon introduced them that she felt her heart tremble. But if he knew of her previous visit to Simon's cabin, or of her meeting with Peter, he gave no evidence of it, and after a casual remark or two about the fire he left her alone with the Scotchman.

A worried look was in McQuarrie's eyes.

"I've found out more about Carter," he said. "He is the best man in this division and is never sent out on minor affairs. Leaving us so quickly right now shows how clever he is. He doesn't want to create suspicion. He dropped in to ask me the best trail northwest, and says he is going to leave in half an hour to make a report on the fire. That's another lie. In the woods he is like a cat, and he won't go half a mile from the settlement. He is wondering where Peter is, and if he once gets on his trail—" Suddenly he drew his hands together, and a grim smile gathered about his mouth. "If Carter goes to that fire, I'm going with him!" he exclaimed. "Five Fingers is interested, and he cannot very well turn me down."

In a few words Mona told of Peter's visit; and then, standing so near that he could not avoid the directness of her eyes, she gave low voice to her suspicion that either he or Peter was planning to kill Aleck Curry.

The effect of her words on Simon startled her. He stood dumb, staring at her. Then one of his bony hands reached out and rested on her shoulder. Its fingers hurt her. "Don't even whisper that anywhere—but here," he said. "You understand? *Don't!* Peter won't kill him. And I'm not worrying about Aleck Curry now. It's Carter."

He left her without another word, and went out to overtake Carter. There was something so grim and foreboding in his movement that it chilled her, and as she dropped a few steps behind him she noticed his boots. At midnight she had seen them in his cabin, clean and freshly oiled. Now they were frosted with half-dried mud to their tops. His sourness, the harshness of his fingers on her shoulder, his silence now and the aggressive hunch of his shoulders, together with the mud on his boots, tightened her breath. Had Simon already accomplished the thing she feared? Was that why he was so anxious to follow Carter, go with him—get him away from Five Fingers? She ran up to him, meaning to demand the truth.

He anticipated her intention and spoke almost roughly. "Don't ask questions, Mona. Carter has stopped, and is looking. Go home—and stay in if you can't keep control of yourself."

The rest of the morning Mona waited anxiously for Peter. At noon, when they were at dinner, Pierre Gourdon talked of little but the fire. It had surely crossed the line of rail thirty miles north, he said, and was traveling steadily eastward. If the wind should quicken and swing into the south there would be danger to the forests about Five Fingers. But the settlement itself was safe, protected as it was by fire-lines and cultivated fields on three sides, and Lake Superior on the other.

He wondered where Simon McQuarrie was, and asked Mona if she had seen Peter. He surmised they had gone back to the crests of the high ridges to make a closer observation of the fire. He had already sent out Jame Clamart and Poleon Dufresne to guard the northern ridges, and if the fire threatened to break coastward, all the men in Five Fingers would go out to fight it. He had made preparations. But he didn't like the way Peter and Simon were missing, without leaving any word behind them. Carter was gone, too.

Afternoon saw smoke settling like a thin fog about the clearing. The sun was entirely hidden. Animals and fowls came up to the buildings, and men and women gave up their work to discuss with one another the possibilities of the next few hours. A dozen times Mona repressed the desire to steal away and go to the little cabin where Donald McRae was hidden. She knew Peter was there, and now that the smoke was thickening she believed he would soon leave for the settlement.

She noticed how hot and sultry it had grown in the last hour. Scarcely a breath of air was stirring, and in the middle of the afternoon Adette Clamart insisted that she go with her for a swim down in the inlet. While they were in the water Peter came up from the lake in a boat. His sail was down and he was rowing. Adette Clamart covered her pretty eyes with her two hands while he bent over to kiss Mona, and in that moment he whispered, "I want to see you in the cabin." He was acting strangely, Mona thought.

A few minutes later she joined him in the cabin.

"Dad is better," Peter said. "But tonight I'm going to get him away— somewhere. I'm afraid of the fire. With a bad wind it would be on us in an hour or two. Right now I want to take some supplies over to Aleck Curry. Then I'll come back and see you before I return to dad. There's a little breeze on the lake, and I can make the island in an hour. Have you seen Carter?"

"This morning. He hasn't been here since then."

"And Simon?"

"He is gone, too."

She got a bundle she had prepared and said good-by to Peter but not until he had promised to return directly from the island by way of the inlet. She watched him until he disappeared in the gray haze that hung over the water, and then looked at the clock to mark the time he would be returning. Scarcely had she done this when a figure stalked past one of the windows. Instantly she recognized it as Simon McQuarrie. He went straight to his cabin, entered it and closed the door. *And Carter was not with him!*

Her heart throbbed as she went outside, determined to follow him. But something held her back. Then she forced herself to follow her first impulse, and a moment later was knocking at Simon's door. There was no answer. She persisted, knocking loudly and calling his name, and still there was no response. Then she tried the door and found it locked. Where there had been fear in her breast there was now conviction. The tiger in the old Scotchman had been at work, and in his own way—*and the only way*—he had solved the great problem of her life and Peter's, and had made the world free again for his old friend Donald McRae. He had rid the island of Aleck Curry, and had done away with Carter. And now he wanted to be alone—alone in his cabin!

Not for a moment did she question the reasonableness of her conviction. It seized upon her like a many-tentacled thing, choking back her doubt and overwhelming her with its certainty. It made her steal pantingly to the edge of the forest, and then to the beginning of the long finger of spruce and cedar that reached away out to the entrance of Middle Finger Inlet. Half an hour later she was on the sand and gravel beach under the big cliff, waiting for Peter's return. And now she noticed a change in the wind. Loose tresses of her hair blew seaward. That meant the fire would come over the ridges!

In another quarter of an hour she could scarcely see the farther side of Middle Finger Inlet. A black pall of smoke was creeping closer in the north and west. Then, very faintly, she saw something creeping up like a ghost out of the smoke gloom of the sea. She knew it was Peter. He was coming with nerve-racking slowness, it seemed to her. Yet she did not want to cry out to him until he was nearer. He was using his oars, and at times there was a half-minute interval between his strokes. Why was he so slow? Was it because of what he had found on the island? Surely Simon would have left no telltale signs. So far as Peter was concerned Aleck Curry could only be *missing*—nothing more!

A shudder ran through her. Then she cried Peter's name. Her voice carried strangely clear. There was silence in the boat. The oars were resting without a sound.

"Peter," she cried again. "Peter! I am here—on the point!"

He must have heard her, and it was unusual that he did not answer. But the oars rattled again, and she could see the shape of the boat turning slowly, and then growing larger as it came toward her. It was odd, too, that Peter did not come directly to the point, but grounded his boat among the big rocks fifty yards below her—a place where he knew it was difficult for her to go. So she stood on the white sand, waiting for him. She could hear his boots on the rocks; then she saw him approaching through a dusk of early twilight thickened by the smoke of the fire.

"Here I am, Peter," she called softly.

It did not seem like Peter, for the figure was grotesquely large, and slower of movement. She held out her arms, and her eyes were glowing. It was the smoke and the dusk that made Peter look like that! And then her heart stopped beating. The figure was within ten feet of her. It was not Peter. *It was Aleck Curry!*

XIX

In that moment Mona felt for the first time in her life the giving way of living tissue under the sudden overwhelming stress of complete shock. Strength left her body, her arms dropped limply, and she felt herself swaying, as if about to fall. Had there been anything near her she would have caught at it. She did not know that to Aleck Curry she was betraying no physical sign of her weakness—that she was standing like a lifeless creature carved out of rock, except that her wide eyes were blazing and her lips parted. What seemed an age to her covered but a few seconds. Then her mind leaped back, fierce in its command of her. She was wrong! Simon had not been to the island! He had not harmed Aleck Curry—and Aleck had returned in Peter's boat. *What had happened to Peter?*

She did not ask the question. It blazed out of her eyes as Aleck advanced until he was almost within arm's reach of her. He had on only shirt and trousers, and he was barefooted. She could see his naked throat. And surprise, joy, the knowledge of his mastery lay in his heavy face. It was transformed. He smiled at her, and his great arms reached out as if he were Peter and she would come into them.

"I made a bargain with Peter," he said, "and he changed places with me. I made him see how much it meant for him, and for his father, and for you. I'd let his father go and forget everything—for something I want. So he changed places with me, and I've come to see you. Lucky you're here. Lucky you called."

It was a clumsy lie, and stumbled on his lips. The menace of him filled her with horror. But she did not let him see it—now. He came a step nearer, and she backed away from him. Suddenly her mind whipped inspirational words from her lips. She looked up swiftly to the top of the cliff. "I don't want Carter to see you here," she cried quickly. "He walked down the point with me, and I think he's up there."

The significance of her words was not lost upon Aleck. He moved nearer to the cliff, so that one above could not see them. She followed him, fighting back her fear.

"Why don't you want Carter to see us?" he asked in a throaty whisper.

"Because—if he saw us—everything would be lost. You would not dare help me then. And you will, Aleck—you will help me, won't you?" He was stunned by the change in her. She had laid a hand on his arm.

Her eyes were shining at him. "But you must tell me the truth. There isn't any need to lie. What did you do to Peter—when he came to the island?" Her fingers pressed his flesh. There was almost a smile on her lips.

"The smoke was thick," said Aleck. "I heard him coming and hid in the water. Then I stunned him with a club. He ain't bad—not badly hurt—but he's safe enough on the island!"

Mona crushed back the little cry of relief that wanted to come to her lips. Her eyes glowed at Aleck, and suddenly one of his big hands closed about the one she had laid on his arm. She could feel his breath as he bent over her. "I told you my time would come," he cried in a husky, exultant voice. *"My day!* And it's here. I got 'em both—safe—one to hang, the other—"

"Sh-h-h!"

She placed a finger to her lips. It was an excuse to draw away from him, get her hand free—and not let him hear the terrified beating of her heart. She looked up again at the cliff.

"Did you hear anything?"

"No. And if anyone hears *us* it's going to be your fault and not mine!"

It was impossible to escape the look in his face and eyes. It was not necessary for him to use words. But Mona did not flinch from her peril. It was not only her danger, but Peter's, and Donald McRae's, and Simon's if he had harmed Carter. It had suddenly and unexpectedly become her fight—all hers, and she knew that Aleck Curry thought she was yielding, and that the brute in him was held in leash only by this belief that was beginning to possess him. If he guessed the truth, guessed that she was fighting to trick him, nothing would save her, not even her assertion that Carter was on the cliff above them. So she smiled again at Aleck, and laughed very softly, with a nervous twisting of her hands. Her eyes had never looked at him as they were looking at him now. They were like glowing stars, velvety-soft—hiding hate and desperation behind them. She had never looked half so beautiful, or so unresisting, to Aleck Curry.

Her fingers pressed his arm again.

"I must get Carter away," she whispered. "I've got to do it, Aleck! He mustn't know. I'll hurry. And then I'll come back. I promise!"

Horror seized her as she felt him drawing her toward him. But still she did not resist. With a low cry his great arms were about her. She felt herself almost broken against him, and then she was helpless, her head bent back, and his thick lips killing her with kisses. Again her strength left her, and she lay limp in his arms, smothered in his passion. Those moments of helpless and agonized passiveness saved her. To Aleck it was surrender. His arms loosened and allowed her to breathe. Weakly she pressed against him, and he allowed her partly to free herself. But she could still feel his hot breath like a poisonous fume in her face. He bent forward and kissed her again—on the mouth. It almost choked her.

"I must—must get Carter away!" she gasped. "Then I'll come back. If you won't let me do that, I'll—I'll scream—and Carter will hear us. But if you'll let me get him away, so he'll never know—never be able to tell Peter—"

It was unnecessary for her to finish. Aleck's face was transformed by an iniquitous joy. He looked close into her face, and she looked back at him, unafraid.

"I'll let you go—and get Carter away," he said. "If you don't come back soon, I'll go to Five Fingers—and you know what that means for Peter and his father."

"I'll come," she lied.

She climbed up the narrow footpath to the top of the cliff, and getting her breath there, she called Carter's name—loudly enough for Aleck to hear.

Then she began to run. She was still weak, and it seemed to her that the poison of Aleck Curry's embraces and kisses followed her. She began to sob under her breath. There was no turning of the ways for her now. She must tell someone the truth—anyone—the first man she met. But Simon first of all. On the little island Peter might be dying. Maybe Aleck had killed him, for it was in his power to do so and still be within the law. She began to moan his name. Then she came to the crest of a high knoll which was bare of trees, and what she saw ahead of her stopped her, gulping for breath and almost falling in her exhaustion.

A wind was in her face. And northward there was no longer a black pall of smoke but a world afire. The glow of the conflagration reached from the earth to the sky. It swept in a great arc, and red seas of flame were leaping from peak to peak of the farther ridges. Pierre Gourdon's fear had become a reality. The fire was racing with the speed of the wind itself upon Five Fingers!

She ran on. Her hair caught in the brush, and she clutched it in front of her. She came at last to the edge of the clearing and staggered across

　　　　　　　　　　JAMES OLIVER CURWOOD

it. There were lights in the cabins, in her own home, in Adette Clamart's, in Dominique Beauvais's and half a dozen others. But Simon's was dark. Yet she swayed toward that, hopeful to the last—and almost at the door she came upon Simon. He was rigid and still, like a shadow. She could see his gray, hard face. Then he heard her panting, heard her trying to gasp out her terrible news, and his arms reached out and gathered her to him—and she told him what had happened to Peter.

Ten minutes later Simon was leaving in a sailboat.

"It's so dark Curry won't see me when I pass through the mouth of the inlet," he said. "And I'll reach Peter in half an hour."

Mona went back to McQuarrie's cabin, climbed to Peter's room and lighted a lamp. In a cedar box she found Peter's thirty-eight-caliber automatic and loaded it with skilful fingers. Then she extinguished the light, descended the ladder and left the cabin in the direction of her tryst with Aleck Curry. There was only one thing for her to do, and her mind was quite fixed. It was her right to be at the end of the point waiting for Simon and Peter. And if Aleck threatened her—or put his hands on her again—she would kill him. That was the one way out. It would save Peter, and Peter's father, and herself.

It was not a monstrous thing but a just and righteous act—this wiping out of existence of a creature who threatened to destroy everything that made her world a fit place to live in.

She had nearly passed the Clamart cabin when a white figure ran out of the gloom, and she had only time to hide the pistol in her dress when Adette Clamart was holding her excitedly by the arm. Adette's lovely face was white, and she was half out of breath from running.

"It is terrible!" she cried. "Jame says the fire will be at your beaver pond within an hour, and he has just started in that direction with Jeremie Poulin and Carter—to keep it from coming over the last ridge—"

"Carter!" gasped Mona.

"Yes. Jame told him about the cabin Peter built, and Carter said it was a shame not to save it, and the beavers. Jame says it is impossible— that a hundred men couldn't keep the fire back—but Carter insisted, and they've gone!"

Mona tried to force words from her lips, and thanked God that Adette hurried on, crying back to her that she was making an effort to overtake Jame before he got out of the clearing, to give him a lunch which he had forgotten. Carter had returned—and was on his way to the cabin in which Peter's father was hidden! And that cabin, Jame said, would be in the heart of the fire within an hour! With Peter dead or wounded on the island, and Simon gone, what hope was there now for Donald McRae? If the fire did not reach his cabin first, Carter would get him, and if the fire beat out Carter—

Mona's dry lips gave a little cry. Through the pitch-filled evergreen forest about the beaver pond the fire would sweep in a destroying inundation which no living creature could outrace if the wind was behind it; and Donald McRae, sick and helpless, would be the first human victim in its descent upon Five Fingers.

The peril which was threatening Peter's father from two directions worked a swift and thrilling change in Mona. She must beat out Carter—and she must beat out the fire! Thought of Aleck Curry became secondary to this more immediate necessity. She could settle with Aleck later. But she must reach the cabin *now*. There was not a minute or a second to lose if she was to get there ahead of Jame and Carter. She began to run again, following a path through the meadow into the strip of forest between the settlement and the shore of the lake. Her feet and Peter's had worn this trail smooth, and she knew that in the thickening gloom of smoke and night she was traveling faster than Carter and Jame Clamart, who were going by the rougher tote-road. In ten minutes she reached the cliff which ran westward along the lake.

Here she was high, and there were no trees to shut out her view of the ridge country. What she saw appalled her. Nowhere in the north was there any longer a wall of blackness. The world was red, with lurid flashings that came and went like mighty explosions. Westward, beyond the beaver pond, she could see the leaping of the flames in the thick spruce and cedar timberlands where ten thousand barrels of pitch and resinous oils were turning sleeping forests into boiling caldrons of fire. The smell of this oil and pitch was heavy in her nostrils, and she could hear the moaning, distant roar of the conflagration as one hears the roar of great furnaces when the fuel doors are opened. But it was the wind that brought quicker fear to her heart. It was beginning to blow strongly from the north and west, and carried with it a heat that was stifling. And with this heat and wind came also a thickening cloud of ash particles, until at last, afraid of their increasing sting, she stopped to take off her skirt and fasten it about her hair and face.

Halfway to the pond, with still another mile to go, she saw the flames leaping over the last ridge, and her heart seemed suddenly to give way in a sobbing cry of agony and despair. She was too late. Between that ridge and Peter's father was less than a mile of spruce and cedar and balsam forest, with pitch-sodden jackpines interspersed so thickly that no power less than God could hold back the speed of the holocaust. With the wind that was behind them the flames would be at the cabin before she could cover a quarter of the distance to Peter's father.

For a few moments she sank down helpless and without strength, sobbing for breath as she stared at the merciless red death which had beaten her—and Carter. And in these moments her agony was greater than when Aleck had told her about Peter, for now she was picturing a man, creeping out on his hands and knees to face that sea of flame—a man, sick and helpless, crying out for Peter, for her, and dying by inches with their names on his lips.

She staggered to her feet and went on, and in her dazed mind lived a prayer that Donald McRae might be given strength to drag himself to the shore of the lake. If that strength had not already come to him, it was now too late, for as she toiled over a high and craggy point in the cliff the wind blew hot in her face, and where the beaver pond should be was a red hell of flames.

The trail descended as she forced herself on—descended from the ramparted ledge to the smooth, sandy level of the beach, and suddenly she was conscious of the crashing of bodies in the thickets and the frenzied sound of living things. A great moose swept so near her that she sprang from his path—a monstrous beast with flaming eyes and snorting nostrils, closely followed by a darker, rounder object that she knew was a bear, racing for the safety of the water. She came to the sandy open where the trail swung straight ridgeward toward the beaver pond, and stopped, knowing she could go no farther unless she defied the death from which all other living creatures were flying.

Piteously Mona cried out—to Peter, to Simon, to Donald McRae, and then to God; and at last she fell down with her face buried in her skirt, ready to welcome death itself in this hour when not only her world but all that she loved in it were doomed to destruction.

It was a sound close to her that uncovered her face, a sound that came strangely above the moaning roar of heat-wind and flame, and staring through the gloom and against the red glare of the burning forests, she saw a grotesque shadow—something that was not moose nor deer nor any four-footed thing she had ever seen in the wilderness; and rising up before it she saw that it was a man bent under a huge, limp burden which he carried. She cried out, and a choking voice answered her—a strange, terrible, unhuman sort of voice, yet the sound of it nearly split her heart, and when the figure deposited its burden in the white sand and stood up she saw that it was Peter. She stumbled toward him. His arms caught her, and she could hear him sobbing under the strain of his fight, and his heart was beating so hard that each throb of it sent a tremor through his body. In his weakness her own strength returned, and in a moment her hands had left his face and she was at the side of the man who lay upon the sand.

It was Donald McRae. Now a great light was flaming in the sky over their heads, and she saw that his face and hands were black, and his eyes were closed, though he was breathing. She tore the skirt from about her head and ran to soak it in water, but when she returned Peter was kneeling beside his father, and held back the dripping cloth.

"Not water," he said. "We must get—something else. He is burned."

She put her arms about Peter, and his face rested for a moment on her shoulder. In that moment he told her that Aleck had tricked him, and had left him on the island. With the aid of a piece of dry driftwood he had managed to swim ashore, but too late to reach the cabin ahead of the flames. He found his father halfway to the lake, fighting his way on hands and knees in the van of the fire. His face and hands were badly burned, but that was all. Another minute and he would have been too late. His voice choked, and Mona's hand stroked his face gently, and she kissed his hot forehead.

Then they carried Donald McRae under the shelter of the cliff, where they were free from smoke and heat, with the water rippling in and out among the stones at their feet. And here Mona told Peter of Aleck's coming to the point, though she kept to herself what happened there, and that Simon McQuarrie had gone to the island in a sailboat and would surely come straight to this beach when he found Peter gone. And as they made Donald easier, and waited in the coolness of the cliff for the fire-storm to burn itself out, she told him also of Carter and that no time must be lost in getting away to a place of greater safety.

Peter knew what that meant as he bent over his father. In scarcely more than a whisper he told Mona. He, too, must go. It would not be for long—maybe a week, a month, or a little longer. It was not for himself. He was not afraid of either Aleck or the law, because he had done at the pool just what he would do again if it were before the eyes of the whole world. But his father needed him, and never would his heart beat the same, nor would she ever again look at him with a bit of the pride and love which made him so strong, if he failed to do what was right in this hour. Without him his father was lost. He hoped Simon would come with the boat, for in that boat they would escape into the wilderness farther west.

Mona made no answer to these things, for it was hard enough for her to breathe with the thickness that was in her throat. But her hand stroked Peter's, and her cheek lay against his, and above the grief in her breast rose a great pride in this man who loved her. And a thought came to her of Sir Nigel, the chivalrous young knight who looked so much like this Peter of hers with his sensitive boyish face, and of how Mary so bravely sent him away to the great wars in which through long years he rose to undying fame; and she subdued her heart, as Sir Nigel's sweetheart must have conquered her own, and at last told Peter it was the thing to do—the one thing to do—and that God and she would love him for it. And even as she did this there was creeping over her an unutterable foreboding, and death seemed to pierce her heart when she heard Simon McQuarrie's boat grounding on the sand. But she smiled, and kissed Peter—and then Simon stood before them. And in another five minutes he was gone again—this time to the settlement for the supplies and medicines which would go with Peter and his father.

For an hour they were alone, and Donald McRae tried to keep back the moans of pain that came to his lips. But he could not open his eyes, and Mona fanned him gently with a piece of her wet skirt, and told him Simon was hurrying with ointments which would make him comfortable. Peter even laughed and spoke of the sudden on-sweep of the fire as if it were an exciting adventure, and it was good that Donald could not see their tense and grief-filled faces in the gloom.

The fire roared through the last of the evergreens and burned itself out against the bare stone knolls and ledges of the lake shore. And then came again the sound of Simon's boat on the sand.

"Carter has returned to the settlement and was preparing to come this way in a boat when I slipped out through the inlet," Simon whispered to Mona.

With Peter she went to the boat, leaving Simon alone for a few moments with his old friend. And it was Simon who came at the end of a brief interval bearing the burden of Peter's father in his arms. Very tenderly he laid him on the blankets in the boat.

"God be with you, Donald," he whispered, a broken note in his voice. "God be with you—always."

The stricken man raised a burned hand to the other's face.

"They have always been with me, Simon," he whispered back. "God—and Helen. And now that you have made such a fine man of Peter I hope I may go to them—soon."

In the darkness Mona crept out of Peter's arms.

"Peter, you must wait no longer. You must go."

"In a little while I will come back, *Ange*."

"And I—by the sweet spirit of Ste. Anne—I promise to be waiting for you when you come, Peter—though I wait until new forests grow where yours and mine have burned. So go—good-by—lover—sweetheart—"

And then she had slipped away from him and he made no effort to follow her into the smoky gloom, though a sobbing cry came back to him faintly.

For a moment Simon stood aside with Peter. Their hands gripped in the darkness and a strain was in the old Scotchman's low voice as he said:

"I've put ointment on your father's face and hands and he is easier. I don't think he is badly burned. Everything is in the boat, lad—provisions, blankets, medicines, a pack and what money I had at hand." He hesitated and the grip of his fingers tightened as he added: "In the bow is your rifle with extra ammunition in the buckskin sack beside it. You'll need it. But don't fight the law unless they force you to it, boy. Remember that. The law finds no excuse, even though scoundrels like Aleck Curry and blood-sucking ferrets like Carter are sometimes a part of it. And let me tell you that I saw with my own eyes when your father killed a man years ago when you were a baby in your mother's arms. It was for your mother he did it and he was right; but in spite of that the law won't rest until it lands him. And it's your job now to beat the law, but without the use of a gun. I love you, lad—but I'd curse you for a coward if you didn't do what you're doing now. For years you and Mona have prayed that God would send your father back to you—and now he has come—and it's God's will behind it. All that is left in a body that was once stronger than my own is his worship for you and his memories of your mother. Take care of him, Peter. And—God bless you both!"

Never had the iron-natured old Scotchman said so much in all the years since Peter had come to live with him as a son. And without a word Peter went to the boat, for his throat was thick and choking, and Simon shoved the craft out into the sea until he was waist-deep in the

JAMES OLIVER CURWOOD

water. Simply he said good-by as if Peter were going only to the nets or the islands outside the mainland, and no tremor in his hard, calm voice betrayed the tears on his cheeks which darkness hid. And as Peter raised the sail McQuarrie waded ashore and was met by a pair of arms and a sobbing voice that cried out in its grief and despair against his shoulder.

Another sound came before they turned to the cliff trail that led along the unburned shore of the lake to Five Fingers. From the direction of the settlement a light skiff bore down swiftly upon the strip of sandy beach.

Carter, who sat in the stern, was old in the service of the provincial police, a ferret on the trail, a fox in his cleverness, cold-blooded, unexcitable and merciless—and when the bow of the skiff ran into the sand and Aleck Curry leaped ashore he remained quietly in his seat and waited. In a moment he heard voices—the cold, unemotional voice of the Scotchman first and then Aleck Curry's in fierce demand and Mona Guyon's in answer. He went ashore, his thin, hard face smiling in the darkness, and heard Simon tell Aleck that the law no longer had a work to do at Five Fingers, for Peter and his father had died somewhere out in the heart of the fire. He heard Mona's sob, close to Simon's shoulder. Then he opened his flashlight, but not upon them. It illumined Aleck's face, thick-lipped and bestial in its disappointment and passion. What he saw was amusing to a man like Carter and a spark of chivalry made him leave the others in darkness. But he stepped back and cast his light upon the wet sand of the shore. And then he said quite casually, as if his discovery was a matter of small significance:

"You lie, McQuarrie! We have come only a quarter of an hour too late. Peter McRae and his father have gone in your boat, and as this breath of wind will scarcely fill a sail, I think Aleck's enthusiasm and a light skiff should make it possible for us to overtake them within an hour!"

He chuckled as he switched off his flashlight, and that chuckle was like the rattle of a snake to Mona, deadlier than all the hate and animal passion she had seen in Aleck Curry's face in the one swift moment when it had flashed out of the darkness into light. For Carter was more than a representative of the law. He was its incarnation, and more than Aleck Curry—more than any other man in the world—she feared him now as the skiff sped in the direction taken by Peter and his father.

XX

For a few minutes after leaving the shore Peter did not trust himself to speak. He could see nothing but a gray chaos except landward, where the red sky and the darker blot of the cliff were visible through the smoke gloom. Even the weather-stained canvas of Simon's boat was indistinguishable, and where his father lay on a pile of blankets at his feet he could make out only a shadow. Now that the fire had burned itself out of the forests between the shore and the ridges the heated winds gave way quickly to a growing calm. The smoke hung like a dense fog and with this change came a strange stillness in which sound seemed to multiply itself until he heard clearly the wailing of a dog at Five Fingers.

Then the faint rattle of oarlocks came to him and his hand tightened on the tiller. It was Aleck Curry again—Aleck and the man-hunter, Carter, hurrying to cut them off before they could leave the shore! And suddenly in fierce passion he wanted to shout back his defiance to them just as years ago—three days before he came to Five Fingers—he had felt the desire to kill the men who had driven his father into the forest. Something in these moments brought that day back to him—a vivid memory of the big log behind which they were sheltered, and armed men in the thickets, the blue jay screeching at them, his thirst and hunger and his father's pale, strong face waiting with courage for darkness to come; then the dusk, their escape on a log in the flooded river and their first fugitive camp in the big woods. How wonderful his father had been in those hours of peril which he as a boy could scarcely understand! And now he was lying at his feet, a pitiable wreck because of that same merciless and unfair law which had pursued him then—

Peter cried out. It was not much more than a throat sound, as if the smoke had made him gasp for breath. But a hand rose out of the darkness and touched him.

"Peter!"

"Yes, dad."

"It has all gone wrong, boy. If only I hadn't been so heartsick to see you—if I had never come back—"

Peter bent over and his hand rested tenderly against the face which Simon had cooled with ointment.

JAMES OLIVER CURWOOD

"If you hadn't come I'd have lost all faith in the God you used to tell me about," he whispered. "I wanted to give up but Mona wouldn't let me. She said you would surely come. And this isn't half as bad as that day behind the log when I was a little kid. Remember how you cared for me then—kept me above water when we went into the river, caught rabbits for me to eat afterward and tucked me into bed every night near the camp-fire? Well, it's *my* turn now. And I'm almost glad you're sick—just so I can show you how much I've grown up since that afternoon you sent me on alone to Five Fingers so many years ago. You lied to me then, dad. You made me believe you'd come back that night, or the next day. Haven't you ever been ashamed of that?"

The strain was gone from his voice. It was his *dad* he was speaking to again, his pal and comrade of the old days, and the thrill of that comradeship was stirring warmly in his blood.

"I knew Simon would give you a good home," said Donald. "And he has made a splendid man of you. But I'm sorry, Peter—sorry I came back. After all those years I was hungry to see you. I just wanted to look on your face and then go away again without letting you know. I didn't mean to break into your life like this—"

His hand was stroking Peter's and for a moment Peter bent down until his face was close to his father's. Donald was silent but his hand continued its caressing touch. After a little he said:

"Did I hear something, Peter?"

"I think it was thunder. A storm must be following in the trail of the fire."

"I mean out there—near at hand. It was like wood striking on wood."

He sank back and Peter reached down and made his head comfortable. "This makes me think of that last night in the woods when you tucked me in my cedar-bough bed and told me to sleep," he whispered gently. "And I'm telling you that now, dad. It's what you need. Try and sleep!"

Even as he spoke he heard the distant sound again and knew it was the clank of oarlocks. He fastened the tiller so that Simon's boat was heading for the open sea. Then he crept forward and returned with a blanket, and this blanket he quietly unfolded in the darkness, taking from it the weapon which Simon had loaded and placed there for his use. And Simon's words were running over and over in his head, as steady as the ticking of a clock. "Take care of him, Peter. It's your job now to beat the law."

As the minutes passed it seemed to Peter that sound became a living, stealthy part of the night, creeping about him in ghostly whispers, hiding behind the canvas sail, rustling where the water moved under the bow, purring at his feet and in the air. This impression of sound by its smallness and its secretiveness served to emphasize the hush which had fallen upon a burned and blasted world. Its muteness bore with it a quality of solemnity and a quickening thrill as if subjugated forces were muffled and bound and might unleash themselves without warning. In this stillness Peter heard the thunder creeping up faintly behind the path of fire. But the sound of the oar did not come again.

He strained his eyes to pierce the gloom even though he knew the effort was futile and senseless. The red line of the fire was steadily receding. In places it was lost. Where he had left the cliff and the sandy strip of beach was a black chaos, and it was this darkness with its silence which seemed to reach into his heart and choke him with its oppression and foreboding.

Through the stillness a sound came to him, floating softly over the sea, sweet and distant. His fingers slowly unclasped and he bowed his head. It was the bell over the little church of logs and Father Albanel was tolling it. Even now in this smoke-filled hour of the night he was calling the people of the settlement together that they might offer up in prayer their gratitude because homes and loved ones had been spared by the red death that had swept the land. It was like a living voice, gently sweet and soothing as it brought him faith and reverence. *There was a God!* Every fiber in his body leaped to that cry of his heart. Without a God his father would have died, the whole world would have burned, there would be no Mona, no hope, no anything for him in the darkness of the freedom which lay ahead. His lips moved with Mona's prayer and he stood up quietly so that he might hear more clearly until the last peal of the bell died away. And when the gray silence shut him in again he felt as if a protecting spirit had come to ride with him in the gloom.

Softly he spoke to his father but there was no answer. Exhaustion and the peace of the open sea had overcome the stricken man and he was asleep.

Encumbered by stillness and smoke, the night passed with appalling slowness. The distant thunder with its promise of rain died away. Half a dozen times Peter lighted matches and looked at his watch. At last it was three o'clock and the horizon of murk and smoke that shut him in receded as dawn advanced. Then came a sudden keen breeze, like the last sweeping of a great broom, and he could see the coast. His own heart was thrilled by the sight of it, for behind the menacing headland of barren rock that rose like a great gargoyle hundreds of feet above the lower cliff was a strip of water which he had once hazarded in a dead calm and which led back half a mile between towering walls of rock and naked ridges into that very chaos of wildness which he had wanted for a hiding-place.

Scarcely had this moment of exultation possessed him when the wind died again. At the same time a clearer light diffused itself over the sea. The horizon drew itself back like a curtain and half a mile away he saw an object that sent his heart into his throat.

For a few moments he neither moved nor seemed to breathe as he stared at a swiftly approaching skiff. Then he looked at his father. Donald McRae had not awakened. A livid scar lay across his eyes as if a red-hot iron had burned out his sight. His hands were blistered, his lips were swollen and his neck and shoulders were scarred and covered with the ointment which Simon had used. Yet—even then—*his father slept*! The horror of it choked Peter and his soul cried out for vengeance against those who had made this wreck of a man. He turned and his hand rested upon his rifle. He no longer feared the law or Aleck Curry or Carter, the ferret. His desire at first was to kill them. With astonishing calmness he waited, watching the approaching skiff. When it was two hundred yards away he picked up his rifle.

He chose the small of Aleck's back for his first shot and raised his gun. In the same moment he observed that with Carter in the stern and Aleck amidships the bow of the skiff was high out of water. It was this situation which saved Aleck and Peter's first bullet crashed through the boat an inch or two below the water line. He followed with two other shots. The effect was almost instantaneous. Aleck Curry lurched away from the oars and the skiff came within an ace of upsetting. In another moment the quick-witted Carter had called Aleck into the stern and there both crouched, their combined weight raising the shattered bow above the water line while Carter stripped himself of his shirt.

The shots roused Donald, and with an effort he drew himself up beside Peter.

"What is it?" he demanded. He turned his scarred face toward Peter and then with a strange cry covered his face with his hands. "My God, I can't see!" he cried. "Peter—I can't see!"

In that darkest moment of his life Peter thanked God the wind came and filled the sail of Simon's boat and that neither Carter nor

Aleck Curry shouted after them or made a sound that his father might hear, and like an inspiration a lie came to his lips—he had done some poor shooting at a flock of mallards! He spoke cheerfully of his father's efforts to see, telling him it would be days before he could hope for vision when his eyes were swollen and scarred by burns. And Donald, seeing nothing of the agony in Peter's bloodless face, smiled cheerfully up at the clearing sky in spite of his pain. He did not mind so much about his hands, he said, but it was a hardship to have his eyes covered as Peter was bandaging them now because he wanted to see as much as he could of his boy in the short time they would be together. There was a note of happiness in his voice which was in strange contrast to the pathos of his appearance and his helplessness.

And Peter fought to keep up that spirit of cheer and of gladness that was in Donald McRae's heart. But his own heart was breaking—for he knew that his father was blind.

Hours later Simon's boat came stealing back to shore in the sunless dusk of the evening. This time the sail was down and with muffled oars Peter rowed cautiously for the break in the cliff. Blended with the deepening shadows of the sea, he worked his boat into the narrow maw of the crevasse whose rock walls rose two hundred feet over their heads. In utter darkness, with the thin streak of light far above, he felt his way for half an hour. Then the fissure widened and after another fifteen minutes of slow progress its walls bulged outward, losing themselves in the gloom, and ahead stretched the hidden inlet, smothered on all sides by precipitous crags and cliffs and towering forest ridges.

On a narrow strip of sand he grounded the boat and lighted the lantern which Simon had placed in the outfit. Its illumination threw up grimly the black shadows about them, and questing among these, he found huge masses of torn and twisted rocks so wildly thrown together that among them were many little caverns and grottoes thickly carpeted with white sand. One of these he chose for a camp, but not until he had gathered an armful of bleached driftwood and had started a fire did he return to the boat. It was then, in the yellow light of flaming cedar and pine, that he noted a strange and startling change had come over his father. Donald McRae no longer bore the appearance of a sick man. He stood straight and was breathing deeply. His lips were smiling as he faced Peter and quite calmly he removed the bandage from his eyes.

"At last we are home," he spoke softly. "And just beyond you—*I see your mother!*" Instantly he seemed to sense the shock of those words to

Peter, for he said: "Don't let that frighten you, lad. Every day and night she is at my side. Only—now—*she is nearer!*"

He reached out his hands and almost fiercely Peter's arms closed about him.

Donald stroked his hair. It was the old caress, and he spoke to Peter as if to a little boy again.

"You're not afraid, Peter?" he asked.

"Afraid—"

Peter's heart stopped beating.

"They can't hurt you," said Donald soothingly. "I won't let them do that, Peter."

Peter drew slowly away. His face was gray in the firelight and in his eyes was a growing horror. He tried to speak but no words came from his lips. Donald's scarred face was strangely tranquil. It seemed to Peter that years had dropped away from it. In it was no fear, no sign of strain, no consciousness of the terrible hours they had passed through or of the tragic future which lay ahead. And the truth came to Peter, a suspicion at first, a whisper, growing and overwhelming him until at last it was a dizzying sickness that set him swaying on his feet. In this hour Donald McRae was not the man who had returned after years of wandering to see his boy. His mind had gone back. It had returned to the days of Peter's childhood and his voice was repeating words almost forgotten—a sacred promise of days when Peter had built mighty castles in the air and his father had helped him plan them with the understanding smile that was on his lips now.

For he was saying: "They won't hurt a boy, Peter. We'll get away. And then we'll go through the big woods to the mountains just as we've always wanted to do."

Peter raised clenched hands to his face to stifle his agony.

In the torturing slowness of the hours which followed Donald McRae lived again in the precious years when Peter was a boy, recalling forgotten incidents as if they had happened yesterday, bringing forth their old dreams, painting their pictures of the future as he had done so often with Peter at his side in the afterglow of evenings long ago. And Peter, with his soul torn and bleeding, talked with him. Together they were hunting again. They followed the old trap-lines. They heard the song of birds and planted seeds and flowers in the little garden back of their cabin home, and Peter was kneeling at his father's knees when he said his prayers at night. These things Peter had dreamed of and treasured in his years at

Five Fingers, but now they were horrors—coming out of the past with a voice that trembled with the thrill and joy of a strange madness.

At last Donald slept. It was after midnight and the last embers of the fire had burned out. Peter rose to his feet and walked up the shore, staring into darkness. The rock walls that inclosed the inlet rose sheer above him, making of the place a deep and sombrous pit. He could see the stars and their distance lent an abysmal solitude to the gloom. About him was no movement and no stir of life; the water lay still; no whisper came from dark forests on the ridge tops; the black walls were dead and in the soft sand his feet alone disturbed the sepulchral quiet.

To Peter this strangeness seemed naturally a part of the change that had come into his life. Everything was changed. His world had gone into atoms and now it was reassembling itself; and with deadened emotions, almost dully, he was beginning to accept it. His yesterdays, it seemed, had existed an infinitely long time ago. Five Fingers was no longer home or a necessity and even Mona seemed a vast distance away from him in these hours when his own soul was remolding itself to fit the grimness of a new existence. His mind no longer questioned the path he was to take and no shadow of revolt rose in it.

One thought was as steadfastly fixed in him now as life itself. He belonged to his father and his father belonged utterly to him. He must go on with him, care for him, fight for him, save him from that one dread brutality of the law if his own life paid the forfeit in the end. That was settled. Even his love for Mona could not change that duty and older love which urged him. It was more than a resolution; it was as immutably a part of him as the beating of his heart and his own flesh and blood.

The stars faded and day broke swiftly above the walls of the inlet. He returned and found his father on his hands and knees groping in the sand. He was gathering sticks and placing them with the remnants of last night's fire, and when he heard Peter's footsteps he paused in his labor and raised a face out of which once more the years of grief and hopelessness seemed to have gone.

"Are you hungry, Peter?" he asked.

And Peter, as he knelt beside him, knew that he was speaking to Peter the boy and not to Peter the man.

Together they built the fire.

JAMES OLIVER CURWOOD

XXI

Nine days Peter and his father spent in their hiding-place under the walls of the lagoon. At the end of that time Donald's burns were healed and his strength had returned. He had taken on flesh and his shoulders were straighter. His eyes were clear again but their vision was strangely shadowed and at a hundred yards the wall of the lagoon was like a dark curtain. For a time it was impossible for Peter to believe that his father's mind was not keeping pace with his physical revivement. Yet with the passing of each day Donald's mental grip concentrated itself more and more on the past until he seemed not to have lived at all beyond those years when Peter was a boy. Together they picked up old threads as if they had never been broken or lost, and in those occasional dark and brooding intervals when Donald's mind dragged itself back into the haunting tragedy of the present Peter found himself praying for the return of that partial amnesia which at first had terrified him.

On the evening of the ninth day Peter once more set out to sea. Fifty miles westward he ran ashore in the illusive, gray dusk of morning and burned Simon's boat.

Now that their flight northward had actually begun there were moments when his father's attitude almost frightened him. At first Donald's mind was keenly alive to the nearness of danger and in his half blindness he became more watchful and alert than Peter. But it was the peril of years ago that haunted him—the menace of the men who had driven them from their cabin home and who had nearly killed them when Peter was a boy.

After the third day Peter began to mark the beginning of the final change in his father. Donald became less watchful and sounds no longer seemed to disturb him. Instincts which warned him of peril became ghosts and at last faded away entirely. By the end of the seventh day there remained only one consciousness of living in Donald's soul; Peter was his little boy, and he was with Peter. Physically he betrayed no sign that his mind had crumbled. His scarred eyes, in which vision had grown even dimmer, held in them a deep and abiding clearness and a strange gentleness grew in his face. And Peter, holding tight to keep his own heart from breaking, knew what it meant. His father was forgetful of all things now but his boy, and was happy.

This change more than anything else killed in Peter's breast his last hope of returning to Five Fingers. Sheer madness with its darkness and its misery might have driven him back to Simon and Father Albanel, taking Donald McRae to asylum doors instead of to the hangman. But this which he saw growing in his father was to him a quietly working miracle of God instead of breaking down of body and soul and brain.

As day followed day and one cool, dark night added itself to another, a warm and thrilling reaction came to replace with new emotions the gloom and desolation in his heart. Not for an hour did he stop thinking of Mona; her face was with him, her voice, the touch of her lips and hands; she walked with him in the thick aisles of the forest, slept near his side at night, wakened with him in the morning and became in each increasing hour of their separation more completely a part of him. But with this thought of her returned also the old passion of his childhood— his love for his father. His heart stirred strangely to the gentle caress of Donald's hand as it had thrilled when he was a boy. The old chumship rose out of its ashes, smoldered for a while and then burned steadily as if the broken years had never been. Home, mother, father, all the joys and dreams of childhood and early boyhood crept upon him a little at a time, until at last he knew that to sacrifice his father was as unthinkable as to surrender that part of his heart which Mona filled.

Between these two loves, encouraged on one side by duty and on the other by desire, lay his grief. Until the end of the third week he did not give up fully his resolution to send word back to Mona. By that time the hazard of such an act had fully impressed itself upon him. He no longer feared Aleck Curry, whose stupidity he had fully measured, but almost as frequently as Mona filled his mind came also dread of Carter. A cold and abiding fear of this man entered into him and he was confident it would not be long before this human ferret of the forests would in some way find their trail. At times he was oppressed by the feeling that Carter was close behind them and he tried to establish in his mind the certainty of his action if his father's enemy should suddenly appear. Thought of what might happen—what probably would happen—made him shudder. For there could be no halfway measures with Carter now.

Always on the alert, with his rifle never far from reach of his hands, he swung still farther north and west. Autumn found him in the Dubaunt River country, and the beginning of winter on the Thelon. Here he traded his watch in a Dogrib camp for a score of traps, blankets and new moccasins, invested the last of his money in flour, sugar, salt and

JAMES OLIVER CURWOOD

tea, and took possession of an abandoned cabin in the neighborhood of Hinde Lake. All through the winter he trapped and set deadfalls and snares.

A hundred times during the long winter he fought against his desire to send a word to Mona. Months had not dulled his caution and as soon as the spring break-up made it possible to travel he led his father into the Artillery Lake country. Through the spring and early summer they were constantly on the move, always making a little southward. By the time August came they had completed two-thirds of an immense circle and south of the Athabasca country found themselves in the unmapped region between the Cree River and the McFarland. Here, in a country of ridges and swamps and deep forests, Peter made up his mind that at last they were safely hidden from Carter and all the rest of the world.

He breathed easier and began the building of a cabin. This was on a dark-watered, silent little stream, with a vast swamp at their back door, ridge country to right and left of them and an illimitable forest reaching out in front. The nearest point of habitation that Peter knew of was a Hudson's Bay Company post sixty miles away.

And this cabin with each log that went into it became a closer and more inseparable part of Donald McRae. Out of that forgetfulness which could scarcely be called madness began to creep memories so warm and vivid that they seemed to breathe with life itself. For Donald was building the old home again, the home of Peter's mother, where the moon had looked in through the window on the night he was born—a home, sweet and whispering with the presence of a woman one had worshiped in the flesh and the other had visioned as an angel in his dreams. After a little it was Donald and not Peter who was building the cabin, and by the time it was finished it seemed to Peter that a strange and unseen spirit of life, gentle as prayer itself, had come to dwell in it with them.

Autumn came again with its paradise of color. The cedars, spruces and balsams took on a deeper, richer green; each sunrise bathed the ridges of poplar and birch in new splendor of red and yellow and gold; the nights grew colder, the days were filled more and more with the autumn tang that made blood run red and warm. God was with them here. Donald said that, as in the days of old. And Peter began to believe—and as faith rose in him hope and dreams returned. *Mona's prayer was answered*—the prayer they had said together for years asking that his father might be returned to him, and that they might all find refuge together somewhere in the wilderness world which they loved. And this was the refuge, given to them through the sweet and charitable guidance of God. All that was needed to complete it was Mona.

He began to thrill with a greater excitement as the first snows came. Would it be safe to return for Mona *now*? There were times when his whole soul cried out in the affirmative and he was almost ready to begin the long journey. But his caution never quite died and he always pulled himself back in time. Sixteen months had seemed an eternity to him but prudence warned him not to hurry. He would wait until spring. By that time, if Carter were on their trail, the climax would surely come. If the winter passed safely, he would go to Five Fingers and bring Mona back with him. Not for a moment did he doubt she would come, and he continued to add to the glorious castles he built in his mind, shadowed only now and then by oppressing thoughts of the many things which might have happened at Five Fingers in almost two years of absence.

Late in February he left for the trading-post with two Indian dogs and a light toboggan to sell his furs. It was not unusual now for Donald to remain alone for several days at a time, for Peter knew the home they had built had become a part of his heart and soul and that nothing short of actual force or his own wishes and plans could drag his father from it. On this trip to the post he expected to be gone five days.

It was very cold. Trees cracked and snapped with the piercing bite of the frost and the snow crackled underfoot. For a long time after Peter had disappeared Donald stood in the little clearing staring over the trail where his boy had gone.

Something unknown to Peter was finding its way into Donald's brain. Through the night it had worked, gnawing its way slowly and stealthily, and now that Peter was gone it grew bolder. Even as he turned the cabin took on a new aspect for Donald. Though the sun was shining and the sky was clear, a shadow seemed to have fallen over it and the welcoming spirit which had always clasped him closely to its heart was missing when he entered through the door. As the day passed a change came in Donald's face. He was restless and uneasy. Sounds startled him again. In the dusk of evening he did not light a candle but sat quietly in a corner, staring into darkness with his half-blind eyes, and all that night he did not go to bed.

The next day there was no sun; the sky was heavy with gloom, the air thick and difficult for Donald to breathe. Mysterious shadows crept about him and at times he tried futilely to seize these with his hands.

As the hours passed his mind became more and more like a broken limb from which the last prop had been taken. A hundred times he whispered Peter's name. Then came the beginning of the storm. It broke in mid-afternoon and by night was a howling blizzard. In darkness the cabin shook and the wind screamed overhead and the snow beat like shot against the window. It would be a long time before the forest people would forget this storm because of its ferocity and the tragedy which it left in its wake, but to Donald it was more than a storm—it was a personal thing. In it was the cumulative chaos of all the evils from which he had been a fugitive through the years, and now, cornering him at last, they were fighting to break through the log walls of the cabin.

He built up the fire until it roared in the chimney and lighted candles until the cabin was aflame with light. And then, suddenly as a bolt of lightning, some thing came to him. It was *voice*—voice screaming at the window, voice howling over the roof logs, voice moaning and wailing and dying away in the sweeping of the wind. *"Peter! Peter! Peter!"* It was crying—nothing but Peter's name, repeating it a thousand times in its laughing, taunting, moaning efforts to make him understand.

A half-savage cry rose out of his breast. He was not afraid, not when his boy needed him—and hatless and coatless he flung up the birchwood bar to the door and faced the storm.

"Peter!" he called. *"Peter! Peter!"*

It all had but one meaning for Donald now. The storm had Peter. It was playing with him, killing him, and these devils in the wind had come to tell him about it in their glee. He could feel them clawing and striking at his breast and face; the snow struck his eyes like tiny spear points and he found it difficult to get his breath in the face of the blast which tried to overwhelm him. He called again as he fought his way out into the blackness and snow. His words drifted away in shreds, whipped to pieces by the wind. Creatures seemed picking up handfuls of snow and hurling it in his face—he could hear their swift movement, the hissing of their breath, their evasion as he struck out at them, and he called Peter's name louder than before to give his boy courage and let him know he was coming.

That Peter was near the cabin, that he had turned back and was making a desperate fight to reach its shelter was as firmly a part of Donald's mind as the conviction that all the forces of the darkness and evil were trying to keep him away from his boy.

His head was bare and his woolen shirt was unbuttoned at the throat, but he did not sense the terrible cold that came with the blizzard. Among the trees his feet found instinctively the beginning of the trail that was blazed through the forest and he reached out his naked hands and plunged knee-deep through windrows of snow that lay in his way. The thickets whipped and beat at him and branches, ambushed in darkness, reached out from twisting trees to strike him, but he did not feel sting or pain.

At last he was sure he heard an answer to his calling but the wind came and roared in his ears and the snow beat so fiercely in his face that he could not locate the quarter from which it came. Then he tricked the wind. He stumbled in the snow behind a tree and lay there until a brief lull followed in the wake of it, when he called again as loudly as he could. But he had the direction of it now and a hundred paces brought him to the edge of a rocky ravine which ran near the trail. Down this he clambered and in the pit-like darkness at the bottom found what he was seeking. Beside a figure rumpled and twisted in the snow he fell upon his knees, moaning Peter's name.

Half an hour later Donald came back to the light in the clearing, staggering under the weight of his burden. He opened the door and together the two crashed in upon the floor. On his hands and knees Donald turned and shut the door against the storm. Then he crept to the younger man whose wide-open eyes were staring at him from a thin, white, strangely contorted face, and put his arms about him, holding his head closely against his breast.

"You're all right now, Peter," he comforted in a broken, gasping voice. "You're all right—" He tried to laugh as his frozen fingers wiped the snow from the other's hair. "We're home and it's warm and I'll get something to eat—"

He crawled to the stove, almost crooning in his joy, and opened the iron door to thrust in more wood. The flames lighted up his face, bloodless from the cold and wet with snow that had already begun to melt and trickle down his cheeks to his bare neck and chest. His hair glistened white—whiter, it seemed, than an hour ago; his breath came huskily as if driven through a sieve; he was a crumpled, frozen, wind-broken wreck, and yet as he turned from the flaming door of the stove to look at the man on the floor there was a strange miracle of triumph and happiness riding over the torture in his face and a smile was on his lips. The storm might beat and howl outside and all the evils of darkness might scream and rage to get in for all he cared now. He had saved his boy!

He rose to his feet and stood swaying for a moment, smiling, trying to speak. Then he fell upon a cot.

The man on the floor had pulled himself to his elbow. He put a mittened hand to his throat as if to free himself from fingers that were gripping him there. His face too was bloodless. It was a thin face, driven white and hard by exhaustion and pain. He was a man who had been close to death and the shadow of it was still in his eyes.

He drew off his mittens and a foot at a time dragged himself across the floor. When he reached the cot he pulled himself up to it and put his arms over the stricken form of the one who had saved him.

Donald felt the nearness and raised a hand weakly to the other's face. "You—Peter?" he asked.

"Yes, it's me."

Donald's blue lips smiled.

"They didn't get us, did they, boy? We got away from them—"

"Yes, we got away."

"And you're warm now—good and warm?"

The head over him bowed itself slowly until almost reverently it touched Donald's breast. It was not Peter's head. It was not Peter's voice that answered. But Donald gave a deep sigh of contentment as his fingers found a hand which he thought was Peter's and for a time neither one nor the other spoke again, while near them the fire crackled merrily in the stove and the candles sputtered and flared as if laughing at the storm which was lashing itself into a wailing madness outside the cabin walls.

FOR THREE DAYS AND NIGHTS no living creature could stand against the storm which swept the Athabasca country, nor could they travel in the intense cold which followed in its wake.

It was the fifth of March, twelve days after he had left the cabin, before Peter crossed the Pipestone on his return into the region where he and his father had made their home.

His mind was a torment of unrest as he visioned a hundred tragic happenings, any one of which might have visited his father during his absence. The last twenty-four hours he traveled without an hour of sleep.

It was midday when he came to a high ridge from which he could look down into a cup of the forest where the cabin stood, a mile away.

For the first time he breathed easily when he saw a spiral of blue smoke rising straight up into the clear sunshine of the day.

He laughed in his gladness as he came to the trail which led past the spring near their home. He would stop and drink there and then give the old-time halloo for his father. He could see Donald hurrying through the sunshine to welcome him as he heard that cry.

As he came round the last turn in the trail he stopped suddenly. Someone was at the spring. The bent figure was less than a hundred yards from him and he could see it rising slowly, lifting a pail filled with water. He shifted his rifle and made a megaphone of his mittened hands at his mouth. It would be a rousing surprise for his dad!

But the cry died before it reached his lips. The man at the spring was not his father. Tall and thin and hooded, and walking with a stick as he advanced, the stranger came toward Peter. He progressed slowly and with difficulty, limping with each step he took. His head was bowed and not until they had approached within a few paces of each other did he raise it so that his face was clearly revealed. And then Peter gave a startled cry and swift as a flash swung the muzzle of his rifle upon the other.

"*Carter!*" he gasped.

A wan smile played over the ferret's face as he raised a hand and thrust back his hood.

"My name is not Carter," he replied. "Since twelve days ago I have been Peter McRae—Donald McRae's son."

Something in his thin face and strangely sunken eyes sent a cold chill to Peter's heart.

Carter had stopped with the muzzle of the rifle touching the pit of his stomach. He made no effort to thrust it aside but stood looking calmly into the other's eyes.

"It happened just that long ago," he said. "I was trailing you when I slipped over a ledge and almost broke a leg among the rocks. The storm came and I was about done for, when your father wandered out into the night, calling your name, and I answered. He got me into the cabin and I've been there ever since. From the beginning he thought I was you. I understand now, McRae. I know what I've done—and I wish you would pull that trigger. I deserve it."

Peter lowered the gun.

"You have not harmed him?"

"*Harmed him!*" A dull look of agony filled Carter's eyes as he turned slowly toward the cabin. "No, I haven't harmed him—not since twelve days ago. It was all done before that. Only God will ever know how gentle and good he was to me, thinking I was you—and if by dying I could return what I've taken away from him I'd kill myself. And if I were in your place, Peter—standing where you are—*I'd shoot!*"

He gave a stifled cry as Peter hurried past him. In it was a note of appeal that choked and died in his throat. But Peter did not hear it nor did he see fully the look of dread that was in Carter's eyes. He unshouldered his pack at the cabin door, laid his rifle beside it and went in. He was no longer afraid of Carter. Something tighter and more terrible was gripping at his heart.

Carter came limping up the trail and when he reached the door he bared his head and quietly followed Peter into the cabin.

Peter was on his knees beside the bunk in which Donald was lying. His arms were spread out and his head was bowed upon Donald's breast.

White-faced, Carter knelt beside him and put both his hands about his shoulders. "Until *he* brought me into this cabin twelve days ago I never believed in God," he said huskily. "But I do now, Peter. For twelve days *your father was my father*. I loved him. And I know, if he could have understood, that from the beginning he would have forgiven me—the man who hunted him to his death. If by any merciful chance *you* can do that, Peter—if you can find it in your heart to let him remain my father and you my brother—" One of his hands found Peter's, clasping it tightly, and the other crept to Donald's face, where it lay cold and lifeless on its pillow. "In God's name say you forgive me!" he whispered.

In answer Peter's fingers returned the pressure of Carter's hand and a sob broke on the man-hunter's lips.

After a moment of silence he said: "It was the terrible cold and exposure of that night in which he was hunting for you. It reached his lungs. Until yesterday I was not afraid. Then the change came—swiftly. He died this morning, Peter, in *your* arms, and the last word on his lips was *your* name—and Mona's."

A long time there was stillness in the cabin as the two men knelt beside their dead.

XXII

In the long days and weeks which followed Peter's return to the cabin and the death of his father a change which seemed to him a little short of a miracle came over the man-hunter. The pitiless Carter, the human ferret, whose years of duty had never been tempered with mercy or conscience, was gone, and in his place was a new Carter, dragging himself a little at a time out of the paths of tragedy and misery which he had followed for so long.

Through those years Peter knew that Carter had been a Nemesis and a destroyer. He had not known pity, but only the grim exultation of achievement. Women, love, the extenuation of circumstance, even motherhood in its most beautiful sacrifice, had not stayed his hand when once the law had set him like a hound upon the scent of his victim. He had broken men and women. He had opened doors of blackness and despair to a hundred human souls. Yet the law had been always at his back, urging him on and exulting in his triumphs; he had committed no crime, no sin, and the world had applauded his exploits when it heard of them, visioning him as a splendid part of that mighty mechanism of legal force which made peace and good will on earth possible among men. Yet Carter, in these strange days of his mental and spiritual transformation, knew differently.

He knew that he had served too well, and for that reason he hated himself, and called himself a fiend. It was now, after he had hunted Peter's father to his death, that his successes began to dig themselves out of their graves and reappear to him as haunting ghosts. And he prayed God to keep Peter, of all men, from hating him.

"I killed your father," he said to him frankly. "I hunted him until his mind and his body broke down and he died. And in the end he accepted me as a son, and I loved him. If I had only known! But I didn't, and my life belongs to you. I give it willingly as the price of a great mistake."

And as the sullen winter's end passed Peter found it impossible to hate Carter. Instead, there grew in him a slow and irresistible feeling of brotherhood for the man who had trailed them to their hiding-place at last, and who, in the hour of his deepest grief, had knelt with him in prayer over the frozen grave of his father. In those moments he had learned that it was not Carter who was accountable. It was the system— the law and its inalienable right to strike and kill.

Now, late in April, they were going home.

Six hundred miles behind them lay the wilderness of the Pipestone and the McFarland, where the hunt had ended and the final tragedy had been enacted.

Ahead of them, beyond four hundred miles of still deeper forests was Five Fingers.

On this night, as they sat in the yellow glow of a birchwood fire which they had built in the chill of sunset, Carter had drawn a rough map in the edge of the ash. The somber depths of a moonless night lay like a curtain of heavy velvet behind him, and against this his thin and hawk-like face was set so vividly that Peter saw the odd twitch of his lips as he said:

"One week for Jackson's Knee, another for the country of Lac St. Joe, two more for the Height of Land, and then you'll be looking down on Five Fingers! They'll all be glad to see you, Peter. And Mona—" He shrugged his shoulders and a little throb came in the pit of his throat when he spoke of Peter's sweetheart. "God knows a man should be happy with a girl like her waiting for him at the end of the trail."

"I've been away two years," replied Peter, for it was always that thought which kept pounding at his heart. "At times I am afraid of what may have happened since that night you and Aleck Curry almost got dad and me in the edge of the burned lands."

Carter made no sign that he had heard. He was staring into the deep, red embers of the fire.

"Your mother was an angel," he said, so quietly and unexpectedly that his words fell upon Peter almost with the effect of a shock. "In the last of those days when your father and I were shut up together by storm and cold in the cabin, and he was accepting me as his son in his madness, he talked of her almost as if she were alive and we were going home to her."

"She has been dead twenty years," said Peter.

"I know. Dead, and yet living. I can scarcely believe that I hunted Donald McRae until I drove him mad—for doing a thing which I would have done had I stood in his shoes that day when he killed a man! It was justice, Peter. My mother I cannot remember. But *your* mother he made very near and real for me in those last days of—I can't call it his madness!—it was—"

"Forgetfulness," said Peter.

Carter bowed his head. "Yes, forgetfulness. Yet some things lived so vividly—things of the past. He made them live and breathe for me—and one picture makes me want to kill!—that picture of the little cabin in the clearing more than twenty years ago—your mother—you in her arms—Donald McRae's homecoming and the vengeance he dealt out to the snake who had come to take advantage of his absence. When I see that vision I want to choke the life out of a human beast I know—Aleck Curry!"

Peter made no answer.

"I can't undo what I've done," Carter went on. "I tracked your father until his mind broke under the strain, but I can't help that now. It is over. All I can do in the way of reparation is to help you—you and Mona Guyon. And between you two—between your happiness and hers—is one man, a slimy, conscienceless serpent, waiting and watching for your return."

"You mean—Aleck Curry?"

"Yes, Aleck Curry."

Carter stood up, his tall, catlike form bathed in the fire glow, and his hard lips were tightly closed as he stared off into the darkness of the forest.

"Sounds queer—that word 'conscienceless' coming from me," he mocked bitterly. "I've never had a conscience or a heart in obeying the word of the law—but I've never thought bad of a woman in the way Aleck Curry thinks of Mona Guyon. He would sell his soul, if he had one, to possess her—even if she came to him for only an hour as the price of your safety and freedom. And you're going home—*an outlaw!*"

"By that you mean Curry will hold me in his power when I reach Five Fingers?"

"Yes."

"And will attempt to force from me a price—"

Peter stood looking straight into Carter's eyes.

"Yes, partly from you, but mostly from Mona. That is why I've been holding you back, a drag from the beginning. Curry's uncle has become a power politically, and Aleck was given a corporalship a year ago. I would stake my life that he is keeping his secret about you and the part you played in your father's escape two years ago. The knowledge is too precious for him to divulge. You assaulted him, almost killed him, and freed your father; you kept him—an officer of the law—a prisoner on an island; later you fired upon Curry and me with the rifle which Simon McQuarrie gave you—and all this means from five to fifteen years in prison for you, and Curry knows it. The fact that your father was almost blind, and that his mind had broken down, won't help you. Law is law, especially in Canada. Our judges and juries go by the code and not by

JAMES OLIVER CURWOOD

emotions. And this law, its inviolability, is why Aleck Curry is a greater menace to you now than all the dangers you have encountered since you led your father into the north.

"He is moved entirely by two passions, one his desire for Mona Guyon and the other his hatred for you. On the night when we almost caught you both in your escape from Five Fingers he offered me a thousand dollars and his uncle's influence in getting me a sergeancy if I would keep the secret of your capture, and turn our prisoners over to him. It was my humor to let him think he had bought me. And then, in the dawn of that morning, you filled our boat full of bullets—and got way. That's the story, Peter. There is no escaping the trap if you return to Five Fingers. Curry will descend upon you, demand marriage of Mona, or probably worse—and if she refuses—"

"She can visit me occasionally in prison," said Peter.

His face reflected no trace of the white heat that had mounted into Carter's; he spoke quietly and his hands had lost their clenched tenseness. For a moment Carter gazed at him in silence.

"You mean that?"

"I do. Aleck Curry holds no power over me that can in any way endanger Mona. If I owe a debt, I am willing to pay it. Neither Mona nor I have anything that we want to sell, and Aleck Curry has nothing that we want to buy."

Carter drew in a deep breath.

"If you look at it in that way—"

"There is no other way."

"But Curry and I are the only two men on earth who can swear that you have done these things. The smallest restitution I can make to you for all the wrong I have done your father is to keep my knowledge secret. Torture could not tear it from me. Now—if we can silence Curry, tie his tongue, break him—"

"None of which we can do," interrupted Peter. "He has hated me since the day we first fought over Mona when we were boys. Only one thing could stop his vengeance. I would have to kill him, and that is inconceivable. For my father I would have done that. I had even prepared myself to kill you, Carter, if such an act became necessary to save him. But for myself—*no!*"

Carter thrust out his hand, but as it gripped Peter's he turned his face away. "You're a lot like your dad," he said. "I see it more every day. I'm going to bed. Good night!"

Caution and habit had made the ferret spread his blankets in the pit of gloom outside the glow of firelight. He disappeared in the darkness and a moment later Peter heard him as he stretched himself out for the night.

But Carter had no idea of sleeping. For days past a thought had been building itself up slowly in his brain, and tonight he had almost revealed that thought to Peter. He watched him now, and in the firelight the drooped figure and pale, sensitive face of the man he had hunted and whose happiness he had helped to destroy tightened something at his heart until he found it hard to breathe. He had never loved a woman, and had never felt the bond of a great friendship for a man, but for Peter something more than the friendship he had known—a thing that was very close to a man's love for a man—had begun to possess him body and soul. In this one warm emotion of his cold and merciless life Carter felt a deeper thrill than in the hour of his greatest man-hunting triumph, and as he lay in stillness, strengthening that thought which was becoming a larger and more definite thing between Peter and Mona and the tragedy which threatened them, his lips parted in the grim and humorless smile which in all the years of his service had made men fear and avoid him.

And with that smile, deadly and uncompromising, Carter whispered to himself: "I guess maybe you needn't worry, Peter. I don't think Aleck Curry and the law are going to get you—not if I can help it."

With this settled, it was easier for Carter to give himself up to sleep.

For a long time Peter sat near the fire. The birch logs burned down into a mass of coals, and as deeper shadows closed in about the camp he felt himself alone except for the visions which came and went in the dying embers. With a clearness that brought almost physical pain the years passed before his eyes, and when they had gone they had taken with them his boyhood, the father he had worshiped, his dreams and happiness, leaving behind in the ash of the fire only memories shadowed with the gloom of tragedy. But calmly and with a courage inspired by his own grief he was ready to accept what lay ahead of him. The fight, as a physical thing, was over—and he was going home. On that point his mind was fixed and no sense of self-preservation could move it. What was to happen to him when he reached Five Fingers was a matter which Fate should decide.

Even in these moments of his decision he felt Mona's nearness and her protest. If in defense of his father he had become an outlaw, there was still a wide world in which he could hide, and Mona would come to him. So the persistent voice of caution whispered to him, and at times that voice was Mona's.

Haggard-faced, Peter went to bed, and in the morning it was Carter, cold and mechanically efficient, who pointed out the same way to him.

But even as he pressed his reasoning home, Peter observed there was a still deeper and more mysterious change in his companion. It lay more in Carter's eyes than in his voice or the unemotional lines of his face.

"You've learned how big the woods are," he said. "Go north, into the Yukon or Alaska. I will see that Mona comes to you—safely."

Peter shook his head.

"I've also learned what it means to run from thicket to thicket, guarding a hunted thing you love. That would be Mona's share—years of it, until the end. And the end would come sometime. I'd rather pay the debt—and have free years left to me afterward."

It was Carter's last effort. From that hour he traveled steadily homeward with Peter, making no protest against this new code which had come into his life of giving, instead of taking, a tooth for a tooth and an eye for an eye.

The middle of May found them halfway between Lac St. Joe and the Height of Land, with Five Fingers still a hundred and eighty miles ahead of them.

"We'll make it in seven days," said Peter.

"Unless the melting snows flood the streams," said Carter.

Spring was breaking gloriously. Scents filled the air. Crushed balsam and cedar gave out a redolence that was tonic. The poplar buds were bursting. Birds were returning. On the sides of slopes where the sun struck warmly the snow was gone, grass sprang up lush green, and flowers that budded while the earth was still white began to bloom. Sap dripped from broken limbs, and the whispered breath of a wakening life, of growing things, and of matehood, hope and happiness, seemed to rise between the earth and the sky, night and day.

Both Peter and Carter sensed the thrill of these things, yet neither felt their joy. The floods held them back, so that at first their loss was in hours, and then in days. Carter was glad, but he gave no betrayal of that fact. His face in these last weeks had grown quietly and splendidly different from the old Carter's. It was cold, deeply lined, austere, but its sharpness was mellowed and there was no longer the ferret-like gleam in his eyes or the grim hardness in his lips and chin. Not a day passed that his hand did not rest on Peter's shoulder or arm, and in his touch was a gentleness that at times was reflected in the look of his eyes. But in the secrecy of his own thoughts was a dread of the day they would arrive at Five Fingers. Dread—and yet not fear.

Peter did not reveal his own fears except as they became a part of his face and eyes in certain moments which a man like Carter could not fail to observe. These fears were not inspired by visions of personal danger, for in adjusting his mind to the necessity of paying his debt to the law he had eliminated the menace of Aleck Curry in so far as it could possibly affect the future of Mona or himself.

What he dreaded were the changes which nearly two years might have brought to Five Fingers, and the evil which Aleck Curry could have accomplished in that time. Just what outrage his enemy could have successfully consummated he had no definite idea. Yet the thought seized upon him at times and held him under a dark and oppressive apprehension.

On the last day before crossing the Height of Land Carter spoke of what he knew to be in Peter's mind.

"You will find Mona safe and well, and as true as the day you left her," he said. "And lovelier, too, Peter, for she needed these two years to round out her glorious womanhood. I'm not worrying about her. I'm putting all my faith in another gamble."

"And that?"

Carter gave his thin shoulders a suggestive shrug.

"Has it occurred to you how nice it will be if—in these two years of change you have anticipated—something has happened to Curry? Death, for instance?"

Peter looked at his companion to see if he was joking. Carter's face was set and unsmiling.

"Why not?" he argued. "Aleck, although a brother of the Devil, isn't calamity-proof. With him under six feet of good, honest dirt, or mysteriously missing, or kicked out of the force by an authority greater than his uncle—you would be a free man, and Father Albanel could ring the wedding bell the day you reach Five Fingers. Maybe it's only a dream I've had—but I seem to see Aleck Curry safely out of your way, now or very soon. If he has tried to take advantage of Mona Guyon during your absence—"

"Simon McQuarrie or Pierre Gourdon would kill him!"

"Exactly!" And Carter lighted his pipe and said no more, nor did he raise his eyes to see the strained look which he knew was in Peter's face.

JAMES OLIVER CURWOOD

That night they slept on the northward slope of the ridge that separated the waterways of a continent.

Two days later, on the first of June, they crossed the southern line of rail and camped in the deep wilderness between it and Lake Superior.

Carter made his bed with more than usual care.

"Our last night," he said. "Tomorrow we should pass the high ridge country before dark and reach Five Fingers in the early light of the moon. Are you a little excited?"

"I should like to go on," said Peter.

Carter smiled a bit wistfully. Now and then this flash of gentleness had crept into his face of late. "I'd be willing to give up the rest of my life if for a few hours I could have someone waiting for me as Mona Guyon is waiting for you," he answered in a low voice. "Strange that I've let all the years go by without thinking of that, isn't it? But I'm thinking now. And I'm sorry—for a lot of things."

"You say you are going to resign from the police as soon as you can," said Peter, looking into the darkness that lay between him and home. "When you do that—come to Five Fingers. Simon McQuarrie and Pierre Gourdon and Joe and Father Albanel and all the others will make it home for you. And Mona and Marie Antoinette and Josette will love you because you were four-square and helped *us*. And after that—somewhere—maybe at Five Fingers—there will be a girl—"

A cough came from the gloom behind Peter, a thick and husky cough as if Carter were choking something back that was in his throat. "One of the few things I remember from years ago is a song called 'The City Four-Square,'" he said. "And when you, of all men, call me four-square—why—" Darkness hid his face. "Good night, Peter!"

"Good night," said Peter.

XXIII

Carter, as usual, had made his bed in deep shadow, and there after a time he slept. The moon rose, but still the shadow enveloped him, while Peter lay in a glow of light when the man-hunter roused himself. He looked at his watch and found the hour a little after midnight. A second time he slept, and a second time he awakened, and thick darkness had come in place of the moonglow. This he knew to be the dark prelude to dawn, and he rose out of his blanket and crept cautiously away from the camp, moving a foot at a time and making no sound. In a quarter of an hour darkness and distance had swallowed him. He waited then. Dawn broke first over the tree-tops and filtered down softly and swiftly into the lower depths of the forest until Carter could see to travel. He lighted a last match to look at his watch and compass and struck due south.

He traveled fast, free of pack and gun. Dawn grew into the grayer softness of day. Peter would be awakening now, he thought, or very soon. In an hour, or two at the most, he would know he had been tricked. Even with his advantage Carter sensed the thrill of an impending race and the tragedy of it, if he should lose. Peter was swift and sure in the woods and it was a long way to Five Fingers.

High up in the sky a fleet of white clouds took on a crimson flush. The sun rose, and it found Carter's face settling into the hard and grim lines of the hunter whose game had so frequently been the lives of men. In a small leather pouch he had stored some food, and a part of this he ate as he traveled. He lost no time in seeking log and driftwood dams to pave his way over streams but plunged waist-deep into water that was still cold with the chill of snow and ice. It was noon before he stopped to rest and eat what was left of the food in the leather pouch.

A second time a miracle of change swept over him, and in his face, his eyes and the lithe swiftness with which he moved he was the ferret again, hot on the trail of game. Late in the afternoon he felt the cool breath of Lake Superior in his face. The sun sank lower. Dusk came. In the beginning of that dusk he emerged from the last rim of the forest and stood with the water of the big inland sea moaning under the dark cliffs at his feet.

A sense of exultation and of triumph swept over him. It was something to have mastered the wilderness in this way and to have come out within half a dozen miles of Five Fingers. Peter could not beat that, even in this country which was his own.

Thickening darkness made these last miles more difficult and for two hours Carter progressed slowly. The sky was beautifully clear, but rocks and slides and ragged cracks and pits at the cliff edge made his feet wary, and countless stars only served to deepen their shadows. When the moon came up he had reached the huge cliff whose sheer walls rose two hundred feet above the sea, less than half a mile from Five Fingers.

A last time he sat down, and with a strange smile on his thin lips watched the full moon as it rose swiftly over the forests, as if eager to reach its higher and more permanent place in the arch of the heavens. He was tired and wet and his clothes were torn. Until now, when the settlement was only a step ahead, he had not realized how exhausted he was or what a fight he had gone through. Surely he had beaten Peter by many miles and could afford to rest for a little while before finishing his task!

His eyes closed in restful stillness. In half a dozen minutes he could have slept, but each time that his body wavered on the rock where he sat he forced himself into rigid wakefulness. The temptation persisted, and at last he gave himself five minutes and slept thirty.

The rattle of a stone roused him, and he gathered himself up, blinking at the moon. Then he heard iron nails scraping on rock. Instantly he was wide awake. Someone was advancing along the face of the cliff from the direction of Five Fingers. He could see first the shadow of that person, growing in the illusive light mist of moon and stars. It was big and grotesque and the tread of its substance was slow and heavy. He heard a cough which was as unpleasantly heavy as the tread, and a few steps more brought the advancing figure to the little plateau of rock where he sat. Not until then did he rise. The other stopped. The moon laughed down into their faces. The stars seemed to send upon them a more brilliant light. A dozen paces separated them. Then, uncertainly, they shortened it to half the distance. Carter's heart gave a great throb. He would not have to go down to Five Fingers now, *for this was his man*!

"Curry!" he greeted.

The other stared, half disbelieving. "Is that you—Carter?" he gasped. He advanced again, peering into the other's face. "By Heaven, *it is*!"

Carter was very white and thin and strange-looking in the moonlight, and Aleck Curry was heavy and huge, even to his neck and face. He thrust out a hand, but Carter did not touch it.

"Yes, it's me," he said, in a voice cold as ice. "Queer why you should be coming this way, Curry. I was going down there to find you."

Aleck's eyes pierced the blanket of moonlight behind him. "What luck?" he asked. His voice thrilled with nervous eagerness. He bent his big shoulders toward Carter, looking into his face, his thick lips parted and his narrow eyes gleaming anxiously as he tried to read an answer before words came. "Any?"

Carter's slowness was an insult, and with that insult his eyes and lips were smiling.

"Yes, I've had luck," he said, when the tenseness of the other's silence seemed about to break. "Donald McRae is dead, and Peter is back there—my prisoner!"

HALF AN HOUR LATER, DOWN in Five Fingers, the bell over the little log church rang out sweetly and softly the good news that Father Albanel had come in from his monthly trip into the farther wilderness, and that services would be held tomorrow, which was Sunday. In the stillness of the night the music of the bell carried far through the forests, creeping in and out and high above the hidden places, bearing with it the peace and gentleness of benediction and prayer to all things.

Peter heard it, far back in the hollows between the ridges, and he paused to offer his gratitude to God for this voice that was welcoming him home.

And at the edge of the cliff where the moonlight and the starlight made a vivid arena of the table of rock its message seemed to beat with the clearness of a silvery drum. Then it stopped. Its echoes melted away, and the two men who had heard it there remained unchanged.

Carter seemed straighter and harder, his face more like carven stone. But he was ready. And Aleck Curry was like a huge gorilla gathering himself for a leap.

"Carter—if you mean that—I'll kill you!" he said in a voice that was thick with passion.

"I mean it," replied Carter, biting his words short. "I've taken the trouble to tell you the whole story. But you can't understand and you never will. You're a snake. You're a traitor to both justice and the law. You think your power over Peter will give you vengeance and something from Mona. But it won't. And I warn you again that if you try to use your knowledge, if you offer Peter as a price to Mona, if you give him up to the law when she strikes you in the face—as she will!—then I shall go to the highest authorities and strip you to the skin. The truth will blast you. I will tell how you offered me bribes, and then threatened; I will tell of your affair in the home of Jacques Gautier and expose the horrible trail you have left wherever your slimy soul has gone. I shall investigate the death of the young Indian girl on the Arrowhead. I—"

He did not finish. Curry, the man who had waited, the fiend who had kept the fires of hatred and passion burning until they were madness, saw more than the threatened ruin for himself. Reputation, family, his place in the service meant nothing to him. What he saw now in the white and almost deathlike face and gleaming eyes of the Ferret was the end of the dream he had built up—the end not only of his power over Peter but of his last chance to possess Mona. If Carter carried out his threat, if he told the story of Gautier's wife and laid naked the truth of the Indian girl's death on the Arrowhead—then all that he might say against Peter would be discounted in the eyes of the law, and punishment would fall upon himself.

But he was not thinking of this punishment. At times the evil mind in his heavy head worked with amazing swiftness—and in this last moment of Carter's threat and defiance he saw the yawning abyss of the cliff behind the Ferret, and its overwhelming temptation. With Carter down there, dead, and Peter walking straight into the trap at Five Fingers, his own power and triumph would be more complete than he had ever dreamed it could be—*for he would make Peter also the Ferret's murderer!*

The moon revealed the monstrous thought that leaped like flame into his face, and it was then Carter cut his words short to meet the avalanche of flesh and fury that descended upon him.

Swift as a flash he sensed Curry's intention of throwing him over the cliff, and twined his arms about his enemy's neck as they crashed upon the rock. For a moment after that a great shadow of fear darkened the Ferret's soul. A hundred times in their associations on the trail he had witnessed the tests and measured the possibilities of Aleck's huge body and herculean strength. And now he was at death grips with it. That day he had seen a wood-mouse in the fangs of a weasel, and he was the wood-mouse now. And then he thought of Peter—of Peter and Mona and the battle at the pool two years ago when they had beaten this great hulk of a man. Fear went out of him. His biggest thrill in life was in the main chance against death. And this was the biggest of all!

A queer thought shot into his head, a surging back of his old pride. He was not the wood-mouse, nor was he the weasel. He was the *ferret*, and Aleck Curry was an unknown beast, ponderous and mighty, but with that vulnerable spot which the ferret always found in its prey. And this time Carter knew he was fighting for more than himself. He was fighting for a man who was dead, and whose spirit was there on the rock watching them. He was fighting for Peter. And he was fighting for a woman.

His thin arms and legs fastened themselves about Aleck like things made of wire steel instead of flesh and bone. Over and over they rolled, twisting, bending, breaking, heads and faces gouging on the rocks, and always Carter's quickness made up for the other's weight and strength.

Their breath came in panting gasps as the nails in their boots struck fire from the rock. A moan of anguish came from Curry when Carter got the terrible thumb gouge in his eye, and a gasp of agony from the Ferret when Aleck bent his head back until his neck nearly broke. There was something merciless and horrible in the struggle.

A little cloud ran under the face of the moon. It was followed by a larger and darker one, as if spirit hands were drawing a curtain between it and the tragedy on the rock. The light of the stars seemed to grow dimmer, as if they, too, shrank from this thing that was happening between the sea and the sky. And over the edge of the cliff came a wailing sob of wind that was already beginning to croon its death song for the victim. Minutes were hours. Gasps, chokings, blows and the panting of breaths were the ticking of the seconds. Moments of stillness, when the two lay crumpled and twisted as if they had died together, were like eternities. And foot by foot they had rolled until they were close to the edge of the cliff.

Then it was that a shudder of deeper horror seemed to creep through the night. A black cloud swept under the moon, hiding entirely what was happening at the cliff's edge, and this cloud moved away with appalling slowness. When the moon looked out again one object remained where there had been two. For a long time it lay crumpled there, sobbing for breath. Then it crawled away slowly, dragging itself painfully over the rock, and disappeared at last into the thick growth of the burned-over lands which reached far to the north.

Under that same moon, hours later, Peter came to the edge of Five Fingers. Out of the sky all sign of cloud was gone and the

JAMES OLIVER CURWOOD

stars glowed in radiant constellations. Peter knew that it was midnight, and as he looked down from the crest of the slope, where he had first walked hand in hand with Mona when he was a boy, a strange and gentle silence rose up from the bottom-lands to greet him. Five Fingers was asleep. He could see no light and at first he heard no sound. Then came to him the old familiar tinkle of silver bells on distant cattle, and the soft murmur of the sea that was never quite still where it ran in and out among the rocks of the Pit at the end of Middle Finger Inlet.

For a space he stood looking down where the dark shadows of the cabins lay in a great pool of mellow light that was like a gossamer mist of silver and gold. His heart beat fast, so fast that he clutched a hand at his breast and swallowed hard to get his breath. Down there, within sound of his voice, was Mona—and all at once his manhood seemed to leave him and he wanted to shout wildly through his hands like a boy, calling her name, rousing her from sleep, shrieking at the top of his voice that he had come back. A sort of thrilling madness possessed him, but of all his desire only a choking sob rose in his throat.

He walked down the slope and he saw Pierre Gourdon's home among the scattered cabins. It was there he would find Mona, if—

His heart skipped a beat. If anything had happened, *anything*—sickness—accident—if she had gone away! Two years was a long time. Two years might have brought—a change.

His feet seemed to stumble, and then suddenly he stopped, and a cry came to his lips. For he had come to the smooth little patch of green meadow where Mona had made the men of Five Fingers bury the scores of marauding porcupines they killed each year, and he saw here and there freshly made little mounds of soil. Near one of these, which was scarcely dried by a day's sun, was a spade. Eagerly he seized it in his hands. It was *their* spade, with its broken edge and the iron rod handle which Simon had put on it to replace the wooden one which porcupines had eaten away. Mona was in Five Fingers! She was alive—well—sleeping in her little room where he had visioned her at prayer every night of his life!

He took off his pack and dropped it near the freshly made mound. Then he went on, and stopped under Mona's window.

It was partly open. He could hear the soft flutter of a curtain in the breath of wind that came up from the shore. Almost afraid to break the stillness he called her name in a low voice.

"Mona!"

The curtain fluttered back at him. It seemed to be laughing at him, seemed to be signaling to him like a hand from the window.

Then he saw on their nails against the log wall the long bamboo poles which Pierre Gourdon used in his fishing. A hundred times when he had come in from the woods late at night he had tapped at Mona's window with one of these poles, and she had thrust out her head to blow him down a kiss and say good night. And now, with two hearts seeming to beat in his breast in place of one, he seized one of the poles and gently tapped the old signal on the window-pane. And all at once the curtain ceased its fluttering and he could hear the two hearts pounding mightily against his ribs.

He tapped again—*tap-tap-tappety-tap!* and stepped back into the deep shadow that hung around the edge of the Gourdon cabin in a heavy fringe.

Someone came to the window. He knew it—yet he could not see straight up above his head. He held himself back, waiting for some response to his signal. In a moment he would step out in the moonlight, and then—

He heard the curtain fluttering again. Sound came from her room. It continued for a few moments, and ceased with the quiet opening of a door. Then he heard footsteps, quick, light, almost frightened footsteps, and a slim figure came around the end of Pierre Gourdon's cabin and stood white-faced and trembling in the moonlight.

It was Mona—Mona as he had left her an hour ago—yesterday—two years ago—unchanged—except that she seemed taller to him, more beautiful. She had thrown a long cloak about her and he could see her hand clutching it at the throat as her wide eyes strained to solve the mystery which the misty chaos of the moonlight was hiding from her. For a space he seemed powerless to move. Then he tried to speak as he revealed himself, ragged and torn and bronzed to Indian darkness by his long fight through the wilderness, but it was only an incoherent cry that stumbled on his lips. Mona saw him. For an instant she swayed like a tall flower, with the whiteness of lily petals in her face as he went to her. And then she gave a cry that even Pierre Gourdon might have heard if he had not slept so deeply—and Peter's arms closed about her.

A minute later she held back his face with her two hands. Her eyes were filled with the glory of the stars and her lips were red with the wild, sweet passion of their kisses. Slowly a shadow came, and with it an unutterable tenderness in the words which she whispered to him:

JAMES OLIVER CURWOOD

"Peter, *I knew*. Carter sent me word—about your father—and *you*—"

She drew his head down until she was holding it against her breast. Her heart beat against his cheek. Her lips kissed his hair.

"Only you—you and God—know how sorry I am," she whispered.

And Peter felt once more like the small boy in the edge of the forest years ago, when Mona had come to him in the dusk of evening to mend his broken heart. For in these first moments of his homecoming it was Mona—again—who thought first of his grief, and not of her own happiness; and holding his head close, pressing his rough cheek in the palm of her soft hand, she told him how Carter had sent word to her all the way down through the wilderness, and how she had kept Carter's message to herself—as he had asked her to do—and had waited night and day for his coming with prayers of gratitude in her heart, and sorrow for him.

"And Carter promised to bring you to me," she whispered, "because he said that in the end he had learned to love your father—and you."

XXIV

Where the shadow of Pierre Gourdon's cabin fell deepest a man had dragged himself and lay like a dark and lifeless blot. Since Peter had tapped at the window this man had scarcely moved, except to breathe and change his position a little as he watched the lovers out in the light of the moon and stars. They were very near to him, so near he might have touched them with a pole less than the length of that which Peter had used. And he heard the girl speak of Carter, and of what Carter had done.

It was then he drew himself slowly away, moving with the stealth and caution of one to whom freedom from discovery meant a great deal. Not until the cabin was fully between him and those he had spied upon did he rise to his feet. This movement was slow and brought a gasp of pain from him. He did not stand straight. His shoulders were bent. He was hatless and ragged and his arms and breast were half stripped of clothing. In his hand he carried a heavy stick, and with this stick he helped himself to walk as he struck out in the moonlight.

He tried to hurry, but at best his progress was not fast, and to make up for lack of speed he kept the cabin between him and the two from whom he was running away. In the shadow of a second cabin he stopped to rest, breathing deeply, as if what he had accomplished had cost him great effort. One at a time he passed the dwellings in the settlement and made his way across the green open to the little log church. Here he rested for a longer period, and in these moments he noted with satisfaction that trees threw a deep and continuous shadow between him and the edge of the forest.

The door of Father Albanel's church was never locked and after a little he opened it and entered. But he bolted it carefully behind him. Then he groped his way through the moonlit seats and opened a window. After that he found the rope which rang the bell.

Never in its history had Five Fingers roused itself to the ringing of the bell as it was rung tonight. It was not the Sabbath message. It was not Father Albanel's sweet, slow tolling of peace on earth and good will toward men, nor was it the sad and slumberous requiem for the dead. It was, instead, a wild exultation, an almost savage triumph, a pealing alarm that called upon every soul in the settlement to rise up in instant wakefulness. It filled the forest until its notes beat one upon another and the hills and ridges caught them up and flung them back as they had never done before. Men rose out of their sleep and stumbled for matches; a light appeared here, another there, and still the bell continued to ring until not a cabin in Five Fingers remained in darkness.

Not until then did the man who had rung the bell drop from the window of the little church and steal through the shadows of the trees into the forest. There he did not pause but went on with the slowness of either age or exhaustion until he was swallowed in the deeper secrecy of the woods.

Pierre Gourdon came first out into the night, bareheaded and in his shirt-sleeves, and in front of his cabin he found Mona ahead of him with her long hair streaming down her back and a strange man's arms tightly about her. Almost fiercely he tore them apart—and then he saw it was Peter.

Jame Clamart came running up a moment later, and it was Jame who first sent the news abroad in a shout which, next to the mad ringing of the bell, was the wildest thing ever heard in Five Fingers between the hour of midnight and one o'clock in the morning.

"Peter McRae has come back!" he yelled. "Peter McRae—has—come—back!"

Swifter almost than men could travel word passed that this was the reason for the ringing of the bell—Peter McRae had come home after two years, and Father Albanel, or some other, had wakened them from their sleep to welcome him.

Pierre's women were first to take Peter away from Mona—Josette, coming first, and then Marie Antoinette. And after them came Adette Clamart. When she saw Peter she gave a little screech and threw her arms around his neck, kissing him before her husband and all, and then she fell upon Mona and cried hard in her gladness. The little group grew larger; voices, glad laughter, tremulous excitement filled the air, but suddenly a hush fell as a tall and gaunt-faced figure stalked up through the silvery haze of the night and old Simon McQuarrie shouldered his way among them.

He said nothing when he came face to face with Peter, but for a moment held him off at arm's length, his stern face working in a strange sort of way, and then, as Mona crept to his side, he clasped them both in his arms and stood for a few moments with his head bowed close down to theirs.

And then a whisper of gladness ran among the women, for Father Albanel stood beside Mona and Peter and the little gray missioner's face was streaming with tears of happiness as he, too, put his arms gently about them.

"It was Father Albanel who rang the bell," the women whispered softly among themselves.

And to this day the people of Five Fingers believe that he did.

But on this night, Father Albanel was neither crooked nor bent, nor did he walk with the aid of a stick.

To PETER IT WAS LIKE a dream, a glorious dream of friendship and of a love that lifted his soul above all thought of fear and tragedy, and not until he was alone with Simon in the cabin which had been his home for so many years before he went away with his father did he think of Aleck Curry or of the payment he had promised himself to be ready to make to the law. But the thing which happiness had held back came out now.

The old Scotchman heard Peter's story from the night of the flight almost two years ago, when the forests were burning in the great fire about Five Fingers. And then Peter learned, in turn, that Aleck Curry had built himself a shack in the edge of the timber and was quite frequently at Five Fingers, usually remaining for a week or two at a time. He was there now. That very evening Simon had met him face to face in company with one of the half-dozen government surveyors who for a year or more had been working up and down the shore. He was surprised that the ringing of the bell and the excitement had not brought Curry upon the scene. Probably he was with the surveyors at their camp. Tomorrow he would show up.

"And you haven't any idea what became of Carter?" Simon asked.

Peter shook his head. "He simply disappeared. I cannot guess why. Maybe he, too, will show up tomorrow."

"Peter, who rang the bell?"

Peter flushed under his darkened skin. "I think Father Albanel saw Mona and me in the moonlight. He always loved to wander about late at night, when the moon was bright."

Simon's gaunt face broke into a strange smile.

"It wasn't Father Albanel who rang the bell," he said.

"No?" Peter looked at him sharply. "Then it was you, Simon! You saw us?"

"No. I was asleep—sound asleep. But I know who rang the bell. It was Carter!"

A little thrill leaped through Peter. "It is impossible. Carter would not have run away from me for *that*. Besides—"

He did not finish, for Simon had risen and was looking out through the window in a way that puzzled him.

"I'm going down to the church," he said. "And I'm going the back way, along the edge of the woods, so that no one will see me. Want to go?"

They stole forth through the moonlight into the shadows of the forest. When they came to the church Simon tried the door.

"Locked!" he said. "That is unusual!"

A few seconds later they stood at the open window. Through this they climbed and one after another the Scotchman lighted a dozen matches until they knew that no one could have remained hidden inside. Simon then closed the window and led the way out through the door, leaving it unlocked.

"Careless of him," he grunted. "We'll leave the place just as he found it. Fewer questions will be asked."

He did not speak again until they were once more in their own cabin. Peter, feeling the completeness of his exhaustion now, was about to ascend the ladder to his own bed when Simon rested a hand on his shoulder.

"Boy," he whispered, "whatever happens after this, forget that Carter came down from the north with you and that he ran away from you back there on the trail. Understand, laddie? *Forget it!* Lie about it if you have to. For I believe it was Carter who rang that bell tonight, and if he did, and it should so turn out that something has happened to Aleck Curry—why—you see—it might be a suspicious circumstance, pointing to a thing which you and I, with God's blessing on us, will always know could never be true!"

Even these words, making significantly clear the suspicion which was in Simon's mind, could not keep Peter from thinking of Mona, and of Mona alone, when he went to bed. But he awoke with the first crowing of Simon McQuarrie's roosters, three hours later. He was going to take breakfast with Mona, he told Simon, and as he was an appalling mess he needed a lot of time to prepare for it. For two hours he scrubbed and shaved and shampooed and manicured himself, and then dressed in the best outfit he had left behind him two years ago.

It was only a quarter of six when he finished, but an hour before, he had seen a light in Mona's room and now smoke was rising from the chimney over Josette Gourdon's kitchen.

He went out the back way, as he and Simon had gone a few hours earlier, and was sure he had succeeded in coming up behind Pierre's cabin without giving any evidence of himself. But Mona's eyes were bright and her cheeks were flushed as he stood very still for a few moments in the doorway, though her back was toward him, and she seemed to be absorbed in a number of purposeless little details at the kitchen table. Peter made no sound, unless the pounding of his heart could be called that.

There was a change after all—a change which the silvery radiance of the moon had veiled from him last night. Mona *was* taller, and—even as he was looking at her now, without clearly seeing her face—she was so much lovelier than when he had left Five Fingers that he was a little frightened. Carter was right. It had taken those two years to make her even more beautiful than Marie Antoinette. And he continued to stand where he was, thinking himself undiscovered, worshiping her in silence from the heels of her little feet to the top of her lustrous head as if a word or a movement from him would destroy the transcendent reality of it all.

Mona's cheeks grew pinker and her eyes brighter.

Then she turned upon him so suddenly and with such an unexpected knowledge of his presence filling her eyes with laughter and joy that in one swift moment Peter had her in his arms, and kissed her so wildly on eyes and lips and hair that she was compelled to hide her face against his breast to get breath.

"You are—breaking me," she protested. "You have grown so strong, Peter. And you are tumbling my hair down that I put up with so much care, because this is Sunday!"

She leaned back and shook her head so that the loosened coils of her hair flooded down about her shoulders in a radiant protest to her words.

"The two happiest days of my life have been Sundays," he said, holding her more gently.

"This is one, Peter?"

"Yes."

"And the other?" she asked, as if she had forgotten it entirely.

"Was that first day you took me to church, when I thought you were a little white angel, and sang with you, and dared to take a tress of your hair in my fingers when I thought you didn't know it."

JAMES OLIVER CURWOOD

"And since that day I've loved you, Peter. Yes, I loved you in that very hour when you bit Aleck Curry's ear!"

He filled his hands with the loosened masses of her hair, crushing the soft coils between his fingers.

"Kiss me."

"Sh-h!" She put a finger to his lips. "It is Aunt Josette! I hear her coming! I must run up the back way and fix my hair!"

"It is unthoughtful of Aunt Josette—"

"But she is coming!"

"Kiss me!"

She pressed her warm lips to his, and he let her go. Scarcely had she escaped when Josette's light footsteps sounded in the dining-room, and a moment later she appeared in the kitchen. Peter was stirring pancake batter.

"Mona gave me this job," he tried to explain. "She'll be back in a minute."

Josette smiled at him sweetly, and then quite innocently picked up several hairpins from the floor. "How careless of me to lose these!" she exclaimed, but there was a roguish light in her dark eyes which did not quite escape Peter as she tucked the pins in her own thick tresses.

To Peter it was as if he had gone away yesterday, and returned today. Pierre came in yawning, and found him helping with the breakfast. When Mona reappeared her hair was in a long braid. Never had he seen such lovely, velvety softness in her eyes or such sweet color in her face.

Josette, with a sly signal to Pierre, maneuvered them to the open door. "When we are ready for you children we'll call you," she said.

They walked toward the forest. And there, in the edge of the beautiful green meadow which had always been hallowed as their playground, he saw for the first time a new cabin nearly finished. Mona was looking at him. She saw the surprise and then the cloud that gathered in his face. She took his hand, and her fingers clung to his.

"You don't like it?" she asked.

"It is a nice cabin, but—"

He did not know how to finish. She looked down, very demurely, so that he could not see her eyes for the long lashes that hid them.

"It is my cabin."

"Yours!"

"Yes, mine. Maybe I shouldn't tell you the secret, Peter, but I'm going to be married."

It seemed impossible that a human heart could rise up and choke one as quickly as Peter's did.

Mona was still looking at the ground.

"You see, Carter told me in his letter to confide in Simon. And when Simon knew you were coming, and would of course have to marry me very soon, we planned this cabin together and Simon is going to give it to me as a wedding present. Then I'm going to let you live in it. Don't you think I'm nice?"

Peter stopped. Mona looked up, frightened.

"Don't, Peter—don't!" she entreated. "Aunt Josette is looking, and Uncle Pierre will see you, and all the rest of Five Fingers—"

But all the rest of the world could not have stopped Peter. He crumpled her in his arms.

THAT DAY WAS ONE IN which Peter could not bring himself to reveal to Mona the uncertainty which had been a part of his homecoming. Her happiness completely possessed him, and as hour after hour passed he found himself further than at the beginning from carrying out his resolution to tell her the price which he fully expected the law would ask of him. That he could expect no mercy from Aleck Curry, he assured himself through Simon. But he did not see Aleck, nor did he mention him to Mona. She sensed no danger. No one in Five Fingers could guess at the menace which hung over him, for he believed that even Simon did not know of that first morning of his father's flight when he had committed the fatal sin of firing upon the law. From the fact that Aleck had kept this crime a secret he realized the nearness and deadliness of the trap which would soon spring upon him.

But Aleck did not appear. It was not until after morning service in the little church that Mona mentioned him quite casually. He was bigger and coarser and more detestable than ever, she told Peter. He had tried to pay some attention to her, and she knew that he and Simon had frequently had words. It was through his uncle, she said, that he had been given this lazy assignment, covering the country between the railroad settlements and Five Fingers.

In the afternoon Peter met Simon alone.

The lines in the old Scotchman's face seemed to have grown deeper since morning. They were like little creases cut in stone.

"I have been over to the surveyors' camp," he said. "Curry hasn't been there since yesterday morning. And he didn't sleep in his bed last night."

JAMES OLIVER CURWOOD

"He has gone to the settlements," suggested Peter.

"His pack and traveling dunnage are in his shack," answered Simon. "He hasn't gone to the settlements." Simon did not once let his eyes meet Peter's squarely. He spoke even carelessly as he looked away. "You haven't forgotten what I told you about Carter?"

"No."

"That is well. I wouldn't be surprised if something happened to Curry last night. I saw him dead drunk at dusk—starting out alone along the cliff to the west. I told him to come back, and he cursed me."

Simon McQuarrie could not hide a lie. And Peter knew he was lying.

A little later Simon struck off into the woods to the east and did not return until after dark. At bedtime Peter asked if he had found anything of interest.

"Only a hungry man. I happened to have a lunch in my pocket. The poor devil was so weak he was hobbling along with a stick."

"Who was he?"

"I didn't ask his name." Simon turned his back to Peter as he prepared for bed. "Queer I didn't ask his name—but I didn't."

On the third day after this night Five Fingers received a stupendous shock. Simon McQuarrie and Father Albanel, in seeking lost net buoys under the Big Cliff, had found the body of a dead man. It was Aleck Curry. He was terribly broken and almost unrecognizable by the pounding of his body in the surf that washed in and out among the rocks. The story of his end was quite clear. He had evidently stumbled over the edge of the cliff while drunk, inasmuch as Simon had seen him staggering in its direction on the night he had disappeared.

"We'll take him to the nearest railroad settlement and let his friends have him," Simon said to the men of Five Fingers.

But to Father Albanel he added, in a voice which others did not hear, "It would be unpleasant, *mon père*, to have him always in our own little cemetery where only those we love are at rest."

And so, on that same day, all that was left of Aleck Curry was borne northward through the hills and ridges to his people.

Three weeks later Mona and Peter were married. Five Fingers will never forget that day. It was in the full glory of June, and the robins and thrushes were singing outside the little church. In spite of Peter's protest Mona teased him by insisting that she would not tell him where she wanted to spend her honeymoon until the little missioner had said the last words, and they were man and wife. And then, putting her soft mouth to Peter's ear, she whispered, "I want to stay in the new cabin which Simon is giving us."

So there, from the beginning, they found their new happiness, and Pierre Gourdon and Josette would walk in the twilights of summer evenings, lovers still, and never grow tired of painting for each other the beautiful and unforgetable pictures of many years ago when they had come through the pathless wilderness to make this paradise in which God, in His great goodness, had made the last of their dreams come true.

IT WAS ON AN AFTERNOON in August that Adette Clamart came to Mona's home with her cousin, Adele, who had come from the French country of Quebec to live with her, and announced that a stranger had arrived in Five Fingers and was talking with Simon in his cabin.

"Adele met him on the settlement trail," she said. "He carried a basket of flowers for her, and was so very nice that she has fallen in love with him. Haven't you, Adele?"

"He was very stiff and frightened every time I looked at him," replied Adele, "and I felt sorry for him. But he was nice—yes. And he had—how do I say it, Adette?—such a strange, stern face, with sadness in it—and—"

"Ugh!" shuddered Adette. "He was dangerously hungry, Adele. I know because Jame gets that way."

"Whoever he is—*he is coming*!" said Mona, looking through the open door.

And so he was, with the old Scotchman on one side of him and Peter on the other, as if they were pulling him along against his will. And as they came nearer Mona's heart gave a sudden flutter, and then a great jump, for this stranger who had carried Adele's flowers was Carter the man-hunter.

She ran out to meet him, and though she said only a few trembling words of welcome a light which Carter saw in her eyes made him draw in a quick breath of gratitude and joy.

"The new superintendent of the mill," announced Simon a little pompously, when Adette and Adele had joined them. "I'm getting lazy and he is taking my place. Quite a surprise! But we've been planning it a long time, haven't we, Carter?" And Simon laughed mysteriously.

Then came a sudden interruption. The bell over the little church began to ring as it had rung on a certain midnight weeks ago. And this time it was surely Father Albanel who was tugging at the rope. In his face was a flush of benevolent joy, and the louder the bell rang the rosier his cheeks grew, and there alone in the church he laughed like a boy.

Nudging Carter, whose face had grown strangely fixed and staring, Simon McQuarrie chuckled softly at his shoulder: "Someone rang the bell like that on the night Peter came home. And *now*, Carter, it is ringing our welcome to *you*!"

Observing Mona a few moments later, Adette wondered what had happened to make her eyelashes wet with tears.

Peter understood, and his hand found Mona's and held it tenderly. With an inspiration born of words which Carter had once said to him about a girl waiting at the end of the trail, he found the opportunity to whisper, "Ask Carter to have supper with us, and also *Adele*."

This Mona did in her own sweet fashion, making sure of Carter first, and after his acceptance calling upon Adele to lend herself to his entertainment in a way which gave her no possible excuse for a refusal, had such a thought come into her mind. Simon looked shrewdly at Mona and Adette. Then he turned toward the green ridges to the north over which billowy white clouds were rising.

"It's going to rain," he said. "I smell it in the air. It will come tonight."

"The crops need it," said Peter.

"And most of all—the flowers," added Adele, looking at Carter.

"Yes, the flowers—and the woods," he nodded. "It is very dry in the timber for this season of the year."

Mona and Peter turned toward their cabin, and Mona's eyes shot a sly signal to Adette. Jame's wife took firm hold of Simon's arm. "If you know what is good for you—come with me!" she whispered, with her back turned to Adele and Carter.

For a moment Carter stood helplessly. Then he moved to Adele's side and they followed Mona and Peter.

"You like flowers, Miss Adele?"

"I love them, Mr. Carter!"

As they passed through the door Mona squeezed her husband's hand.

"It was a wonderful thought, Peter. Do you think you can kiss me very quickly before they come in?"

"I am sure that I can," replied Peter—and kissed her.

The End

A Note About the Author

James Oliver Curwood (1878–1927) was an American writer and conservationist popular in the action-adventure genre. Curwood began his career as a journalist, and was hired by the Canadian government to travel around Northern Canada and publish travel journals in order to encourage tourism. This served as a catalyst for his works of fiction, which were often set in Alaska or the Hudson Bay area in Canada. Curwood was among the top ten best-selling authors in the United States during the early and mid 1920s. Over one-hundred and eighty films have been inspired by or based on his work. With these deals paired with his record book sales, Curwood earned an impressive amount of wealth from his work. As he grew older, Curwood became an advocate for conservationism and environmentalism, giving up his hunting hobby and serving on conservation committees. Between his activism and his literary work, Curwood helped shape the popular perception of the natural world.

A Note from the Publisher

Spanning many genres, from non-fiction essays to literature classics to children's books and lyric poetry, Mint Edition books showcase the master works of our time in a modern new package. The text is freshly typeset, is clean and easy to read, and features a new note about the author in each volume. Many books also include exclusive new introductory material. Every book boasts a striking new cover, which makes it as appropriate for collecting as it is for gift giving. Mint Edition books are only printed when a reader orders them, so natural resources are not wasted. We're proud that our books are never manufactured in excess and exist only in the exact quantity they need to be read and enjoyed. To learn more and view our library, go to minteditionbooks.com